Paul Curtis is a works director for a firm of cold-forging engineers. He has travelled extensively in Eastern Europe and Russia during the Cold-war years – once being arrested and interrogated by the K.G.B. in the former Soviet Union.

He now lives in Surrey. His interests are Eastern European and Russian History – political and military. He is an animal lover and supporter of Compassion in World Farming and The Donkey Sanctuary.

Books by the same author

The Shock Tube (Vanguard Press) 2004
ISBN 978 1 84386 146 1

The Border (Vanguard Press) 2006
ISBN 978 1 84386 227 1

The Fall of Sir Winyard Hall

Paul Curtis

The Fall of Sir Winyard Hall

Vanguard Press

VANGUARD PAPERBACK

A CIP catalogue record for this title is
available from the British Library.

ISBN 978 1 84386 895 8

The front cover has been designed by David Shenton, the cartoonist.

Vanguard Press is an imprint of
Pegasus Elliot MacKenzie Publishers Ltd.
www.pegasuspublishers.com

First Published in 2012

Vanguard Press
Sheraton House Castle Park
Cambridge England

Printed & Bound in Great Britain

In loving memory of Alberta Jones;
30th October 1906 to 17th March 2008

CHAPTER 1

Lichtenstein: small principality to the east of Switzerland, population 24,000 – plus me and Norman, makes 24,002. Note: has its own Chapter.

CHAPTER 2

Rayners Lane: suburban area in the environs of Harrow and Wealdstone – population 103,200. Note: doesn't have its own chapter; has to share it with all sorts of other comings and goings needed to explain what I was up to in Lichtenstein with Norman – starting with…

…Me skipping home from school at the start of the 1987 summer vacation in absurdly high spirits, brandishing my school report proudly, which I was confident would inform my parents that not only was I greatly esteemed, revered, loved even by the entire contingent of my schoolmastery, but would also inform them that a unique destiny awaited me. "Not since Gladstone…" Is how I imagined it would start.

My father frowned with mild consternation; the burden of fathering a child prodigy evidently weighed heavily upon him, he being such a humble man himself. I saw him struggling with words to express himself. He even looked mildly embarrassed. I felt sorry for him; I loved my dad, I loved most people, but particularly my dad. He patted me gently on one shoulder, the left I think, but it might have been the right; it is after all a long time ago now. He sort of smiled.

"Time we had a little chat, son."

I was always ready for a little chat with my dad. Eclectic is the word for these little chats: how you could create your own car wash by cultivating two privet hedges along the edges of a narrow driveway and drive your car up and down on a wet day; how you could drink as much as you like and drive, providing you confined yourself to the back garden; how socialists were not allowed to keep bees because of their allegiance to their queen – but were allowed to keep wasps, who admittedly still had a queen but no one curtsied to her, and, besides, they could be attracted into one's attic space using an electric shaver…

But it wasn't that sort of a chat. I could tell by the way he cleared his throat. He only did this when imparting unwelcome information; e.g. telling my mother that her new hairdo was without doubt very fashionable and fetching, but that he rather preferred it as it was. And I have to tell you, as a bit of an aside, that this was my dad putting his foot down; my mother being, in general, the Alpha Female. But strangely, after the statutory fit of hysterical sobbing and bitter recriminations, Mum would take herself off to the hairdresser and have her 1950s' style restored to its former magnificence, which left us with the unanswered question as to how deep her commitment to feminism really was.

Dad cleared his throat. "Erm – what was it you fancied doing after school, son?"

I enlightened him; nice of him to take such an interest. It involved a can of Tizer, some rolling tobacco, some mud, lots of mud… But apparently he meant after school in a different sense. This was more difficult; proprietor of a Greek shipping line I thought would be good, because it would allow me time pursue my other ambitions which would probably take a certain amount of time to get off the ground financially – a general problem encountered by jungle explorers, experimental film directors and high-altitude balloonists. But it was also true that I hadn't given the subject a lot of thought. The world was, after all, my oyster. Even my mathematics tutor had had to admit that. "I suppose you think the world's your oyster, Curtis?" I knew it was; I knew it would fall over itself to accommodate me without having to be rubbed three times. Anyway, if the worst came to the worst, I could always marry into royalty. It was a bit of a last resort, but it would please my mum, as did anything that put one over the neighbours. Of course I realised that I would have to go through the formality of university, which would occupy a lot of my spare time, what with the regattas, summer balls and snogging.

Something in my father's eye alerted me. He handed me the report solemnly, and I was afflicted with an unusual doubt.

I'll skip the first few paragraphs if you don't mind. They contained nothing substantial, just filling a bit of space with generalities on character and personality. I told my dad that all the other boys' reports were almost certainly just the same – "word for word," I explained, to make sure he got the point.

The next bit wasn't really worth repeating either: very dry; dealing with grades mainly, and over-using the rear end of the Greek alphabet. They did this, I explained to my dad, just to show off – everyone knows Alpha Beta Gamma Delta, but who has heard of Phi Chi and Psi?

This left the last section, dealing with my career prospects. I was going to skip this too, because it was poorly written I felt, but the proofing editor who has a red felt-tip pen that she is particularly proud of and likes to find any old excuse to use, exhibited a rare moment of enthusiasm in the form of, "OH GO ON". So here goes…

"Bringing us to the matter of future career (using the word loosely). This school is no stranger to failure; we have, since our establishment in 1473, produced an investment banker, a popular musician, a rugby player, several politicians (including one prime minister), three estate agents and, to our long-lasting shame, a television sports commentator!"

I'll interrupt there if you don't mind, just to say grudgingly that old Anstruther (the headmaster writing this stuff) did have a point here. I have noticed since reading this remark that if you see someone looking particularly gormless on your TV or even moronic or vacuous, the chances are that they are telling you that Sidmouth Athletic beat Sutton Coldfield Dynamo 4-2 in a tense game that had everyone on the edges of their seats, and holds out the promise of an even more important match in two weeks' time that could see Sidmouth elevated to the sixth division. It's the use of the word "important" that disturbs me – as if it mattered! You get my point. But to continue…

"We certainly have higher hopes for Curtis insofar as they could not be lower. I am sure that he is capable of obtaining the minimum entry requirements to one of our lesser universities such as, erm, Cambridge." (Another note here: Anstruther was an Oxford man.) "Indeed, with Curtis' remarkable parrot-like ability to mimic his schoolmasters, he should find no problem in regurgitating the mindless inanities required to achieve success in subjects such as politics, business management and literary criticism. And, of course, with his negligible intellect, lack of grasp of the world around him, entire absence of common sense, and ability to talk childlike nonsense with conviction, he should not rule out a career in economics…"

We'll stop there I think. Anstruther went into a long diatribe identifying further features of my character and intellect that qualified me to become an economist and although, strangely, many of these appeared unflattering, he did at least have the decency to concede that were I to become an economist, I could become a world-class one, and he spent a further twelve pages discussing my particular suitability to deliver a Reith Lecture. He seemed to have a bee in his bonnet on this subject.

In fact, this school report of mine went on to become famous in its own way. A disgraceful leak from the staff room referred to it as an "all time stinker", and unfortunately, due to grave character defects in both my brothers (no doubt a defective gene which I consider myself fortunate to have escaped) the sordid truth is that the report was stolen from my father's bureau and sold at private auction. My father himself had been holding dinner parties solely as an excuse to read the report aloud as an amusement to his guests. I could hear them all screeching with laughter late into the night, which I think determines the origin of the defective gene in my brothers. My school report went on to change hands on a regular basis, appreciating considerably in value each time it was sold. While it was in my opinion poorly conceived and lacking in any inherent merit; quite worthless in fact; it acquired value purely as an investment, rather as a Damien Hirst; no one particularly wanted the thing, but as long as there were gullible collectors around, they could flog it on and make a killing. The last I heard of it, it was into five figures, and had been translated into fourteen foreign languages including Arabic and Finnish, which did make me a little proud I must admit. But then of course came the stock market collapse, and I've not heard of it since.

Suffice to say, I ended up at ████ University [name deleted following a threatening letter, postmarked Durham] from the Dean to my cowardly lawyers ████, ████, ████ & Simpson [names deleted due to more threats – except for Simpson who is a bit of a sport and says she couldn't give diddly-squat about those two-bit mothers, (she's American)] reading economics! I came to find that in spite of the fact that Anstruther was such a pathetically poor judge of character, he was right about this subject – it was, and probably still is, unless it has pulled its socks up dramatically, absolute rubbish. I spent the first few weeks studying the effect of supply and demand on turnips. The point about turnips is that they are seasonal and some people like them and others don't – so they are of particular interest to economists because of the complexity of the demand patterns. Unscrupulous farmers dig them up and re-plant carrots to limit supply and push the prices up. All very simple really; in fact I volunteered this to my tutor as an explanation for the inflated value of my school report: its limited supply, i.e. just the one, but he just gave me a funny look and sniffed. As if this wasn't bad enough, being sniffed at by a bloke in a sports jacket with appalling breath and a ginger beard, but then I learnt that the whole business of turnips wasn't actually that simple. Apparently there were other theories by other economists, Keynes, Friedman and Fisher – probably all with ginger beards and bad breath – and they evidently hated each other and devoted themselves to rubbishing each other's theories and putting forward their own (a bit like the forwards to James Joyce's *Ulysses* – "Oh no, Stanley Weintraub has that quite wrong; the River Liffey actually represents a vagina…"). Apart from the fact that these theories were the sort of nonsense your average six-year-old would come up with if it weren't for the threat of a wooden spoon on the back of the legs, we had to learn the mantra of these prima donnas. They won't have it that some people like turnips and others don't; they want to tell you why! They stray into the realms of psychology, where they make a quantum leap to a new level of ignorance. They claim that a child doesn't like turnips because he or she wasn't exposed to them at the critical early formative years and, in turn, the child's mother was deprived of turnips going back fourteen generations to the great turnip disturbances of 1433 – leading to an entirely new subject known as Economic History. Which believe it or not, is surpassed in its nonsensical value by Economic Geography!

Suffice to say, I wasn't fooled by any of it. I saw it for what it was. I knew all about supply and demand, I had been exposed to it at an early age when a brush salesman had turned up on our doorstep and enquired of my mother:

"Would you like a brush, Miss?"

At which point my mother giggled, because she liked being called Miss, and replied:

"I'd love one."

"They're one and six," said the man doubtfully.

"One and six it is then."

Keynes and Freidman wouldn't have liked this. Even Fisher, who disagreed with them both as a matter of principle, would have clicked his tongue. In rare agreement they would have sent everyone involved in this shameful transaction that threatened the very being of economics on some dreadful degree course just to complicate things unnecessarily.

I started having dreams about economists. I strangled Keynes until his eyes bulged and a sort of gurgling noise came from his throat. I planted a bomb in the luggage compartment of Friedman's private plane and watched it plummet into a mountain in a ball of flames. I booked Fisher on a transatlantic cruise ship with Kate Winslet and Leonardo DiCaprio. I enjoyed these dreams immensely, which worried me, so I took myself off to a psychologist – nervously because I thought she would start making a big thing about dressing up in my mother's underwear when I was six. But apparently it was quite normal to have a pathological hatred of economists, just enjoy it, she told me – but try to refrain from actually killing any. While this was not in itself in any way wrong, due to some sort of legal loophole, economists were treated by law as if they were human beings. I'm better now. As part of my therapy I had to listen to a lecture from an economist on the subject of global extinction and its effect on the stock market. It is true that the blood drained from my face and all my knuckles turned white, but I just commented mildly that an economist was perhaps not the best qualified person to be giving lectures on the subject of science, a subject of which he was spectacularly ignorant. But I shrugged it off as more whimsical than annoying; I even laughed – although my psychologist suggested I should stop after half an hour.

So it was that I left university with a degree in a completely useless subject, and entered by default the world of accountancy. True, I didn't sit at a high desk and scratch away with a quill pen, but I did find a position working for a firm owned and run by a miserable and sinister bastard by the name of Poulter, who was a bit like Uriah Heep but without the redeeming features.

He took a dislike to me on sight. In spite of my degree, my position was the lowest of the low. I had to start my education all over again to study for accountancy exams, and my salary, in the words of Poulter (or Poultice as we called him for some unknown reason) "was commensurate with my position in the firm."

Everyone was petrified of Poulter. The liftman, an ex-serviceman with a game leg, had something wrong with his mouth, which, it took me a while to work out, was linked in a Pavlovian-type way to the utterance of Poulter's name. I'm ashamed to tell that I took advantage of this to get a cheap laugh. I made sure every time I was in the lift to mention Poulter by name. The liftman's mouth began to work. I would stay in the lift many floors past my destination just to get as many "Poulters" in as possible; usually after six, sometimes seven, the poor beggar would begin to froth at the mouth. It became a kind of party trick to ride the lift shotgun in turn with other members of the firm, leaving the poor old boy foaming furiously while I escaped with my associate, both of us desperately trying to contain our laughter until the lift was safely on the next floor.

I suppose I'd better tell you a bit about Poulter just in case you start developing an unhealthy sympathy for him. His wife and son were afraid of him. He had an evil temper which he vented on the least valuable staff. He resented having to treat the senior members of staff with a minimum of civility, and made up for it in his treatment of the juniors. Being five minutes late for work resulted in a threat of dismissal and the loss of an hour's pay. He had a clique of favourite clients who were like him: sinister, bullying, odious crooks. He employed attractive unmarried secretaries who were fired if they objected to his grubby hands straying where they shouldn't or got pregnant, married or even took up with a boyfriend.

But to return to the liftman (about time too, you might say, and I wouldn't entirely disagree with you). George. Who says you can't have a sentence without a verb and a thing and a thingummy? She with the red pen evidently. The liftman's name was George, is what I am telling you so succinctly, and George and I became friends. Like my father, George had served in the

Royal Navy during the War. I asked him timidly about his service. I knew that my father and many of his generation didn't talk about it. George was it seemed one of them, although this changed after I had asked him the question. Slowly but inexorably he began to talk of the terrifying actions he had been in, which culminated in a great opening of the floodgates to his soul, causing us to stop the lift somewhere between the sixth floor (Featherstonehaugh, Tweedle, Gilbert and son – the son was a particularly useless specimen who wore flamboyant silk shirts and laughed like a horse) and the seventh (Barking, Fenwick & Cox – nothing much to report here except that Mr Cox wore a wig) until George recovered his composure. Strangely and embarrassingly, I put my hand on his sleeve, which I wouldn't normally do. It was one of those rare moments where the human animal reverts to a time before words. And writing, "OH FOR GOD'S SAKE!" in bold red capitals will not deter me from telling you this.

From this moment on, a special friendship existed between me and George. We smiled at each other on an impulse, we were pleased to see each other, we liked each other – and we respected each other. This last point is important because it made me feel queer. I don't think anyone had ever respected me before and I was in awe of it; it made me feel intensely uncomfortable and proud at the same time.

I got it out of George why he hated Poulter so much. Unlike me, George's job was important to him. It was the work ethic I suppose. He spoke with dread of disability benefit and the dole because they had the smell of charity about them. George was a humble man but had immense pride, and Poulter (nasty little shit) played on this. He took a sadistic pleasure in finding fault with George and hinting that his job was on the line. It is doubtful if Poulter actually had any such power because George was employed by the freeholders, but Poulter was the sort of creep who had unhealthy influence in all sorts of places where his nose didn't belong; and George was afraid of him. All this came together in a strange way one day in the lift.

I was late for work that day. I'd overslept and missed my train. It occurred to me that Poulter was quite likely to fire me. I had just passed my Part 1 (PE 1) exams. It seemed unlikely that Poulter would want to give me a promotion, and he didn't like waiting until people left. That gave them a moment of power which I suspect he was afraid of. He liked to get in first with dismissal on some trumped-up charge, and in my case, on this particular morning, I would be providing him with a perfect opportunity.

I turned into the building with this thought in my mind, and suffered a moment of trepidation followed by a sudden dazzling feeling of liberation. █████ is what I thought, and then again ██████████!!! I've tried to slip this in a few times but it's been deleted in red pen, in spite of which you get my drift I'm sure. It was a similar feeling experienced at school while sabotaging the music master's bicycle; caution just gets thrown to the wind, followed by a great rush of euphoria. Some people I am told have visions of gurus in orange robes floating somewhere around shoulder height and humming to themselves. The universe slips a cog and whatever it is that has been bottled up for so long comes bursting out: a woman tells her husband that he snores, his toenails are revolting, he has an excessive growth of nasal hair and consequently she will be divorcing him. Or it could be that a man on his fiftieth birthday announces to his mother that he won't be needing sandwiches today because he'll be eating out, he also won't be wearing any gloves, vest or even a scarf, and don't bother waiting up because he'll be spending the night with a girl called Daisy who does night work around the Portsmouth Docks.

In my case, I had the sudden compulsion to enlighten Poulter on the subject of him being a little shit. As I walked into the lift, it seemed that destiny had spoken for there he was festering in the corner. The door closed. George's mouth worked furiously. My hovering, shoulder-high guru hummed himself into a frenzy. This was my moment… And I flunked it! It's all well and good looking down your noses and sniffing or writing "HA" in red felt-tip; you weren't stuck in a lift with the Eye of Sauron blazing into you. You will be disgusted but probably not surprised to learn that I was relieved when the stare rotated past me, like a slow-motion sinister lighthouse, to rest upon George.

George began to froth lightly at the corners of the mouth; just a few small bubbles to start the show. I have to explain that this was the week before Remembrance Day – the one week in the year when George wore his medals. I knew all about George's medals. He had shyly but with great pleasure showed them to me: the 39-45 Campaign Medal, the Atlantic Star from his days on escort duty – and the one that made him chuckle with amusement: the Africa Star from having docked just the once at Tripoli; and at this moment, it was this particular medal that was being glared at with hostility by Poulter. Perhaps he had wanted to go to Libya as a child but had not been allowed?

"You'll take those baubles off, Cartwright – this is a place of work, not a dog show."

That did it! I felt the rage well up inside of me. Strangely, although I was fond of George, this insult was against all of his generation; against my father, against my uncle who had fallen – all sneered at and insulted by this loathsome piece of excrement. I don't think I had ever lost my temper before. I rather admired people who did, just because they had some extra faculty that was denied to me: a button on their keyboard with "rage" written on it in red capitals.

I became slowly aware that George and Poulter were staring at me. My fists were clenched so tightly that my nails were cutting into my palms. George told me afterwards that I had turned a deep shade of crimson – very similar to some curtains his wife had bought just after the War, he said – and my eyes were bulging out of their sockets, presumably not resembling any sort of indoor furnishing, or I am sure he would have shared this with me.

I roared at the top of my voice: "HOW DARE YOU!!!!"

This would probably be written off as small beer by the world's great orators. But looking back I'm rather proud of it. Who wants to listen to hysterical tirades that go on for hours anyway? This was modelled more on the lines of "J'accuse": short, thought-provoking and delivered at high volume somewhere between the eleventh floor (Price, Kopperburg and Weatherspoon – chartered surveyors – three well-dressed and polite gentlemen but amazingly short, giving them a commercial edge on other surveyors possibly by allowing them to survey all sorts of nooks and crannies denied to other more substantially built surveyors) and the twelfth (shared between Fotheringay and Phipps – graphic designers – and Metcalf, Spooner and Foster – import agents. There was some sort of a quarrel between this lot; they hadn't spoken for years. The trouble had started between Foster and Metcalf, and of course, Spooner had been under pressure to take sides as is so often… Quite why the rest of this should have been crossed through in red, I'm not sure). Delivered, as I was saying, somewhere around there, and received loud and clear on the twentieth (there are three firms on the twentieth, all with interesting backgrounds, but perhaps I'll tell you about them some other time) and also in the basement, where the caretaker was having a private moment with a publication entitled: *Mistress* – and just at the critical moment, approaching a guilt-ridden climax, he heard a disjointed command bellowed down the lift-shaft and echoing around the basement: "How dare you!" Which he said was peculiarly apposite because he was at that moment changing places in his head with a young man in the picture strip caught peeping up the tight pencil skirt of his schoolmistress. Apparently that did it for him. In the domain of explosive ejaculations this was a particularly devastating one, vaulting effortlessly over a storage radiator and a rolled-up carpet, and splashing down in the middle of a tea chest full of archived accounts. More information perhaps than I required at the time, but I was pleased for him, and double-pleased, some time later, when the Inland Revenue in a vindictive mood opened a BD (backdated) enquiry on the accounts of a firm that just happened to be sitting at the top of that very same tea chest.

But to return to the lift shaft, which was somewhere around the thirteenth floor by now (Travis, Woodruff & Montmorency – and you can jolly well whistle if you want to know what they do); all was silent, except for the gentle creaking of lift cables, and an echo in my head of: "How dare you, you, you, you, you, you, you…" (I could go on; those of you with Obsessive-Compulsive Disorder will know how difficult it is not to).

George's mouth was completely still, but the effect on Poulter was peculiar. He swallowed awkwardly, fiddled with his tie and concentrated his gaze at a stain on the floor. He coughed.

"Here please, George."

Very curious. Firstly, Poulter never called his subordinates by their first names, secondly he never said, please, and thirdly, he couldn't possibly have any reason to visit the seventeenth floor (the whole business of listening to echoes in my head, Poulter coughing and George stopping the lift, had taken us past three firms of accountants, two chartered and one certified, a Danish travel company, a market research bureau and a fashion label company) to the seventeenth floor. This had been solely occupied by Hymenburger, Goldstein and Horrowitz, who had cleared out after a raid by HM Customs and Excise.

George opened the lift door to an office covered in dust sheets and, as the door closed, the last sight we had of Poulter was of him pottering in a bemused sort of way into a cleaning cupboard.

George and I descended in a silence that lasted about four floors. Then George began to tremble. His mouth worked. He sank slowly to his knees with his hands clutching at his face. He began to laugh. I didn't realise this at first; in fact, I was just remonstrating with myself: "Now look what you have done," (which is definitely what my mother would have said to me under the circumstances) when the truth began to dawn on me. No one had ever heard George laugh, but there were certain telltale signs: the rolling on the back, the tears streaming down his face, the gasping for breath only to let it out again in a series of yips – and of course this set me off.

We spent something like ten minutes parked up on the thirteenth. The lift call lights were flashing like a disco. Presumably Messrs Travis, Woodruff, Fotheringay, Phipps, Metcalf, Spooner and Foster all took it into their heads that they fancied milling around on other floors – but they all had to wait.

I kept my job. It may have been as simple as the adage that all bullies are cowards, or it may be that in the twisted workings of Poulter's brain, my outburst only made sense if I had in some way got the goods on him. I even got an unexpected promotion and pay rise, but this was all relayed to me by one of the other partners – Poulter never spoke to me again.

CHAPTER 3

Poulter died suddenly and unexpectedly. There was a phone call one morning from Mrs Poulter. Her husband would not be in today (which was a strange way of putting it, because he was unlikely to be in on the following either). He had died of a heart attack in the night. Mrs Poulter sounded far more animated than was usual for the announcement of bereavement. The receptionist suggested somewhat inappropriately that it was a merciful release – and Mrs Poulter agreed quite gaily that she thought so too.

In fairness to the staff of Poulter, Grimshaw and Mugertroyd, they did pay their respects with a moment's silence, but I'm afraid that it didn't achieve the customary two minutes; just the five seconds before a great cheer went up followed by a protracted burst of applause. A fitting assortment of office paraphernalia was thrown into the air: staplers, paper punchers, rubbers, rulers, reams of copy paper, coffee mugs and ring binders – all in memoriam of course. Ties were ripped off in respect, although a certain lack of decorum was shown by those affiliated to the world of football who started punching the air to cries of: "yes!" and "result!"

A bottle of champagne appeared from nowhere (one uses these expressions, but Poulter's drinks cabinet door had been wrenched off its hinges which gives us a bit of a clue) and the memory of our much unesteemed former leader was toasted. For some reason the assembled ranks seemed to look to me for a speech. I felt my coat sleeves plucked in an encouraging sort of way. Someone placed a large glass of champagne in one hand and a lighted cigar in the other. I rose reluctantly to my feet.

"Gentlemen, and indeed, ladies; dearly beloved in fact…" I seem to remember faltering at this point, having come unexpectedly to the bottom of my glass. Someone thoughtfully replaced my glass with a full magnum, and I was able to continue.

"Thank you, most kind – and a splendid cigar, one of Poultice's finest from the rosewood box that in his lifetime was always locked and now it would appear… isn't. I'm sure, indeed I know, it is what he would have wanted…" I was interrupted at this point by a long spell of laughter. I smiled at them all gratefully and swigged at the rare and incredibly expensive vintage Bollinger. It was probably surprised to find itself being drunk from its bottle. I almost wished Poulter was alive just to witness this. My audience was now piping down and looked at me expectantly.

"In the midst of life, gentlemen and of course, still the ladies, not to exclude anyone, you get my drift I'm sure – we are, and I hope you won't be offended by my saying so… in death. Yesterday, our departed benefactor was amongst us – and yet today, just one day later than yesterday in fact – he appears not to be. He is in fact conspicuous by his absence. One might almost say that he cometh up like a flower, albeit a somewhat poisonous and parasitic one, and is cutteth down, and has even signally failed to continueth in one stay, which might even count against him. One should continueth in one stay as we all know, and if one doesn't it's quite likely to be frowned upon up there, and indeed… down there."

I remember taking a particularly large swig at this point, and exhaled a cloud of cigar smoke.

"Nothing personal ladies – and of course the gentlemen, but I have to say this: we are but dust. I know I am and I have every reason to suspect that you are. All in fact at Poulter, Grimshaw and Murgatroyd, along with a large assortment of other firms in this building, with particular emphasis on Metcalf, Spooner and Foster, who, let's face it, are no spring chickens – have but a short time to live – that's my point. I fully expect us and them to flee like a shadow. Indeed, like a shadow… I have it on the highest authority. Murgatroyd did it a while ago and not to be outdone, Poultice has joined him; not only fleed, but audaciously failed to continueth, what with being cut down like a flower of the field and whatnot, when the wind bloweth over, gone as it were – and being known no more by its place, which is only right and proper when you think about it. And of course, not having stopped or stayed – that's the worst of it." An adjacent secretary helped me with the champagne bottle; apparently I wasn't lifting it high enough. "There you have it, dearly beloved, but the question remains: Do you, Poultice, take this woman, Murgatroyd, to be your lawful wedded doodah – even if she turns out to be a man, which may well be the case. If anyone knows of any just reason… I know I don't; seeing as you have all been commended to the deep… Bless this ship and all who sail in her…"

I don't remember any more but I am told that I went on to perform a baptism, a blessing and an excommunication, before passing out attempting to exorcise a filing cabinet. All I remember is waking up the next day with a massive hangover and a pang of conscience about my lack of reverence for the dead. But this passed when the awful truth about Poulter came out in the next few days. Not only had he systematically robbed his clients' pension schemes but it turned out that he was a wife beater. This particularly incensed us. Nowadays, such behaviour seems tolerated if you are a footballer or something on the television. Back then, such a man was just scum. And this provoked much animated discussion on the subject. Someone, one of the secretaries I think, said: "I'd like to dance on his grave." It was one of those remarks that wasn't intended literally, but the mood in Poulter, Grimshaw and Mugertroyd was rather peculiar at that time, and significant glances were exchanged.

So it was that a week later we found ourselves in a pub conveniently close to Mill Hill cemetery, which shall remain nameless for the sake of propriety – suffice to say that the sign outside depicted a duck and a dog, but not necessarily in that order.

We sneaked out after last orders, filing down a dark lane towards the cemetery. The gates were open and we crept in. All our bravado had evaporated. We filed past effigies of angels, raised vaults and tombstones with epitaphs to old soldiers and families. We passed the tragic shrunken graves of children taken before their time. In our hearts every one of us knew this was terribly wrong.

"Here it is," announced a junior partner in a loud whisper.

A dozen torches shone on the headstone. "Here lies Douglas Edward Poulter 1938–2004. May the Lord take him and bear him away." A curious epitaph, I thought, made less enigmatic by "TOSSER" written diagonally across in chalk.

This cheered us up. Beer was passed around and a transistor radio tuned in. Strangely, Radio Three was playing Verdi's *Requiem* – quite inappropriate for our requirements. We tuned past to *Boogie Nights* – perfect. We limbered up, half-heartedly at first, but gradually worked up to party mood, and proceeded to groove with that spectacular lack of rhythm that only accountants can achieve.

We formed up in two columns – logical I suppose; accountants being naturally attuned to double-entry book-keeping.

We were so absorbed in our dancing that we failed until the last moment to see the approach of two lights sweeping towards us in an eerie fashion. The dancing faltered and the radio was kicked into silence. We unknowingly huddled together, seriously frightened. A nearby secretary cuddled me which was enjoyable. The lights were now swinging in two arcs, up towards us and then back – then stopped suddenly still, outlining two faces that were turned towards us. I gulped – it was Poulter's wife and son. I was seriously mortified; our insult was intended against Poulter, not his poor wife and son, with whom we had always had a warm feeling of camaraderie in adversity.

No one spoke. The silent figures around me were desperately trying to look like statues. Mrs Poulter turned to her son, her face an inscrutable mask. I noticed that the boy held what looked like a small suitcase. He placed this at the head of the grave and started fumbling with it. Suddenly, a wild Irish jig rang out at incredible volume. Mrs Poulter raised her arms, let out a whoop of delight and shrieked:

"And, riverdance."

We did as ordered, attempting to follow her lead and failing miserably. Mrs Poulter on the other hand was magnificent. We gave of our best. Some of the girls weren't bad; the rest of us were rubbish, but it was a sincere effort, anyone could see – except perhaps for one of the senior partners whose dancing had evolved in the days of Bill Haley. He planted his legs firmly apart, pivoted at the waist with his arms akimbo and rotated furiously back and forth; Michael Flatley, he wasn't. Poulter Junior wasn't much better. He started a half-hearted jig, but I'm afraid emotions got the better of him and the prancing steps regressed into a sort of stomp that ended up with him jumping up and down with maximum possible force on a place directly above the head of his sadly missed father, six feet below.

Funny the things that make you laugh, if you know what I mean. The sight of a senior partner frugging away like a demented old Hell's Angel, and Poulter's boy trying to crush his old man's head could have been sad, bizarre, disturbing; in fact it definitely should have been, but somebody started laughing and that was how the night ended: with everyone having a good laugh. Somehow I don't think it was "what he would have wanted" but it was certainly what he damn well deserved.

CHAPTER 4

This next bit is rather embarrassing. I have to explain how I ended up in the Directorate General for Economic and Financial Affairs (DGECFIN) office of the European Union. I was going to leave a gap and hope that no one would notice. Being a delicate matter, I discussed it with my editor and she was most reassuring. She said that having read my manuscript, she could categorically assure me that no one of any significance was likely to read it, and accordingly any damage to my reputation would be negligible. She patted me on the head repeatedly during this conversation. She is a tall woman and does this a lot. I find it patronising but I'm sure she means well; in fact, I think she likes me, because she is always smiling and laughing when I am around.

Anyway, I'd better get on with it. I settled back into Poulter, Grimshaw and Mugertroyd. I failed my PE2 on the third and final attempt and had Paul Curtis A.C.A. embroidered on my underpants as a gesture of defiance. I was not in the same position as my higher flying colleagues who were so valuable to the firm that they held the partners to ransom with steely-eyed demands for pay rises. This resulted in a lot of peacocking by the young turks, a growing alcohol dependency on behalf of the senior partners, and me just knowing my place and getting on with my work.

I was content except for one thing: I didn't have a girlfriend. This was partly due to a tendency to swallow my lower lip and put my head under my armpit whenever any female came anywhere near me.

I answered an advert. What sort of advert? Funny how suddenly you're all so interested. Very well then: it was an advert in a certain magazine, which, yes, I did borrow from the caretaker at work – and, yes, was entitled *Mistress*. I thought I needed a lady who would take charge of things. Otherwise, with my excessive shyness, I would start inspecting under my arms and the whole thing would amount to nothing. The advert featured an extremely tall lady (my editor would like me to point out that it was not her) and invited correspondence rather imperiously I thought: "Worm required – on your knees and submit to your mistress." I duly corresponded. "Dear Madam…" very formal – with a picture of my naked buttocks as ordered, which was perhaps not so formal.

Apparently this (or these) was to her satisfaction and a liaison was arranged. I remember walking down seven stone steps to a basement (she with the red pen suggested: "Are you sure you don't mean abasement?" No I don't – and the number of steps has no link to Goethe's *Faust*, just to make that quite clear – nobody likes a smart arse).

I didn't know it at the time but apparently all such ladies live in basements. An estate agent has since told me that whenever a basement flat comes onto the market, their offices are filled with tall imperious beauties in catsuits planting leather boots with ten-inch heels on chairs and making low offers while half-strangling a negotiator by his tie. Not such a bad way to treat an estate agent you might think and who am I to argue.

But to return to the basement steps; they know their business these girls; there is something about descending concrete steps knowing that there is something leather-clad and lethal at the bottom. I don't think I've ever been so scared and excited at the same time, which put me in a peculiar sort of anatomical dilemma. I would like to have leant forward to relieve the pressure in the front trouser area, but dare not, due to the associated perils to the rear trouser area.

The door opened. I leaned forward slightly as a result of a rapid risk assessment in the altered circumstances. A tall, tightly leathered, curvaceous being with long auburn hair and a whip (the whip was also long but not particularly auburn), ordered me in with a crooked finger. The door closed behind me.

So began my relationship with Donna – perhaps a little different from most people's relationships. Romance for Donna entailed a vicious beating, which was strenuous for her, and she found the need to relax afterwards, by sitting astride my face, smoking a cigarette, using my navel as an ashtray, and watching television. Donna watched a lot of television; quite what sort of programmes she liked, I'm not too sure because the sound was somewhat muffled. I got to see mainly Channel One and just occasionally, when she turned round to read a magazine, Channel Two, if you follow my meaning.

At first I thought this was wonderful; I mean, this all happened on the first night, within about two minutes of meeting her in fact. This was my kind of girl I decided, even though it was all very different from what I had expected. I'd been brought up on Jane Austen and it seemed that an awful lot of foreplay had been avoided in the way of quadrilles, meaningful glances across cucumber sandwiches, starchy but witty conversations while embroidering furiously, painful misunderstandings, tears and rejected marriage proposals – fortunate indeed for the world of nineteenth century literature that Donna wasn't around at the time: "Oh do come in Mr Darcy and lie on the floor while I arrange myself (saucy titter) on your face." THE END.

Marvellous. (There you go: another sentence with no whatsits.) But I assumed that this was a prelude to some seriously passionate lovemaking and unfortunately it was more often than not a prelude to a seriously passionate beating – with just an occasional rather perfunctory bit of something or other that has been struck through with a red pen – and I think the only purpose of this was to keep me interested. It was the beating that did it for Donna. My yelps of pain and the purple stripes across my buttocks after she'd let rip with a riding crop would fire her up into a state of supreme ecstasy. Funny thing the mating game; you've probably seen these nature programmes where a lady baboon with a particularly vivid red bottom has the gentlemen baboons all of a twitter. Their lonely hearts columns are full of ads with hardly a mention of a "GSOH", but feature heavily a "RRRA" (really really red arse).

Donna so enjoyed beating me, she confided with a slight blush some weeks after we had been together, that it gave her the most intense multiple orgasms. I was pleased for her of course, having being bought up as a gentleman, but for me it brought only intense multiple contusions.

True we did go out, but to specialist functions, where men wore chains and women wore leather. There was a sort of protocol whereby the men would wait in an anteroom until called for. The other men tended to be weak-looking specimens, some tall and thin, others short and fat, but all with one thing in common: they were almost demented with anticipation at their coming humiliation. I remember one short fat bald-headed man being in a particularly frenzied state. He was a bank manager and apparently had been so desperate to get away from work in time for the party that he'd just granted a £50,000 loan to a known benefits scrounger. His time came; his mistress sent a maid to collect him. I'd seen his mistress – a six-foot Amazon in a catsuit stretched across the sort of thighs that if she ever got herself pregnant, the attendant midwife should not tell her to "push". But I digress, which is not like me at all. The little bald-headed man came back in a terrible state. It was customary on these occasions for buttocks to be shown, and we admired the damage in awe;

they were truly ripped to shreds. He was heaving for breath and finally gave way to tears. We consoled him standing up, for obvious reasons, and finally his sobbing began to abate; he turned his tearstained face towards us and announced in a trembling voice: “I don’t deserve her,” before lapsing into another fit of hysterics. At which point I realised that there was a subtle separation between me and these other chaps. While I appreciated the strict and powerful woman, didn’t mind a bit of chastisement and quite enjoyed the humiliation, I rather felt (timidly and without any wish to cause offence of course) that this should be more in the realms of foreplay than a substitute for things that will have a red pen struck through them however I describe them.

The crisis came at one of these parties. I was sitting in the waiting room, smoking nervously, when a maid in a rather fetching outfit came for me (when I say fetching, I don’t just mean that she had come to fetch me, although apparently she had – I refer to her uniform which was modest when viewed from the front but took one’s breath away when she turned for me to follow her). Imagine my surprise to find the six-foot Amazon awaiting me, brandishing a riding crop with which she pointed to a nearby trestle. I knew the etiquette for these occasions; while it is generally considered good manners to keep your trousers on in front of a lady, here it was frowned upon.

I’ve never known pain like it. It was stunning. I tottered from the room in a daze, bumping into walls, lapsing in and out of consciousness. I am told that I crawled into the waiting room on my hands and knees. It took about ten minutes to realise how much pain I was in, and a further ten to do anything about it – i.e. burst into tears. The men comforted me; I felt a moment of intense bonding with them, probably similar to that of hardened SAS soldiers when they throw in stun grenades and pull one of their number free from a grisly fate at the hands of a brutal enemy. These were the very best of men. The moment was only slightly spoilt by one of them being so impressed with the state of my bottom that he started to stimulate himself.

Donna went ballistic! To understand this is to understand that Donna was not, in the conventional sense, jealous. True, she would beat me if I looked at another woman, but only because it provided her with an excuse to beat me – along with, playing with myself, staring at her bust, fidgeting, sniffing or indeed if nothing else came to mind, that good old trusted act of impertinence: breathing. But to allow myself to be beaten by another woman!!!! (yes I know this is not a good sentence but it purveys dramatic effect if you don't mind, and who is writing this anyway I'd like to know?). This time her anger was for real; she was too angry even to beat me. And after the heart-rending recrimination: "How could you?" she burst into tears. There is something particularly appalling about a proud beauty in a leather catsuit sobbing her heart out. I tried to comfort her, at which point she broke down completely and told me that she was in love with me, even though she added: "you worm," out of sheer force of habit.

I left her with an ache that was not in its usual place. I admired Donna, but it hadn't occurred to me for a moment that she could feel this way about me, and the sad truth was that what I felt for her now was pity rather than love.

I wrote her a letter explaining this. I didn't hear anything for a week, then, arriving home after work one day, I found a large bunch of magnificent black tulips. I think they had started out life as another colour because there were traces of overspray on the leaves and stems. My mum gave a knowing look.

"A girl on a motorbike in a leather suit delivered them, dear – I think she was one of those dominatrixes."

"Dominatrices, dear." This was my father's only fault: to be extremely pedantic about spelling and grammar. On the very rare occasions that he had a row with my mother, and her diction was prone to slip on such occasions, he would never fail to correct her

– for which I felt another medal should be struck that could sit proudly between his Atlantic and Pacific Star.

"Dominatrixes," repeated my mother determinedly. "Just the type he likes."

I studied my mother carefully but she was busying herself looking innocent. How on earth did she know this? Mothers – honestly! And to make matters worse, my father was definitely smirking. If my father has a fault (other than a mild case of pedantry) it is a tendency to smirk inappropriately.

Donna was what we would call today a stalker. At first it was flowers, then chocolates, all in black and decorated with a sinister motif of a whip, a chain and a peach-shaped object coloured in crudely in red, which I took to be either my bottom or an extremely aroused lady baboon. And she started following me. A statuesque woman in a leather catsuit with a pair of opera glasses around her neck doesn't blend easily into the suburban setting of Rayners Lane. She cruised past me, head held high, in shops. I saw her silhouette against streetlights at night in atmospheric scenes reminiscent of Vienna in Orson Welles' *The Third Man*. On my way to work one morning, I heard the roar of a motorbike and a leather-clad figure streaked past, her helmetless hair blown back like a witch's hat at a particularly rakish angle.

These fly-pasts became more frequent and extreme. She was evidently lying in wait for me every morning now. She would wait until I was halfway up the high street, and then would appear, storming up the narrow road, opening up to full throttle; people turning to stare. I was frightened now.

One morning, she came past faster than ever. I stopped to watch. The high street was on a hill, with traffic lights at the top. She was still accelerating as she came to the lights, which were red. Both wheels were off the ground as she went through. I got the message: Donna was trying to kill herself.

Three days later I was in Brussels. I had explained to the partners of Poulter, Grimshaw and Mugertroyd that I was particularly interested in transferring to their Brussels office. They replied politely that they'd rather I didn't, on the flimsy grounds that I provided considerable entertainment to the London office (nothing to do with the quality of my work was mentioned, which I found rather hurtful). I had to explain that I had an ex-girlfriend dedicated to ending her life spectacularly in front of me. They saw my point, which was decent of them, and fixed up my transfer.

There was something peculiar about the Brussels office. It was run by a Mr Burger. He greeted me with a complicated handshake which involved stroking the back of my hand with his first finger, while staring intensely into my eyes. I twiddled back as best I could. He coughed and withdrew his hand suddenly. This of course is the danger of not knowing the Masonic code; I had quite possibly accused his sister of being on the game.

There was a lot of coming and going of clients, far more than in London. And they seemed peculiar too; shy to the point of furtive, with turned-up coat collars and dark glasses. I wasn't given any proper work to do, just checking accounts that had already been filed. Often, when I walked into the office, I could hear the rustle of papers being bundled rapidly away, and people started looking out of the window and whistling. I began to feel uneasy.

Things came to a head one afternoon, only a week after my arrival. Four clients turned up at the office with felt hats pulled down low and carrying violin cases. Somehow I didn't suspect them of being musicians. They announced themselves as the directors of the Estonian Cement Company. Mr Burger was on the telephone. He spent most of his time whispering down the telephone. The four men waited in the outer office. They sat stiffly chewing gum and staring in front of them. One appeared to be looking at me, which I didn't enjoy. Apart from the gum chewing, which was revolting in itself, he had a cold evil stare from bright blue psychotic eyes, reminding me of Frank Sinatra crooning one of his love songs. Suddenly there was a minor explosion from outside; I think it was a car backfiring. I was distracted by a sudden blur of movement; the main board of the Estonian Cement Company had all pulled guns on each other, which made me suspect that their real business was something other than purveying top quality cement products, including aggregate, sand, ready-mixed and pre-formed concrete products within, and indeed without, the state of Estonia. The car outside backfired again, and the directors of the ECC (as I shall call them for brevity in case I have to refer to them again) relaxed and started putting their guns away. Well, three of them did; but Frank Sinatra just sat there with his gun pointing at his fellow directors, chewing gum and twitching his upper lip periodically. The mechanism had stuck. The others had to prize the gun out of his hand and replace it in a holster in his jacket, but he continued to stare with hostility at no one in particular. I suspect that to this day, one of the directors of the ECC (you see, it came in handy) can be found staring fixedly in front of him, scaring the living daylights out of junior members of the ECC (Ha) and putting them off their business of purveying concrete and cement products to the hoi polloi in and around Estonia.

All this led me to the conclusion that the clients of Poulter, Grimshaw and Mugertroyd were more overtly criminal in Brussels than in London. One comes to realise after working on company accounts for a while that all company directors are criminals, but some more so than others.

However, in spite of this revelation, I was still surprised to roll into work a few days later and find our offices overrun by Inspector Clouseau-type characters and to hear that Mr Burger and his senior staff had been marched off in handcuffs, accused of an assortment of serious crimes, but with particular emphasis on the money-laundering ones.

I turned back to my digs feeling decidedly gloomy. I liked Brussels. The bit I lived in was close to Leuven, home to a certain famous brewery and loads of giggling flirty university students who had a particular liking for gangly English accountants – or so I managed to persuade myself after the third pint of Madame Artois' hallucinatory brew (they brew it stronger over there).

I rang home. Maybe Donna had given up the chase. But in her first sentence, my mother complained about gangs of motorcyclists who had taken to tearing up and down the road at night; I suspected there was only one of them.

My dad insisted on taking the phone to tell me what a nuisance the slugs were this year. I remained tight lipped; he was fooling no one. The old man was a soft touch and the slugs knew it. He stoutly refused all lethal forms of slug control on the basis that they were inhumane (which doesn't sound right anyway, slugs not being themselves human as it were). Anyway, now they were openly taking the piss. Word had got around, making front page news on *L'Escargot* and other less reputable publications. They were probably holding fêtes, garden parties and discoing into the night. If my father has a fault…

I went for a walk around Leuven that night. Belgian beer is spectacularly strong, and after a few glasses I perked up a bit. I noticed two chaps at the next table. They seemed to be peering at me in an intense but concerned way. One was tall and grey-haired, the other short, bald and Asian-looking. I'd noticed them in the last bar and, come to think of it, in the bar before that. I smiled at them; they looked decent enough chaps. They took this as an invitation to join me. There's no need to stiffen in a British-type way at this. There's much more of this sort of relaxed chumminess on the continent – nothing to be worried about unless handlebar moustaches and leather mule caps are involved.

They introduced themselves as Mr Jones and Mr Patel – fellow Brits by the sound of them. They shook my hand. I was slightly suspicious of Mr Patel's handshake – it reminded me of

Mr Burger's – but Mr Jones' handshake was an experience in itself. The man was undoubtedly a Grand Elk Pursuivant or a Deputy Water Buffalo, if not a Worshipful Master (I'm not too hot on Masonic titles). His handshake was as good as a day at Alton Towers; fingers and thumbs convoluted themselves into a high-speed peristaltic caress. What was most admirable was that in amongst all this frenzied activity his face remained completely impassive and his eyes stared over my shoulder a couple of blocks into the distance. This handshake was so complicated that I suspect even Alan Turing would have needed a week or two to get to the bottom of it.

They insisted on buying me a beer. They told me I'd like it. Mr Jones explained that it was a brew formulated by an ancient order of monks and had remained unchanged for at least seven hundred years. Mr Patel thought eight hundred, but Mr Jones told him that he was fairly certain it was seven hundred, at which point Mr Patel just pursed his lips. I tried it. All I can say is that somewhere in the thirteenth century (or the twelfth if Mr Patel had his way) there was an order of monks who were regularly up before the abbot for slurred chanting and sloppy beekeeping – but be that as it may, a dawning consciousness came over me that Mr Patel and Mr Jones were my best ever mates. Like a large proportion of the population of Brussels, they worked for the European Union. Our conversation strayed into the personal. They were very sorry to hear that I had lost my job. Mr Jones said that he was sorry, and Mr Patel said that he was even sorrier, although Mr Jones corrected him by saying that this was unlikely due to the extremity of his own sorrow, and they both ended up agreeing that their degree of sorrow was probably there or thereabouts in the same bracket as it were. They professed themselves to be interested in the details of the financial shenanigans, and shook their head in unison for some considerable time. Mr Jones patted me on the back consolingly, and Mr Patel took over from him while Mr Jones went to buy me another beer.

It turned out by a strange coincidence that they not only knew of Mr Burger, but had had official business with him. Small world, I thought to myself as I worked my way through the next beer. The other thought I had (sometimes I can manage two at once – unusual in a man I am told) was a sort of revelation as to why Belgian monks had turned to religion. Strange things were happening in my head. There was a buzzing noise which sounded as though it might be some kind of chant, but it was not a language I recognised, and I wondered if the Lord had taken this opportunity to converse with me in tongues, but it turned out only to be Mr Patel. Mr Patel's English was rather heavily accented. He explained to me later that he was descended from impressed labour on the Kenyan tea plantations, although having listened to how they had been treated I found it hard to understand why they had been impressed. I suppose some people are more easily pleased than others. I think I'll stick to having one thought at a time in future.

Mr Patel was asking me if I had any particular knowledge of any financial irregularities with my former clients. What splendid chaps, I thought, taking such an interest in the fortunes of someone who was only an hour ago a complete stranger. I explained that in my position at P. G. & M., I had been entrusted only with work that quite frankly (and I had only just realised this somewhere towards the bottom of this last glass of beer) was considerably below my capabilities.

My new friends agreed with me heartily; in fact they seemed quite affronted to think that someone whom they had evidently taken to their bosom had been so poorly treated, and they said so.

"Shameful, Mr Jones, don't you think?" This was Mr Patel speaking.

"Indeed I do Mr Patel, in fact I would go so far as to describe it as shabby." And this was Mr Jones. You had probably worked this out for yourself. It was a little more difficult for me under the influence of this last beer in particular. Mouths opened, words came out, faces smiled, my back was being massaged. It wasn't that simple.

"Deserves better, Mr Jones."

"Quite so, Mr Patel."

"I don't suppose – no, no, too presumptuous of me I'm sure, don't you think, Mr Jones."

"I do, Mr Patel of course, but on the other hand."

"I see your point, Mr Jones."

Which was more than I did.

"Let me put it this way to Mr Curtis, Mr Patel."

"I'm sure I can rely on you to, Mr Jones."

"The EU is very short of ACA's, Mr Curtis. In short, Mr Curtis, we need accountants – men like you, Mr Curtis."

"But, Mr Patel, doesn't it seem likely to you that a man such as Mr Curtis has a wealth of opportunities in the wider world of commerce?"

"Sadly Mr Jones…"

I held up my hand. Even in my drunken state, where repetitive drivelling is the order of the day, I felt obliged to interrupt.

"Gentlemen, gentlemen – that's one for each of you – allow me to disabuse you – let me say that again, the syntax is a bit tricky." I tried again and failed so resorted to shaking my head. "It's no good you going on about your need for splendid chaps like myself. I, gentlemen" (here I took a slight bow) "am a part-qualified accountant – a P.E.1 if you will – an A.C.A. I am not."

Mr Patel and Mr Jones looked at each other significantly and smiled. Mr Jones held out his arms towards me. Mr Patel held out his arms even wider. They looked like a pair of proud Godfathers in a Mafia movie who had just been told that their youngest sons (who had been such a worry to the family, dressing up in frilly shirts and telling local businessmen not to worry if they were late with their protection money) had just committed their first brutal murders at the age of nine.

Mr Jones leant forward confidentially. "I can't believe our fortune, Mr Patel."

"Indeed, Mr Jones – a P.E.1 – I can hardly credit it."

"The very thing – Mr Curtis probably doesn't know how particularly short of P.E.1s we are, Mr Patel."

"Possibly not, Mr Jones – possibly not."

"Hang on a minute." This was me. This conversation was perplexing me. "Why should you value part-qualified accountants more than the genuine article – well, ones who have got their genuine articles if you quite follow me."

Mr Patel and Mr Jones studied me doubtfully.

"Shall I explain, Mr Patel?" asked Mr Jones, rather uncertainly I thought.

"I'd rather you did, Mr Jones. I'm sure I can rely on you to explain the situation far better than I ever could." Mr Patel smiled, and Mr Jones gave him a look that appeared quizzical to me, but I kept the thought to myself, because this was another word I would not have liked to attempt in my current condition.

"The EU values creative thinkers, Mr Curtis," said Mr Jones.

"Indeed it does," agreed Mr Patel with what appeared to me, an unnatural enthusiasm.

"Freethinkers," continued Mr Jones, "may stumble over the first fence that is PE1, but find themselves unable to comprehend the regimented thought that is PE2."

I beamed at Mr Jones. This made sense to me. I realised even as he spoke, how absolutely spot on he was, and indeed what a damned cheek it was that people should go around lording it about in a superior fashion… just because… when in fact…

My train of thought was interrupted again by a loud buzzing noise. I wondered if this was some sort of resonance from the twelfth or thirteenth century (depending on if you were to believe Mr Jones or Mr Patel) from those Belgian monks of old winding up the inhabitants of their hives while beekeeping clumsily under the influence of "Couvent de tonsure bourre – 13% a.b.v." – although in fact it turned out to be Mr Patel again.

"The level of qualification is in fact inversely proportional to the intelligence of the candidate."

I took this opportunity to shake Mr Jones' hand because he was nearer than Mr Patel and I didn't want him to feel left out.

"Quite right," I said, "like economics you mean."

Mr Jones appeared to wince and relaxed his grip on my hand suddenly. His place was immediately taken by Mr Patel who pumped it enthusiastically. Even in my drunken state, it occurred to me that Mr Jones was probably an economist and Mr Patel definitely wasn't.

Mr Jones coughed. "Serendipity, Mr Curtis," (which impressed me because he'd been matching me beer for beer and there was no way I would have attempted that one) "brought you to our table, with your gifts that we so admire and value in accountants: imagination, flair, boldness. I may even say: panache." (I wouldn't have done.) "Should you accept our offer…"

"Ahem," I didn't want to spoil the party, but…

Mr Jones laughed and Mr Patel joined in.

"Listen to me, Mr Patel; see how I have gotten in front of myself. Think of a figure, Mr Patel – a salary for Mr Curtis."

"I have one in mind, Mr Jones."

"Then double it, Mr Patel."

"I've doubled it, Mr Jones."

Mr Jones leant forward and spoke in a loud conspiratorial whisper. "And double it again – no, wait!" He held up his hand as if perplexed by some inner conflict. "It is Mr Curtis – an exceptional case, Mr Patel – triple it!"

I remember much congratulation, back-slapping, hand-shaking and a general party mood that followed, so I assume I must have accepted. And when at last, everyone was calming down, I remember Mr Jones draping his arm around my shoulder.

"We need creative accountants in the EU, Mr Curtis."

"Thank you," I said rather irrelevantly.

"Let me get you another drink," said Mr Jones.

I don't remember anything after that. Suffice to say that I had accepted a job at some fantastic salary working in the finance department of the EU Directorate General for Economic and Financial Affairs.

CHAPTER 5

I turned up the next day with a couple of trepidations. First trepidation: in my state of advanced intoxication, had I imagined the whole thing? Second trepidation: were my new employers in fact a couple of pranksters? You may have read the Sherlock Holmes story *The Red-headed League* where a chap was enticed away from his shop by an advertisement seeking out blokes with flaming red hair – just so that they could use his cellar to tunnel into the nearby bank vaults while he was away. Substitute the unlikely requirement for a PE1 qualification for the arguably more likely requirement for ginger locks and you will understand my concern. Third trepidation: yes, I know I only mentioned two, but another one crept in when I wasn't expecting it. It was in the way of a non-specific trepidation: that feeling I used to get after a night out with Donna, when she would slip into something less comfortable and beckon me into the bedroom with a horse whip.

My knock on the door of the ECFIN finance department was answered by a sort of muffled grunt – which was explained by the sight of a chap in early middle age (a bit ginger if you're still allowed to mention these things) half buried in a white cardboard box with an announcement around the side in startling red: "Chicken Tonite". The inhabitant of the box answered to the name of Norman.

Norman nodded to me in a chummy sort of way but continued worrying at his chicken in silence. Let me rephrase that: not so much silence as the sound of an attempt to change gear without the use of the clutch in a pre-synchromesh gearbox, accompanied by a heavy chewing and gnawing noise which alternated between sub-theme and main theme as Norman opened and closed his mouth.

Norman beamed at me. He was enjoying his chicken and, as I have come to learn, Norman enjoys company when eating. He feels that people shouldn't rush off so politely when he is eating; they should stay for a chat.

"This is a particularly good chicken," said Norman with a great deal of gravity, accompanied by an eruption of breadcrumbs, fragments of goose-pimpled skin and shards of the assorted body parts of one of God's creatures that most of us would rather see wandering around ruminating – if indeed a chicken can be said to ruminate. I seem to be managing it quite well, so why can't a chicken? That's what I think.

We sort of bonded from that moment. I suspect it to be the same process whereby people who survive terrible disasters or witness horrific incidents, become bound by their shared experience: in this case, Norman eating a chicken. This was certainly for the best, since it turned out that Norman was to be my assistant. I'd better tell you a bit about Norman. It seems to be the done thing in the world of, ahem, literature.

In a former life, Norman was a Labrador. He has that unique mixture of bonhomie, lack of judgment and keen interest in food that one finds in the breed (particularly the heavy-set black ones). Norman's ex-wives (totalling six to date) have their own opinions: something with a little less ground clearance and more legs, loads more legs, or none at all, depending on which wife you happen to be discussing the matter with at the time.

Norman has an unaddressed food habit. It all started in his twenties when he fell in love with a dinner lady. It ended in tears I'm afraid, but when she took off, she left a particularly delicious pie in his fridge to remind him of what he was missing. To this day, Norman remembers the contents of that pie in intimate detail;

and I have to say they were peculiar: pork, ham, turkey gammon, grouse, spring lamb, cranberry jelly, paprika, nutmeg, watercress, red onion, curry powder, chilli, reconstituted egg yolk, chives and a brace of E numbers. But – watercress!!! Norman never mentioned that his dinner lady was pregnant but I have my suspicions. Norman felt that in the scheme of things, destiny had spoken, commanded him to move to Melton Mowbray and dedicate himself to search for that particular pie rather in the way that Prince Charming sought Cinderella's slipper (which was OK in those days, but would nowadays be stigmatised as obsessive behaviour, stalking and foot-fetishism).

My first few days at ECFIN were spent learning how to fill in expenses forms. After a week, I was looking forward to getting into my proper job. After a month I began to wonder; one form of expenses followed another; they seemed endless; and, wandering around the office complex, I came to realise that the whole department, all day and every day, was devoted to filling in expenses forms! When I mentioned this to Norman, he looked surprised and slightly offended, and I suspect he repeated my remark to my superiors, because the next day I found myself called into Mr Patel and Mr Jones' office.

"How are you getting on, Mr Curtis?" asked Mr Jones.

"Fine," I said.

"Good, good – we're pleased with your progress."

This puzzled me since I wasn't aware that I had made any.

"Very pleased," agreed Mr Patel.

"I think you are almost ready for your first assignment," said Mr Jones, and Mr Patel chuckled in agreement.

Some impishness of mood took me. "Don't tell me – you want me to fill in a monthly expenses claim for travel, subsistence, entertainment and miscellaneous expenditure?"

Mr Jones and Mr Patel stared at me.

“I see you have considerable ambition, Mr Curtis,” said Mr Jones. “Commendable – really most commendable.”

“Commendable indeed,” agreed Mr Patel. “But let us not run before we can walk.”

“You took the words right out of my mouth, Mr Patel,” said Mr Jones.

This went on for about an hour – four pages of dialogue, all with a red line through them and a curt note: “summarise.” Very well… Mr Patel and Mr Jones felt that given several months training I could look forward to a time when I could single-handedly make expenses returns for miscellaneous expenditure, subsistence and entertainment. But – and they tried to break this to me gently – travel expenses were much more complicated. In view of my enthusiasm and ambition, they would do everything in their power in the coming months to prepare me for this. I had to bear in mind that with no actual travel costs, I would be using a system of fixed allowances, although they promised that as soon as I had mastered these, I would be sent monthly to the European Parliament in Strasbourg, and this would liven things up considerably. I liked this idea and asked brightly what I would be doing there. This question was greeted by blank stares, which Norman filled in for me afterwards. Apparently I would be doing the same as everyone else in Strasbourg: clocking up expenses. That, according to Norman, was the sole function of Strasbourg.

This intrigued me; I decided to tax Norman on the subject over a meal. I want you to remember this meal; make a note of it, it is of some significance. It was a typically Norman selection. Buried deep in even the most expensive menus, you can usually find fish and chips. Most of us with plebeian tastes seek these items out discreetly, furtively working on the encryption – e.g.: “Scallops of wild deep ocean mullet served with golden roast chisel-chased sun-drenched Maris Pipers.” Norman doesn’t. Norman leans back in his chair, summons the head waiter with a crooked finger, thrusts both hands deep into his pockets, looks expansive and announces: "I think I'll have the fish and chips my good man."

In this instance, we were in a particularly expensive restaurant, served by a particularly superior-looking waiter, who duly looked absolutely appalled and sniffed haughtily in French. Norman took this as approval of his choice and consequently beamed at the poor man with pure benevolence, which put the poor chap off his stride. These superior waiters go on six-month training courses on how to appear demeaning to any type of clientele, including royalty. It's subtle stuff consisting of strategic sniffs, staring fixedly at small blemishes in shirt fronts, shifting loose change in trouser pockets in a disapproving manner – but it would need the eighteen-month residential course to prepare them for Norman. Hauteur is lost on Norman; anyone who brings Norman his dinner is a top quality bloke and deserves an encouraging smile. Being smiled at by Norman is an undermining experience. This poor chap started to look uneasy; he shifted weight from one foot to another. In a desperate final effort, he raised his chin, remembering his feudal ancestors who had served Napoleon a particularly tasty boeuf bourguignon in his tent on the field of Quatre-Bras. But just as he was regaining the upper hand, Norman insisted on shaking him by the hand and the poor man was now completely out of his depth and slunk off shamefully.

I suggested to Norman that from what I had seen, the main purpose of the EU was to accrue expenses for the benefit of its employees. Norman nodded in agreement and then frowned as if at an afterthought. He gnawed and gnashed for a while before announcing in a shower of delicious batter debris.

"And money laundering."

"Money laundering!"

"Infrastructure," said Norman – and I'd rather he hadn't because there was something about the "fr" part of the word that resulted in a major eruption of the fish volcano.

"Infrastructure?" I repeated, moving swiftly out of range – just in time as it happened.

"Infrastructure – money laundering," agreed Norman. This is a fairly typical conversation with Norman when eating; he tends to content himself with the main theme, but he did go on to enlighten me.

"Same thing."

"Ah," I said

"Yes," he said, and explained that until the EU was allowed to levy taxes directly, which was its true raison d'être, they had to make do with the meagre billions paid by national governments, and the problem was to find something to do with it that allowed a large part of it to be diverted back to its proper purpose: expenses.

"Which is where you come in, Curtis," said Norman emphasising his point with a heavy wink, a prod in the chest and a lava flow of half-chewed chips.

This was a revelation to me, although it explained why on my regular evenings out with Mr Patel and Mr Jones, the conversation always seemed to turn to the subject of my previous employer's misdemeanours, and, lubricated with local brews of escalating alcohol content, I was invariably encouraged to hold forth. They evidently believed that my association with Mr Burger (who they spoke of with a respect that bordered on reverence) made me an expert on the subject. My denials were met with what I can only describe as dubious cynicism. This was confirmed one evening in what I can best describe as a curious incident.

My hosts seemed keen that evening for me to sample a particularly potent local brew, and by mid-evening I was in that semi-religious state that seems to be inspired by Belgian beer. On the way home, we passed through one of the seedier parts of Brussels. We paused at the gaudily lit door of a massage parlour. Mr Patel and Mr Jones virtually manhandled me inside, explaining that an exceptionally good massage could be obtained here.

"And you seem tense tonight, Mr Curtis. Don't you think so, Mr Patel?"

"I do, Mr Jones. It is in fact the first point that struck me at the very beginning of the evening. Mr Curtis, I said to myself, seems tense."

"Ah," said Mr Jones significantly. "It's not just me then. I mean to say…"

At which point the masseuse appeared. At first I thought I was seeing double, which was not a surprise to me, but after shutting each eye in turn, I came to see that there was in fact only one Madame Wong, it was just that there was rather a lot of her, considerably above the average in terms of size for a Chinese – definitely Chinese; you could tell from the long half-closed eyes, orientated perhaps fifteen degrees from the horizontal (the Duke of Edinburgh could learn something from this sentence).

I was duly impressed and struggled to put my admiration into words, but found this unnecessary because I had already been grabbed by Madame Wong and was being led through the door.

"You want massage." You will notice the lack of a question mark after this remark.

The door closed on a debate between Mr Patel and Mr Jones.

"Indeed, good lady – you have evidently recognised at a glance the innate tensions that beset our friend…"

Madame Wong explained, while undoing my trousers, that she was half French and half Chinese. This particular subspecies, as it turned out, evidently produces a particularly uninhibited and rampant sex maniac.

She stuck a lighted cigarette in my mouth; a considerate woman, I was already fond of her.

The massage was what is described in the back of most local papers (just after the arts review in the case of the *Harrow and Pinner Gazette*) as, "intimate." Under some circumstances it might have been a little embarrassing, requiring some soft background music or a gentle humming or whistling. But

Madame Wong was a conversational lady – definitely half French and half Chinese, because she alternated between the two accents and occasionally wandered around a bit in the middle. Geographically, I think I am right in saying that this should have been somewhere in the Balkans, but it sounded remarkably like Canvey Island. I suppose one has to allow for continental drift when considering these matters. But allowing for drift and returning to the matter in hand, if you'll pardon the expression, Madame Wong explained to me that I looked like a financial gentleman. Madame Wong liked financial gentlemen; they made her excited, and she make things "velly nice" for me if she get excited.

"Talk financial things," she encouraged deftly, not so much with her words as with her hands.

I got the message. "I don't suppose you're interested in money laundering at all by any chance – it's a bit of a hobby of mine?" My voice sounded strange to me, several octaves higher than usual and somewhat cracked.

She gave me a look that I can only describe as pure sex: hard, teasing and determined. She breathed in sharply and hissed:

"Money raundeling."

History has produced a few examples of inspired thought: Newton and his apple, Izal and his medicated toilet paper, Garibaldi and his biscuit – and I'm fairly sure that Heisenberg's Uncertainty Principle would have come to nothing if he had been a more confident young man. I'm not entirely sure of the relevance of this last example but I rather like it so I think I'll keep it thank you very much. Now, where was I? It's enough to make you lose your train of thought having people with red felt tips hovering in the background. Ah yes – this was my moment. I'd never known anything like it. Put yourself in a lady's hands and anything can happen: some tinker around with it out of a sense of duty, some lose concentration and start chatting about kittens and shopping and the neighbour being no better than she ought to be, some start giggling – and some know exactly what they are doing but wait until the vital moment before casually introducing into the conversation the fact that the old sofa is last year's model and needs replacing. Madame Wong belonged to this last category. These are the women that rule the human race. They have temples erected to them and are worshipped on a regular basis (twice on Thursdays). I needed to keep Madame Wong interested and off the subject of kittens, neighbours and above all, sofas.

"Money laundering," I said.

Her eyes glinted. "Money raundeling." She appeared to correct me.

"Interesting business…" I started strongly but broke off into a series of high-pitched squeaks. I was completely at her mercy.

"Money raundeling." She slowed her hands to the speed of the Queen Mum waving to the masses at the Cenotaph. I had to keep things going.

"You have to use a special machine you know – to launder the money in."

"Where you get machine?" she asked suspiciously, but raising her pace slightly as if giving me the benefit of the doubt – for now. But there was a steely look in her eye and I knew I would have to do better.

"Oh – specialist outlets," I explained in a high falsetto.

The Queen Mum was now waving at the masses with an enthusiasm that seemed inappropriate for such a sombre occasion. I opened my mouth to speak but she held a finger to my lips (not the Queen Mum, obviously). She lifted the lid of a lacquered box and pressed something inside that made a clicking and a whirring noise. She smiled at me without a trace of embarrassment.

"I switch on tape lecorder."

"Oh," I said. At which point it seemed that the Queen Mum had just spotted some of her very best chums in the crowd and I groaned loudly.

"You were saying?"

My mind worked furiously, Specialist outlets – it needed to be a long list…

"Argos, Bentalls, Currys… I started strongly and made it through to the Ps and Qs. The Ts, Us and Vs were worrying me; let us not even mention the Ws. I reached the Rs.

"Rumbelows."

"Lumberows."

"Rumbelows."

"Lumberows."

What a bit of luck! She liked the sound of this word and started repeating it obsessively. What a marvellous time to discover that your Chinese/French/Caney Island masseuse suffers from obsessive compulsive disorder.

"Lumberows, lumberows, lumberows," she cooed softly and lovingly as if a term of the warmest endearment, while the Queen Mum stripped off her gloves and stage dived off the Cenotaph into the throng.

I will always remember Madame Wong. Every time I pass a shop window selling white goods, I get a sort of tingling in my groin. But on a more serious note, I learnt from Madame Wong that my peers at ECFIN were pumping me for the low-down on money laundering. I was going to add at this point that Madame Wong also pumped me and got nothing out of me, but this would not strictly be true. They were of course wasting their time; I was only part qualified to PE1 (no doubt money laundering occupies a good part of the PE2 syllabus) and Mr Burger who we know had a masters in the subject had only ever passed eight words with me: three were, "good," three were, "morning" and the remaining two were, "you're late." I had the uncomfortable feeling that my appointment to ECFIN was based on presumed knowledge that I didn't have.

Disaster struck when I came to fill in my expenses on my own for the first time. I stared moodily at the forms in front of me and the words just swam around accusingly: subsistence, travel, entertainment… All I could come up with was Norman's fish and chips, a few rounds of beers for Mr Patel and Mr Jones and a bus fare. That was it. I sat for the rest of the day twiddling my thumbs while the swots around me scribbled furiously with their tongues hanging half-way out of their mouths as swots do the world over. You could hear them grunting as the inspiration took them. I hadn't felt like this since my O level French paper had demanded an essay on the Loire Valley. "*C'est une vallée très magnifique*." Need I have said more? Apparently, yes.

Next day I was summoned to Mr Jones' and Mr Patel's office. My expenses claim lay on Mr Jones' desk. Mr Jones glanced at it with disdain and handed it gingerly to Mr Patel. Mr Patel had evidently not seen the detail before (or lack of) and stared at it with an expression of shock and confusion. I had seen such an expression once before – on the face of my baby nephew, Toby. His mum, Auntie Clara, was just giving him his early evening suckle, from the right breast I seem to remember, when Uncle Stan staggered home from an emotional day at the office. They'd asked him to make a speech for a retiring colleague. The problem was that my uncle was also retiring (by nature I mean) and, in an effort to brace him up a bit, some of his workmates had laced his tea heavily with gin. Uncle Stan, a lifetime teetotaller, came home in a rather peculiar state. At the sight of Auntie Clara feeding baby Toby, he had dropped to his knees, padded across the room, and latched himself onto the available bosom, which I am almost sure was the left one. Aunt Clara, being an accommodating 1950s' housewife, "helped him on" complacently. But baby Toby disapproved strongly of horn-rimmed spectacles and sable moustaches at the dinner table and expressed himself with a look of outrage that so many years later

Mr Patel found himself duplicating while inspecting my expenses claim. It's a small world.

As for Mr Jones; well, he had a particular mannerism that expressed his disapproval: he stared past and beyond me, into space. When I say, space, I don't mean the usual point over the horizon a mere three hours by train – I mean deep space. Possibly when considering an expenses claim of, say, five thousand euros, Mr Jones would have contented himself with searching around for remote supernovae just in range of the Hubble Telescope in infra-red, but when confronted with a claim for fish and chips and a bus ticket, Mr Jones was moved to scan those places on the very fringe of the retreating universe that you can only see by locking the most powerful telescopes in the world onto a particular spot in the night sky where they pick up light that has been refracted around a couple of intervening galaxies and several black holes (acting as a secondary telescope, called gravitational lensing if you are interested and didn't know already) from places that are only a few nanoseconds from the creation of the universe. And bear in mind when considering this, that Mr Jones was using only his naked eye; which is not only a remarkable feat of ocular accommodation, but most disconcerting for an intervening object such as myself whose left shoulder appeared to be being used itself as a secondary telescope – so disconcerting in fact that I felt some sort of comment was due.

"Erm, I'm terribly sorry."

Mr Jones shuddered, possibly from the fact that the place he was studying had so far only achieved three nano-degrees Kelvin above Absolute Zero, although, on the other hand, possibly not. He switched focus suddenly from the very beginnings of time to the subordinate in front of him – quite a shock to the suspensory ligaments I should imagine.

"Mr Curtis. Have you ever considered how it is that the Commission attracts the quality of staff you find yourself amongst here at ECFIN?"

This could be a trick question. The obvious answer was that they had surpassed the exacting standards of incompetence, vindictiveness and corruption required for local government and had gone on to better things, but I felt silence would be a wiser response, particularly after my disappointment with the Loire Valley in my French exam. Mr Jones seemed content to answer his own question (ignoring Mr Patel who had his hand up and was bursting to answer).

"Talent and vision, is the answer, Mr Curtis. These men and women are able to cultivate from a desert of meagre expenditure, a fertile field of burgeoning claims. It is only by fulfilling this potential for personal advancement that we can utilise our budgets to the maximum, Mr Curtis. This is the grand task that we have embarked upon..."

Mr Jones was set to continue for some while yet I suspect, but at this point Norman giggled. I don't think for one moment that he was being subversive; it was just a difficult time of day for him – around eleven o'clock – sort of in between mealtimes when his cholesterol levels sank to a dangerous low, leaving him prone to bouts of emotional instability. I was grateful to him though. Mr Jones' and Mr Patel's disapproval were turned on him. Norman beamed at them happily in consequence.

"Consider, Mr Curtis," continued Mr Jones, realising that he was wasting his disapproval on Norman, after having stared past his right shoulder at some point that would take the average space ship several decades with the foot down, to reach, "the achievements of the European Union." Nothing sprang to mind (or is it sprung?) "What we have achieved, Mr Curtis, is a significant increase in bureaucracy and regulation. I admit that we have a way to go yet; there is a persistent culture of thought whereby nation states have their own ideas outside the Commission and end up doing things that are irrelevant. We have made significant advances in taxation. While we cannot yet levy taxes directly, we are now diverting increasing amounts from national budgets. Taxation deflates people, Mr Curtis; it eats away at the wayward and arrogant private sector, bringing more people into the state sector which will in time become our domain. Taxation brings people to heel, and dare I say – I know it is unfashionable at present – it subjugates people."

Mr Patel applauded; he had been bursting to interrupt for some time now.

"Oh bravo! Well put, Mr Jones."

"Thank you, Mr Patel."

"It's just that you put it so well."

"Indeed."

Norman sighed irrelevantly and everyone stared at him. One glance told us that his mind was turned in on some food-related meditation – crisps I would guess; possibly cheese and onion but from the wistful nature of the sigh, I suspected something exotic and entrancing from over the water: cheesy enchilada with sour cream or habanero and guacamole. Who knows? Mr Jones frowned briefly in the direction of Canis Minor before returning his disapproval to me.

"It is a noble venture, Mr Curtis. We have to absorb ever increasing funds. Our annual budget currently stands at sixty billion euros. Can you imagine how hard it is for us to spend that sort of money?"

I would have suggested one of my mum's shopping trips in the West End, but didn't think this would be helpful.

Mr Jones puffed out his chest. "Over the years, Mr Curtis, we have put together a team of people unsurpassed in specialist areas of incompetence, wastefulness and corruption."

I wished now that I had given my first answer. Mr Jones would have been impressed.

"You may wonder why we put so much emphasis on expenses claims?"

I tried to look blank. I think I succeeded.

“It is a vital part of the training. The calibre of person we require can claim for a plane trip instead of two stops on a bus, a week in a five star hotel in Honolulu when he’s been at home with his wife in Luxembourg – and look you straight in the eye and sign without a tremor, with a throwaway remark, such as: ‘I tried to be as economical as possible this month.’ That person, Mr Curtis, is destined for great things. That person will be able to lose a 200 million euro budget for an airport in Bucharest without a cent of it leaving our account. That person will tearfully pledge three hundred million euros for disaster relief in the Gambia and send a single truckload of Austrian wine adulterated with anti-freeze.”

“I see,” I said contritely, and swallowed hard. “You don’t think I’m cut out for it, do you?”

Mr Patel and Mr Jones shook their heads sadly in unison, rather like two nodding dogs in the back window of a car with their heads pivoted in the wrong axis. Mr Jones looked over my left shoulder at a nearby planet with something approaching kindliness.

“I’m sorry, Mr Curtis. I had hopes, but it wasn’t to be; you are not, and never will be, corrupt. I am sorry to have to be so blunt about it, but honesty is best in the long run.”

“Except of course in matters of expenses,” interjected Mr Patel hastily. He also smiled at me sadly.

Mr Jones coughed. “We do not sack people in the Commission, Mr Curtis, except of course in cases of blatant competence or morality.”

“And we see no traces of these in you,” interrupted Mr Patel reassuringly.

“Or of course, whistle-blowing,” added Mr Jones with a frown.

Mr Patel coughed. “You’re not a whistle-blower are you, Mr Curtis?”

"Certainly not," I denied indignantly. One learns certain things at public school.

"No one likes a whistle-blower," said Mr Patel gravely.

"No indeed," agreed Mr Jones, "and thank you for that, Mr Patel."

"My pleasure." Mr Patel looked pleased.

"Very well then," continued Mr Jones, "in which case we have a rather delicate task for you – particularly suited for your, erm, qualities." He studied the nails on one hand carefully (which just goes to prove really what I was saying about Mr Jones' extraordinary ocular accommodation: from the extreme fringes of space one moment to a few inches in front of his nose the next).

"Indeed," agreed Mr Patel, studying his own fingernails also carefully. This is how trends and fashions become established.

"One of the important functions of the EU, Mr Curtis," continued Mr Jones, "is the diversion of funds. You might call it money laundering – we wouldn't; we'd call it the diversion of funds – but you might."

"I see," I said.

"Your previous employer was of some assistance in this matter."

"Ah," I said, and tried not to make it sound too significant. Mr Patel and Mr Jones both looked at me in a disappointed sort of way that told more than words: that it was a great shame that I was not.

"You were not," said Mr Jones bluntly, while studying the nails on his other hand. Mr Patel followed suit. "However, you may yet assist us in this matter. Have you ever heard of a small state by the name of the Latvian Fish Isles?"

I shook my head, and Mr Jones looked mildly gratified, as if he would have been disappointed if I had heard of it.

"You might suppose that this place would be somewhere off the Baltic Coast, but you'd be wrong."

"Ah," I said.

"They are in fact hidden under a staple in the alpine region of Europe."

"Ah," I said again.

"The Latvian Fish Isles," continued Mr Jones, "are a major repository for EU funds being as they are off-shore – for erm tax purposes." Mr Jones now studied the nails of both hands together, as did Mr Patel. "It is merely a technicality of course, seeing as all European maps are positioned so that the lower staple in the alpine regions completely conceals the existence of the LFI – subject of a directive in fact."

"2007/2/EC/GIS4EU/annexe23," said Mr Patel, rather smugly I thought.

"Quite," said Mr Jones inspecting his right-hand thumbnail with some irritation. "A technicality as I say, but it would be best if the public at large were not made aware of the fact that the LFI is, in a manner of speaking, inland, and completely land-locked to boot. The fact is: a rather delicate complication has arisen." Mr Jones looked across at Mr Patel who had opened his mouth to speak, but decided to study the nail of his index finger instead. "They have applied to join the EU."

Cats and pigeons came to mind.

"We'd rather they didn't," said Mr Patel. "It would be – how can I put this best? Inconvenient."

"Fortunately," continued Mr Jones, "they are significantly divided on the issue. Their president – life president I understand, a somewhat under-rated political appointment in my opinion – Mr Alexander Hohensteil-Schwangau, is implacably opposed to the idea, and there the matter should end, but there is a certain Sir Winyard Hall, nominally the leader of the municipal council, but in reality, a pretender to the presidency, and his is the impetus behind the application. It is I'm afraid an all too familiar story: some petty official with delusions of grandeur."

Fortunately, at this point, Mr Jones expressed his disapproval by staring a couple of million light years into space towards the

NGC 752 cluster so that he didn't notice Norman staring at him intently with an ironical grimace. One of the many peculiarities about Norman is that he has absolutely no insight whatsoever into his own character deficiencies but is immensely alert to them in others, and he had just picked up on Mr Jones' last remark as a piece of blatant hypocrisy.

Mr Jones fired up the main engines and returned to planet Earth rapidly. "Which brings us to you, Mr Curtis." I wasn't sure how I felt about this. Mr Jones smiled at me, which added to my unease. "We feel – Mr Patel and myself…"

"Having discussed the matter with the Directorate General for Enlargement," added Mr Patel.

"…That you would make an excellent special commissioner, to visit the LFI and to invite and consider their application to join the Union, and we feel confident, Mr Curtis, that with your particular qualities, and without the need to play too much of an active role, you will dissuade the euro enthusiasts from pursuing their application."

Mr Patel smiled, glanced at his nails and then thrust both hands into his pockets. "We feel, Mr Curtis, that after a short time in your company, you will put them off."

"You will dishearten them, Mr Curtis," Mr Jones was smiling broadly at me now. "You will make them question the benefits of membership. You will make them think themselves best off as they are. And you will not be alone, Mr Curtis."

Norman looked up nervously, alerted too late to the dreadful truth.

"You will take Norman."

CHAPTER 6

…Which is how I found myself in Lichtenstein. Strange place, Lichtenstein, I thought, surveying the inhabitants of a local bar. Norman, sitting next to me, might have been thinking something different, although since he was foraging in a bag of crisps with a picture of a pig and an onion depicted on the front cover, he probably wasn't thinking of much at all.

I downed half a pint of Weissbier in one go – which wasn't a good idea since I took it by surprise, and it responded by releasing an explosive cloud of dissolved carbon dioxide into my ears – and approached the locals. They didn't look encouraging. I know we all have a common ancestor and all that, but most of us feel quietly confident that ours led a fulfilling life mucking around in the Messel Shale Pit near Frankfurt some forty-seven million years ago, before becoming sadly fossilised and leaving the likes of Professor Gingrich of the University of Michigan to muse on whether it was or wasn't a type of lemur and whether it did or did not have a wet nose (hard to tell after all that time I would have thought; I mean surely it would have completely dried out, unless of course… Never mind).

Whereas, in this bar, I suspected the common ancestor not only of being completely unfossilised, but wearing denim and working in the field of marketing – or indeed just a field.

"Excuse me."

They all turned to stare out of a window. I tried French, German, Italian, and Latin (just in case). They winced collectively and turned grudgingly towards me, evidently to get me to stop.

"Can you tell me how to get to the border from here?"

They shook their heads. A cuckoo clock whirred into life and joined in. I don't mean that it actually shook its head – that would be absurd – but it looked uncomfortable and evasive and refused to look me in the eye.

Mr Patel and Mr Jones' words echoed in my ears as we left the bar, "They like to pretend it doesn't exist – you'll just have to use you initiative, Curtis." This was followed by a moment of embarrassment immediately following the word, "initiative." Mr Patel had developed a coughing fit and Mr Jones had stared out of the window towards the Monoceros Constellation and whistled an aria from *Don Giovanni*.

We reached the end of the village and I studied a map while Norman finished his crisps.

"Strange," I said.

"Pork and onion with sage and dill," agreed Norman.

We had come to a clump of signposts. One pointed east along the road we had entered into the village on, and read: "Buchs 29 KM." Another pointed in the opposite direction and read: "Postamt, Bahnhof & Polizei." A third pointed towards a path across a muddy field (the very direction of the staple on my map) and "Norway" was painted crudely in red letters on it. I call that strange.

"That's strange," said Norman. Give Norman long enough… "I'm not mad on Norway, Curtis… They eat a lot of fish."

Norway, I tried to explain to Norman, was a red herring, but Norman looked unconvinced and told me that although Geography wasn't his strong point, he was fairly certain it was a country rather than a herring and he thought that I might have got confused by him mentioning that they eat a lot of fish.

I had to admit to a slight doubt as we headed down a dirt track towards what was evidently a pig farm. But I smelt a rat (amongst other things); I sensed a distinct attempt to discourage the casual visitor, starting modestly with a sign: "Access to pig farm only," then: "No through road" and progressing to unnecessary belligerence (rather like demands from the TV license authority) "Trespassers will be shot." At which point Norman coughed and broke wind simultaneously, resulting in a look of exaggerated innocence from a nearby pig.

"Er – Curtis?" Norman pointed towards a sign sporting a skull and crossbones and a picture of a land-mine. "Are you sure this is the right way? Paaaaarp."

"Oh quite," I said. I led the way, Norman followed. He appeared to be attempting long strides on points – sort of *Swan Lake* meets Pork Farm.

We made our way across a field to what now definitely looked like a border. The smell of pigs seemed to be following us. Norman and I looked at each other accusingly since the pig was out of sight, probably still trying to look innocent – almost certainly wasted on his family and friends. I say "his" because originally, not being too sure on the matter, I wrote: "its" – But this was crossed out in red felt-tip and replaced with "his" along with an explanatory note in the margin: "all men are pigs" which just goes to show that we all make mistakes. "all pigs are men," she meant to say… obviously. Perhaps if she was a little less liberal with the red pen, she wouldn't make these FOOLISH (one of her favourite words) mistakes; but I don't want to rub it in.

There was a final attempt to dissuade us in the form of a radiation hazard warning next to a signpost with "Norway" facing back the way we came. As we crested a hill we saw a wire fence stretching across the horizon, and what looked like a large industrial warehouse directly before us.

Norman nodded knowingly. "I thought as much."

Our path led directly to a door set into the side of the warehouse. The Latvian flag flew above it: red, white and red triband; you know the one. But, in a departure from the norm, this one was emblazoned with "The Latvian Fish Isles" in gold lettering, and had a large fish swimming across it. What sort of fish, I hear you ask? And I'm afraid I can't help you there: a silver one, possibly a sardine; unlikely to be a kipper.

Norman opened the door; he's better at that sort of thing. Inside was in some ways what you would expect to find at a border crossing point: two lanes lit with illuminated signs – "Latvian Fish Isles Passport Holders" and, "Other Aliens." Norman whinged a bit at this but I didn't mind; after all, one of my favourite games as a child was to walk around with a bucket over my head and greet assorted members of my family contemptuously as "earthlings".

A uniformed official looked up at us from a desk. I wasn't sure that the dark glasses were necessary in the artificial light, and his cap had an excessively long peak and an absurd amount of gold braid.

When I said that the customs hall was in some ways what you would expect to find, there were other ways in which it wasn't. A line of uniformed men stood bolt upright against the wall in front of us, each dressed in an antique military uniform, ranging from a French hussar from the Napoleonic Wars to a First World War Russian cavalry officer.

I was about to politely enquire as to the reason for this when I noticed that I was being looked at from over the top of the dark glasses and fixed with a stare that those of you who have led a sheltered life would describe as quizzical, and the rest of us would describe as rampantly homosexual. Norman, being of the former, took a firm grasp of the situation, explaining that we were the official delegation from Brussels. The reply mixed bitchiness and petulance in a single word.

"Passport."

Norman presented both our passports, which were examined by a critical eye. By this I don't mean the sort of fierce laser-like hostility you get on the North Korean border – this was a critical eye that said, "That tie with that shirt!"

Mr Customs Man looked suddenly bored (I rest my case) and waved us impatiently through with a remarkably supple wrist (told you).

Another official approached us with a huge black moustache. Yes, he was wearing one I mean of course (I don't think the red felt-tip was necessary there). He escorted us towards the line of uniformed men who it seemed to me were behaving strangely. They all stood rigidly to attention with their backs against the wall, evidently under strict instruction not to move a muscle. They stared fixedly into space, appearing not to breathe; but the point I'm coming to, with all possible delicacy, is that I use the word "rigidly" in a rather specific way to describe a sort of tent-pole effect in front of their trousers. I was surprised – perhaps not as surprised as I ought to have been, having been a regular at some strange parties in my youth – but it wasn't what one expected from a guard of honour. I studied their faces more closely and recognised the symptoms: the eyes rolling upwards, the pent-up expression, the blown-out cheeks and the scarlet flush around the face and neck.

A cavalier's waxed moustaches began to vibrate. Interestingly, this was not a simple oscillation, but a standing wave pattern with a maximum amplitude just before the ends of the moustache, which caused me to consider the whole matter of resonance and harmonics as applied to facial hair. I became distracted by another vibration at the tip of a nearby French hussar's busby. Fascinating – my study would have to be widened. A low groan escaped from a Russian dragoon, and a magnificent nineteenth century Spanish Grenadier started to sway from side to side. His eyes bulged, his cheeks turned bright red, his legs shook and finally, with an explosion of exhaled breath, he staggered forwards, panting heavily. His comrades broke ranks, their arms around his shoulders, shaking his hands as if to congratulate him or console him – I wasn't sure which. In matters of archaic military protocol, I didn't know if it was an honour or a disgrace to ejaculate into one's trousers. I have since asked a friend who served in the Black Watch and he explained that in the British Army such things were generally frowned upon – except of course in the Household Cavalry.

The customs officer turned at this point and shook his head. "Bless." He gave us a look that was half critical and half indulgent. "They've been waiting for you since yesterday – it's quite a big thing for them," he mouthed, "visitors."

Norman now looked positively bewildered, or perhaps, in the case of Norman, negatively bewildered. I was just trying to decide between the two when a door opened at the far end of the customs hall and two women entered; two rather impressive women, in very different ways. One was tall slender and dark with an athletic graceful body and the sort of classical beauty that used to get up the noses of Helen of Troy's school chums. The other impressed in a different way; she appeared to have been formed by some sort of continental drift: the collision of one immense land mass into another, resulting in an enormous pair of hips and a colossal upheaval in the chest area, although the two were separated by a surprisingly narrow isthmus, giving her something like an hour-glass figure. I say something like, because any such device manufactured to scale would contain enough sand to run for considerably more than an hour. In fact I was just trying to work this out to the nearest century, and wishing that I'd paid more attention to calculus at school, when I became aware that I was being scrutinised by a look of utter contempt delivered across an enormous expanse of bosoms.

This is an important moment if you don't mind me mentioning it, because afterwards, when I look back, I think this was that special moment when I fell in love. And it's no good people making disparaging remarks in red pen, although it is fair to say that at this moment delicate emotion expressed itself in a way that would have required some people to stand to attention in an antique military uniform for several hours. I prayed for her to turn away; I could see myself being consoled and having my hand shaken by a bunch of men in bushy moustaches at any moment now. And as if answering my prayer, she wrinkled her nose in disgust, and turned to Norman.

"You must be the Special Commissioner?"

Norman looked pleased. He attempted to puff out his chest but unfortunately only managed to relax his stomach. As for me, I wasn't offended. This was a regular occurrence. It's not just that Norman has a certain gravitas (which I suspect to be food-related) it is also that I don't have any at all. If gravitas is G, then Norman is G +4 and I am, say, G -5, so that you put the two of us next to each other, you have a differential of 9G, which is an unusually high value for G, impressing all the attractive lady Gs and leading in due course to a family of small Gs. It was more than sufficient to explain the misunderstanding that Norman was at this moment correcting.

In turn the two ladies introduced themselves; the goddess as Maria Shine, secretary to the President of the Latvian Fish Isles; and Helen of Troy as Margaret Naing, secretary to Sir Winyard Hall, the leader of the Latvian Fish Isles Municipal Council.

At which point, completely unmanned by an imperious look of sheer contempt from Ms Shine and the general proximity of such large bosoms, I began to gibber.

"That's an unusual name."

"I'm half Burmese," Ms Naing replied.

"Oh," I said brightly. "We had a cat…" I paused for a moment. I had just started digging a large hole. "Lovely cat – lovely nature." Six foot long by two foot wide is a good size for a hole. "Called Suki." I thought I'd go down about two metres; one should do these things properly. "Lovely coat she had, and very playful." I jumped into the hole. "She lived to nearly sixteen." I started shovelling the earth on top of myself. "They live longer you know – the half-breeds." At which point the whole thing caved in and the headstone fell neatly into place.

I was rescued from my embarrassment by a minor explosion – which turned out to be Norman. He had been working his way through a packet of Bovril and Tomato crisps, with accompanying sound effects – a large detachment of troops marching around a parade ground – and having come to the end of the bag, he blew it up and burst it. He looked pleased with himself. He told me afterwards that he thought everyone looked a bit tense and he felt that this might help take their minds off whatever it was that was troubling them. This was Norman in thoughtful and sensitive mode.

Because everyone persisted in looking so serious, Norman laughed. He didn't mean to be patronising but experience had shown him that people were often slow on the uptake in the appreciation of humour, so he thought he would start the ball rolling. And strangely enough, Ms Shine, who I would have expected to be threatening the delicate equilibrium in my trousers with a hostile glare, was definitely smirking. She had a small delicate beautiful mouth – and just a word here: I like big mouths on girls which is just as well because most of the ones I know have got them – it's just that Ms Shine had a small one; and it was particularly shaped with a downturn at each corner to look both beautiful and disapproving simultaneously, so I was quite surprised to see it smirking.

You will note that I refer to this goddess as Ms, but at this moment, as she raised her hand to cover her smirk, I noticed with a sinking heart (which she with the red pen has crossed out and replaced with something crude – quite erroneously as it happens, so I've changed it back) that her wedding finger was adorned with a plain gold band. There was then a Mr Shine and I wasn't that keen on him. I didn't like his smugness, his sickening indulgent smile and the detestable pity with which he treated the rest of mankind deprived of marital bliss with Mrs Shine. In short, sigh, I hated Mr Shine. His wife should be mine, and he had no right whatsoever to have courted her in the first place. And it's all very well people writing, "Exodus 20 verse 17" in red letters, but as far as I am concerned, Mr Shine's maid-servant is safe, his ox I have no problems with, he has no need for any concerns with regard to his ass – but…

At this point in my consideration of Mr Shine, my feelings towards him thawed suddenly as a devastating truth dawned upon me. This man albeit smug and bald as a coot (I'd decided he was) had courted Mrs Shine in her maiden days; not just courted, but probably wooed, and almost certainly maintained his gaze in her general direction while conversing about this that and the other: it being unusually chilly for this time of year, time for thicker socks perhaps, and hopefully no early shoots will be damaged too severely by the unseasonable frost – that sort of thing. In short, he had chatted her up. I grudgingly high-fived him in my imagination…

"Mr. Curtis."

"Oh, erm, yes – quite." I kicked one shoe against the other, grinned stupidly and offered my hand.

You've probably gathered from this that I'm not at ease with the opposite sex; cruel of you, but fair. And you're probably laughing because you're one of these fellows who slide up to imperious-looking beauties you've never met before in your life, slip an arm around their waist and impress them by reciting Japanese love poetry in between outbreaks of nauseating salsa dancing. I, on the other hand, have always believed in the strength of my personality. As a youth, I would select the victim of my desires, drift past her, lost in thought, turn on an apparent whim, and fix a stare briefly in her direction, but slightly to one side and above her head. My eyes would express a brief quizzical intensity, but then I would pass on and out of her life for ever – so that stung by intrigue and rebuff, she would seek me out on some pretext and challenge me with bitter tears, that only a night of the fiercest passion… I have to stop here because she with the red pen tells me that to proceed would infringe somebody's copyright, which is blatant nonsense. Personally I think she is afraid of raw emotion. I've found this with women before. Anyway, this was only a partial success. The intrigue seemed to work, but only resulted in my being asked on several occasions if I was feeling sick. So, I had to refer to a superior authority: my older brother. Bear in mind that even Sherlock Holmes had to refer to brother Mycroft when confronted with a particularly sticky one. I don't think my brother actually knew any girls but he did have a first class honours in mathematics, so he evidently knew a thing or two. I asked him. He listened to me and looked knowledgeable and sympathetic. He smiled reassuringly. He knew where I was going wrong and he was going to help me; I was, after all, his brother.

Apparently, what I needed was a bicycle, which cheered me up because I already had one, but my brother shook his head condescendingly. It had to be incredibly fast with gearing so high that you could only pedal it while slipstreaming a bus. In this way you would get up to about fifty miles an hour, and, at the critical moment, break out of the slipstream, head down with a stern grimace, and just as you went screaming past the bus-stop, you flicked a switch on the handlebars that operated an extremely loud electric bell in the saddlebag. The snag was that the object of your desires had to be conveniently waiting at the bus stop, which worked for my brother because he had been spent the last two years impressing Fiona Cartwright who took the bus every day. Two years! Surely by now she should have been putty in his hands? But my brother explained that it was a subtle business; it wasn't just the speed, but the bell-tone pitch was critical. It was only a matter of time, he said, and Fiona Cartwright would be his. Quite! I will say no more on the subject.

As for kicking one shoe against the other while grinning foolishly, there is no convincing research to suggest that this is attractive to women but I found myself doing it anyway. Margaret caught my eye and looked away appalled and, as a sort of reaction I suppose, turned to Norman with a smile. I groaned inwardly. Norman's six ex-wives have written a manual on the subject of Norman which contains a code of conduct and, "Never smile at Norman," is written on the first page in block capitals. I would have added, "particularly when he is in between wives." The trouble is that Norman is an optimist. Norman requires no encouragement; on the contrary, Norman requires discouragement, preferably with something sharp and electrified; anything short of this, Norman takes as an invitation to retire into a dark corner and treat the victim to his life story, which takes most of the night and several bottles of something stimulating – red or white. There is an abridged version of Norman's life story which could be covered in less than three minutes, but Norman feels that the major events in his life – his numerous operations for example – are best related against the background of what he had for dinner the preceding night.

And Margaret had smiled at him! Fortunately, at this point Maria began to lead out of the customs hall. Just in time I suspect, because Norman had switched to main beam and had that conversational look about him.

Margaret announced, with what I took to be a certain pride, that we would be taking the train. I hoped that the train station was a few miles away. You see, Maria was walking directly in front of me. The estate agent's brochure might read, "As well as an impressive frontage with a magnificent view over rolling hills, the rear aspect is also sensational and well appointed." It was this rear aspect that was occupying my attention.

I don't know if you've ever watched one of those re-enactment-type documentaries about earthquakes: where everything starts heaving and pitching and yawing… You're probably with me by now. I refer, my sharp-witted readers, to the sheer magnificence and grace of the rear-end movement of a woman of a certain girth and tonnage. Thinking of which, I rather lost myself in a reverie about supertankers manoeuvring in an Atlantic swell…

CHAPTER 7

Due to a superb feat of authorship I returned to consciousness at the very moment that the ocean-going hips in front of me began to change their rhythm. We were approaching a train station and Maria, being one assumed in charge of the docking manoeuvre, began to slow down; wisely I thought, in view of the fact that momentum equals mass times velocity

What appeared to be a modern train waited at a nearby platform. Margaret stood aside with a look that you see on a mother's face after little Timmy has completed a successful trip to the potty – a sort of indulgent pride; and I admit to being impressed. One doesn't expect a country completely concealed under a size 26-6 staple to have its own railway. Not only that, but I noticed that the locomotive was particularly massive, the sort you would expect to find heaving a reluctant front breakfast car into Vancouver while the rear carriages are having a nightcap watching the sun go down over Fort Collins. Surprising then, I thought, to find this monster hitched up to a single first class carriage.

Our arrival appeared to surprise the driver and conductor. First, a red-faced man appeared at the driver's window looking flustered, then disappeared for a moment and reappeared wearing an expression of officialdom under a peaked cap. Moments later, another man appeared looking quizzical and cupping his chin in his hand. The door opened and the first man minced petulantly down the platform towards us waving a green flag from side to side as if swatting a fly. He straightened his uniform, adjusted his cap and gave us an irritated look.

"Tickets?"

Margaret and Maria fixed him with an icy stare. The guard looked even more petulant.

"Suit yourselves."

Once in the carriage, Norman trod heavily on Margaret's foot, causing her to frown at him, which Norman took as an invitation to sit next to her. See what I mean about the Labrador theme to Norm's personality? I sat opposite them and Maria took the seat next to me with a look of distaste.

A heavily accented voice announced: "The train leaving platform fourteen will depart in four minutes. It will be stopping at…"

Another voice interrupted: "Oh for God's sake…"

The first voice continued with a new note of defiance: "Stopping at, The Latvian Fish Isles West, The Latvian Fish Isles West Central, The Latvian Fish Isles Central Valley…"

The announcement continued but I rather stopped listening.

"Platform fourteen?" exclaimed Norman.

Margaret looked out of the window. "The other platforms are out of service."

"But there aren't any other platforms." Norman isn't tactful. Norman tells it how it is. Norman would have been first up with the line, "The Emperor isn't wearing any clothes."

Margaret pursed her lips and said nothing.

The more I saw of this place, the stranger it became. Out of the window, I could see and hear the conductor blowing a whistle pointedly in the direction of the driver's cab. An extended finger was extended obscenely from within. This was followed by the most appalling din of a massive engine starting up.

Margaret looked smug. "The power unit is a DDA40X turbo charged sixteen-cylinder double diesel, developing 6,600 horsepower, with a swept cylinder displacement of 338 litres."

A loudspeaker crackled into life. “Ladies and gentlemen, we are now starting the main compressor.” A background voice added waspishly, “Starting the compressor,” and then in an easily audible hissed whisper, “Don’t you dare make any more of my announcements.”

The revving engine slowed and strained, the lights dimmed; a slow heavy pulse started, first a single stroke followed by a loud hiss of expelled gas, then another, slowly growing into a massive thudding pant.

Margaret looked smug again – actually she was still looking smug from the last time she had looked smug a few moments ago. It takes time for smugness to wear off entirely.

“The compressor is a model SM 7000, with a capacity of 46,000 cubic metres per hour, and a maximum discharge pressure of twenty-five bar.”

Now I was seriously puzzled. Why should the compressor, being merely an ancillary device, sound as though it was running an ice-making machine for the North Pole? Even Norman looked surprised, and, having done so, decided that, what with the effort of it all, not to mention the emotional stress, there was only one possible remedy… a snack. To translate food-related thought into food-related action is one of the few responses Norman has hard-wired into his autonomic system, causing his hand to transfer robotically towards his pocket.

A psychologist let loose on Norman would have a field day; starting with comfort eating derived from childhood insecurities; a mother who clicked her tongue while wiping crumbs from the infant’s face, a father who looked aghast as the young Norman determinedly hammered a square plastic peg into a triangular hole. The problem is that the rules of psychology have been made up for the human race at large – they don’t apply to Norman. Norman just likes food. He has no shame about it. True, the top of his wardrobe is littered with empty packets of jammy dodgers, and his bed is raised into a dome shape due to the sheer volume of

Kentucky Fried Chicken party buckets stuffed under there – but this isn't an attempt at concealment. It's just that the rest of the floor space is taken.

As he sat in front of me now, releasing a pie from its coloured cellophane wrapper depicting a nervous-looking cranberry surrounded by a semicircle of ducks posing mid-quack for the camera, he completely failed to register the look of abject horror on Margaret and Maria's faces. In fact he grinned at them, gnawed into the side of the pie, looked up and announced:

"Damn good pie, this – cranberry and duck."

The silence that greeted this remark was broken by the noise of a fan starting up. Just as I was getting used to the percussion of the diesels and beat of the compressor, the wind section cut in. A howling gale roared out of vents in the floor and ceiling – and it was absolutely freezing.

The loudspeaker crackled back to life and our guard, who I suspected of having those special pink-coloured regions on chromosomes seven eight and ten so recently in the press, announced proudly:

"The air conditioning is now on." He then added defiantly and rather tartly as if to forestall any contradiction: "Now on – yes it is – thank you. And should you have any comments about the quality or composition of any of these announcements, you'll find a suggestion box next to the ticket office on your exit platform. You may feel for example, that SOME announcers are much more informative than OTHERS. Thank you so much."

Norman appeared distracted. He paused in mid delivery of pie to mouth and peered at Margaret curiously.

"It's a bit parky in here, don't you think?"

Margaret gave him a look that went rather nicely with an even icier blast of air. "This is a municipal train. It has the most powerful air conditioning of any in Europe."

"Why should you want the most powerful air conditioning in Europe?" I asked irritably – I was bloody freezing.

"Regulations – all railway carriages in the LFI must be able to maintain a temperature of minus twenty-eight degrees centigrade in an ambient temperature of up to forty-two degrees and to deliver an air-flow of 500 cubic feet per minute."

"Oh." That shut me up. The diesels were now racing, the compressor was pounding like a steam hammer and the fan had wound up to the pitch of a jet engine. Norman's teeth began to chatter, which was helpful because he was nibbling his way around the perimeter of his pie crust like an electric tin-opener, but I suspected that we would all be encased in ice by the time we reached LFI Central East, or wherever our destination lay, and we hadn't even moved yet.

Suddenly the diesels slowed, the compressor thudded to a wheezing halt, and the shriek of the fan subsided. The significance of this escaped me for the moment because I was lost in a reverie on the subject of nipples. You see, the effect of the icy blast had revealed profound physiological differences on the persons of the two ladies. Margaret's blouse displayed two small protrusions in a forward-facing position – a conventional and, in my opinion, a rather uninspiring place for a woman to keep her nipples. Maria on the other hand, in company with sixty-seven percent of other Western European women over the age of thirty-six and with cup sizes in excess of H, wore hers in a more relaxed position. They were also enormous. In the world of heraldry, they would be referred to as: double tressure crest rampant blazon recumbent (I think). This subject is a bit of a study of mine. I don't know if you have ever seen any of these dating advertisements in newspapers: e.g. "Man (67) substantial hair at sides of pate (will comb over if required) owns teeth (plus two spare sets). Fashionable dresser (sports casual, rally jackets etc. etc.) seeks woman 35-45 with GSOH, for evenings in – no dogs." Or even: "Vindictive man-hating Josephine (married twelve dreadful years) seeks Napoleon to take his bone apart." Very odd what people are looking for in life, but I would not cast aspersions. My own ad would have to read: “Ladies with recumbent nipples preferred.”

My thoughts were interrupted by another announcement over the loudspeaker:

“The train arriving at platform fourteen is from…” and we went through all the stations of the Latvian Fish Isles again in reverse. “The train terminates here; all passengers please disembark.”

Our two escorts began rearranging hair and straightening skirts, but showed no surprise at this announcement. It was left to Norman to articulate mild indignation, severely muffled through a mouthful of pie. Strange business, the passage of sound waves: they spread themselves out effortlessly around the Albert Hall and yet allow themselves to be hampered by a mere cranberry and a brace of duck. Anyway, these sound waves struggled through and regrouped themselves in a typically Norman announcement:

“But we haven’t moved.”

Out of the mouths of babes and sucklings… I felt again that impression of a divergence between the two ladies. Maria smirked whereas Margaret appeared irritated.

“I’m sure you will appreciate that this train, even though it has such a powerful engine…”

“A DDA40X turbo-charged sixteen-cylinder double diesel, developing 6,600 horsepower, with a swept cylinder displacement of 338 litres,” I volunteered helpfully.

“Quite.” Her eyes met mine with cold disapproval. “Obviously they cannot power the train as well as the air-conditioning unit, seeing that it is powered by…”

“A model SM 7000, with a capacity of 46,000 cubic metres per hour, and a maximum discharge pressure of twenty-five bar,” I volunteered even more helpfully I thought, although Margaret looked even less impressed.

“Ah,” said Norman.

“You couldn’t sort of… well, maybe a little less air-conditioning in favour of a little more forward motion?” I asked, probably foolishly.

Maria stared out of the window with a sort of faked innocence. Margaret looked rather how I would imagine a nun might if you snapped her garter. You might argue that nuns don’t wear garters but I know they do because I saw this film… It was left to me to fidget a bit and stare at the floor.

“Regulations?” I suggested

Maria now definitely snorted. “Municipal regulations.”

“Oh,” I said.

Norman evidently agreed with me because he said, “Oh” as well. At first I thought, ‘It’s nice to have the backing of your pals at these difficult moments,’ but I then realised that Norman’s, “Oh,” was prompted by the last remnants of his duck and cranberry making a bid for freedom onto the track as we exited the carriage. Quite whether the duck was the architect of this suicidally heroic action or the cranberry, we will probably never know – and, some might add, or care. Personally, I suspect the duck. Ducks, for all their apparent innocence, are natural troublemakers, whereas cranberries…

I was still musing on this matter as we emerged onto the platform. I mean to say, ducks are at least animate, and definitely capable of bravery. I remember once trying to feed a duckling with a piece of bread and its mother completely misunderstood my intentions and… Whereas a cranberry… My thoughts were interrupted by a platform announcement in a very camp voice.

“Ladies and gentlemen. Welcome to Platform Fourteen. L.F.I. trains hope that you enjoyed your journey and we sincerely hope that you will travel with us again.” This was followed by a coarse laugh; not from the announcer, because you could hear him protest in a forced whisper, “Get off, this is my announcement.” He returned to full volume in a voice cracking with emotion. “On behalf of L.F.I. trains, I cannot tell you what it means to us that you chose this train company, this platform, and above all, THIS TRAIN, to travel with. You… just… don't… know… how much this means to us…" At which point the voice burst into sobbing – and we could see the burly, moustached figure of the engine driver consoling the weeping figure of the guard, with an arm around his shoulder.

I shrugged. This was a peculiar place even by my standards. I was now deeply suspicious as to the motives of my superiors in sending me on this assignment. I could imagine them now, sharing an incredibly expensive bottle of Chateaux Neuf de something or other and lapsing into hysterical laughter in a haze of Cuban cigar smoke at the thought of yours truly on this mission. I sighed and reminded myself that in spite of all this there were certain compensations: I was five or six steps behind Maria, and it was having a profound effect on me. Rather than describing this in detail (she with the red pen has told me in no uncertain terms that she would rather I didn't), it will suffice to tell you that I found walking difficult. I had to stoop forwards and keep my legs straight. This made me nervous because women aren't stupid. Poor Douglas Bader was attacked several times in the street by women with rolled up newspapers, and I bet you anything you like that had these women been apprehended and searched they would have been found laden with red marker pens.

It wasn't just the magnificent oscillations at work: Maria's legs were shapely. They started out from decidedly dainty feet and ankles, having early expectations of tripping around on points in a Darcey Bussell-type fashion, but as they rose upwards, they soon had to take life more seriously in view of the sheer amount of woman up above. By the kneecaps, they were sturdy and by the time they disappeared into the skirt hem… I have to stop somewhere. My point is that they were shapely and muscular legs. There was a flounce to her walk and a significant percussion with every step. Each impact created an aftershock in her nether regions which interacted with the swing of her hips to produce this peculiar, almost rotational rippling of her backside. Walking was becoming increasingly difficult.

When starting out from the railway station, I had observed that we were on a broad open boulevard that led along the bottom of a deep mountain valley. It was a picturesque scene, with a bubbling mountain stream on one side and the railway line on the other. A small town nestled into the valley some mile or so along the boulevard.

Since leaving the station, not a single vehicle had passed, not even a bicycle. When questioned on this, Margaret explained that all vehicular traffic had been banned under municipal health and safety regulations. But, happening to turn around, I noticed a huge stretched limousine following some distance behind us at walking pace. Two pennants on the wings sported what appeared to be heraldic shields. The occupants were hidden behind blackened glass. I caught up with Margaret and Maria and pointed it out to them. Maria pursed her lips, which appeared to irritate Margaret, and she explained frostily:

"Municipal vehicles are of course permitted."

I stared at the car disapprovingly. It seemed decidedly sinister to me. I remembered Mr Jones' comments and wondered if behind the glass lurked Sir Winyard Hall.

At this moment... You might wish to pay attention here. You might even think that there is some sort of typographical error, but I can assure you that she with the red pen won't allow any of that sort of nonsense. I'm just trying to prepare you for the unexpected. At this moment then, appearing as a speck on the horizon, but bearing down on us fast with a sort of popping and buzzing noise was what appeared to be... a motorised wheelie-bin (and don't try to pretend you'd guessed); a red one with slightly larger than usual wheels and a chrome pipe that rose up to what I can only describe as an ostentatious exhaust stack, rather like an American truck. This was the giveaway: wheelie-bins vary in size and colour but they don't usually have exhaust pipes – or large stick-on black moustaches glued to the front for that matter. This one did. As it popped past at some twenty miles an hour, rocking dangerously, I saw a hand holding the lid open a fraction, and the glint of a pair of eyes staring at us. Strangely, even in that brief glimpse, it struck me that the eyes looked anxious.

And as if this wasn't bizarre enough, and I think you'll agree with me… I'll stop there; two months in the employ of Mr Patel and Mr Jones take their toll I'm afraid. Bizarre is quite sufficient to describe a motorised wheelie-bin with a chrome exhaust pipe, sporting large black moustaches – but even stranger was that as it disappeared into the distance, I definitely saw Maria, briefly and surreptitiously, wave at it. I fully understood why Alice, at a similar moment (when high as a kite on mind-bending recreational drugs) had coined the phrase: "curiouser and curiouser."

"Someone you know?" I asked innocently.

Maria shrugged non-committally.

I had to admire the girl. To manage to look non-committal when you've just been caught waving at a speeding wheelie-bin sporting a bushy black moustache, is something of an achievement.

We passed what appeared to be the main centre of the LFI: shops, banks, hotels etc. all spread on each side of the main road with side roads leading up to scattered chalets, sprawling picturesquely in the foothills. We passed right through until there was only one chalet left in front of us, larger than the others but of the same simple wooden construction; our destination I presumed.

CHAPTER 8

I noticed as we drew near that the road in front of the building was littered with a plethora of signposts bearing rather peculiar and forbidding notices: 'No Smoking'. 'Use your bath water twice'. 'Keep away from the railings'. 'Do not exceed the prescribed dose and always complete the course'. 'Walk, don't run'. 'Fish oil must be taken twice daily'. And as if in protest at the authoritarian tone of these signs, someone had disfigured each one with some explicit graffiti which I was going to repeat to you, but found that a certain person (who knows who she is) has herself performed the most outrageous graffiti on my manuscript with a red pen.

A clue to the identity of the artist was found neatly painted in the top right hand corner of each sign; not quite the sign of Zorro but equally distinctive: a single large black moustache. I say single, but there was one exception. The largest sign of all, at the entrance to the drive, read: "No Cats" in very large letters – and this was particularly savagely defaced with moustaches. I counted fourteen in total, and they were considerably bushier than the other moustaches.

We proceeded up the drive. The door was opened by a maid who curtsied politely but rather spoilt the moment by giggling and blowing a bubble with some gum, which earned her a frosty glance from Margaret, but it seemed to me that Maria smirked. I can't keep writing curiouser and curiouser, so I will content myself with… odd.

"This is the President's private residence," announced Maria. "You are to stay as his guests." The subtext to this remark was provided by a look at Margaret that only just stopped short of a tongue being stuck out and two raised fingers – to which Margaret replied stiffly:

"And tomorrow you will meet the Leader of the Municipal Council."

Maria led us into a spacious room. A different maid served us drinks, but she too seemed to have some difficulty maintaining any semblance of servility. She twirled one leg around another, one arm akimbo while holding a cigarette in her other hand, inhaled deeply, then blew the smoke into my face before elegantly flicking her ash onto the carpet.

Maria perched herself on a chair at some distance from me and announced in a frigid tone.

"The President will be with us shortly."

At this moment I heard a sound that probably only half an hour ago I would have struggled to place, but could now name with some certainty, as an approaching motorised wheelie-bin, and if those of you trained as barristers start making tricky remarks such as, "So you actually saw this alleged motorised bin did you?" I will reply, "No, you smarmy little stuck-up git, I did not; but I heard the same distinctive noise as a few minutes ago, which was then caused by a motorised wheelie-bin and even though you may have scraped a grade A French O level due to a sickening familiarity with the Loire Valley, at least I know the sound of a motorised wheelie-bin when I hear one, you smug hypocrite. And besides, before you open your fatuous gob again, just after the motor stopped I heard the noise of a wheelie-bin lid closing – not a window or a car door, definitely a wheelie-bin – you, bumptious, overfed, self-righteous parasite, whose only interest in the law is that it entitles you to line your own pocket."

I'm not mad on barristers.

Moments later, the door flew open and a figure appeared. To save further unpleasantness, please accept my word for it that this was both the President and recent occupant of a wheelie-bin. These two qualities would seem to require their possessor to be both dynamic and eccentric. The figure before us was neither of these things – but his trousers were. I have seen a few pairs of dynamic trousers in my time, and I have actually owned some fairly eccentric ones, but never in my life have I seen a pair of trousers being quite so dynamic and eccentric at the same time. They looked a bit like jodhpurs; they were that sort of cream colour with a high fit around the waist but sleek around the flanks. They were the sort of trouser who out of hours would be found drinking with a horsewhip and a pair of tight leather boots. So what? I hear you say. What's the big deal about a pair of cream jodhpurs? Well I'll tell you: these things flared out below the waist… I haven't finished if you don't mind… to approximately four foot in diameter! This is approximately 12.68 feet in circumference, providing you are happy not to take Pi to more than five decimal places – and I think you should be.

There is no doubt in my mind that this effect was not from the cut of the trouser or the physiology of the wearer. It must be that there was some sort of framework within the trouser. While ruminating on the nature of such an apparatus, I became aware of an intense stare in my direction, and met my host's gaze with an embarrassed smile, knowing that in polite society it isn't the done thing to stare too intently at a chap's trousers. But staring at his face turned out to be equally fraught with problems. It was the massive black bristling moustaches that were the problem. Doubtless they were magnificent, but they could not be real; they were pure comedy moustaches in the best music-hall tradition, and they were beginning to work their spell on me. I felt the laughter welling up inside just as it always does at inappropriate moments; funerals are the worst, closely followed by marriages, final payment demands and any film with Brad Pitt in it. I desperately averted my gaze, and, as luck would have it, was saved by a teapot. You may require some explanation for this. You see, while I had been fighting back laughter and trying to think of desperately unfunny things such as Billy Connolly, Ricky Gervais or Lenny Henry laughing at their own jokes, the President appeared suddenly uneasy. His attention had been drawn to a white china tea-service on a side table. He was transfixed, his expression changed to one of fearfulness. He beckoned to Maria and she hurried over to him.

"The teapot – it's staring at me again."

The President had a point; the teapot was undoubtedly looking at him. It was one of those teapots with a particularly long spout which was pointing at him in a supercilious fashion, and evidently he objected. Most people wouldn't, most people would not suspect a teapot of having any sort of intent other than the usual; i.e. containing tea and perhaps employment of some useful thermal properties to avoid unnecessarily steep temperature gradients. Further conflict was avoided by Maria rotating the offending spout towards the wall. We all relaxed, except for Norman who hadn't tensed up in the first place. The President relaxed; the President's trousers relaxed. The President introduced himself as, "The President," which we sort of knew by now, and gave myself and Norman dynamic handshakes which caused his moustaches and trouser apparatus to oscillate, although at considerably different amplitudes.

We duly introduced ourselves and the President responded by telling us that we could call him Alex. We followed him into what looked like a dining hall. One wall was lined with portraits which Alex led us along, pointing out each proudly:

"Napoleon, Genghis Khan, Ivan the Terrible, Henry the Navigator…" I'll interrupt the President's narrative at this point to tell you a little about some of the more obscure members of the line-up – starting with King Ludwig of Bavaria: always nice to his mum but nutty as a fruitcake, hobbies included saluting trees and drowning in Lake Starnberg. Alexander Stambolüski: liked to lead Bulgarian peasant uprisings and enthusiastic about keeping out of the way of Tsar Boris III; fairly violent but not in the same league as Pedro the Cruel. Oh well, since you ask… Pedro the Cruel: King of Castile 1350-1369; shy in battle but courageous in having his wife and the Archbishop of Santiago murdered. Liked cooking; particularly his enemies.

The theme to this gallery, I'm sure you've guessed, was that the portraits were all of cruel and bloody dictators, excepting Henry the Navigator whose main purpose, Alex explained, was to cover a damp patch in the wall, and possibly Kim Jong-Il, who was a sort of hero to all golfers in his own right, having achieved seven successive holes-in-one at the Pyongyang Golf Club (members only).

A secondary theme was that all the subjects sported bushy black moustaches, and although history was one of the subjects that old Anstruther was particularly rude about in my school report, even I suspected that these had been painted on rather than being naturally occurring.

The President coughed. "The world's great men, Mr Curtis."

I wasn't too sure about this: great in the sense of moustaches or mass murder?

Alex finally reached the end of the line where I was startled to see his own portrait peering out between Stalin and Darius the Great, all sporting massive moustaches of course. Alex pointed a presidential finger at his own portrait. He looked at me shyly but swallowed uncertainly rather than speaking. He attempted to recover himself with an arrogant stare, but the presidential finger quivered slightly and the arrogance of the stare was rendered unconvincing by an underlying diffidence. The man was hamming it up. This was Pedro the Cruel on a charity benefit; this was Henry the Navigator all at sea. There was a moment's awkward silence. I like to think that I know how to behave in a difficult situation; my nervous and hysterical laugh was designed to put the President at ease.

At this moment, the most beautiful cat wandered towards us. It was a chocolate-point Siamese, definitely a female; you could tell by the Portsmouth-dock-girl swagger – not that I have any personal experience of Portsmouth dock-girls you understand. Well, not recently anyway; back in 1994… Actually I'm not sure that she was a girl in a strict anatomical sense, but it is not a matter I care to dwell upon.

Anyway, this magnificent creature ambled with an apparent lack of direction that was obviously faked, directly towards our host, and proceeded to rub herself against the presidential trousers. Alex turned to me with an intense stare. "This cat has failed me on several levels."

Cats, being perverse creatures, enjoy criticism. I have an uncle the same; the ruder people are to him, the more tickled and delighted he becomes. The cat's tickledness and delight emitted as a loud purr and she did that thing that cats do: rubbed her neck lower and lower down his trousers until she fell over onto her back, all four paws in the air. She looked at us for the first time with mild surprise, and covered her embarrassment by patting suddenly at the nearest presidential trouser leg. The President glared at her and wagged an admonishing finger.

The cat looked up at the President with a look that I can only describe as pure love, blinking her eyes as she did so. Incidentally, all similarity with Portsmouth dock-girls ends here. They just yawn and ask if you're done yet, although maybe if they were one hundred percent female, the whole disgraceful business wouldn't take so long – or so I would imagine.

The President faltered and turned rapidly on his heel to lead away, stooping quickly to tickle the cat under the chin, glancing at us surreptitiously, evidently anxious in case we had noticed – and at that moment I decided that I liked this man. The cat looked surprised. Perhaps I was hasty in ending the similarity with

Portsmouth dock-girls. I imagine a certain "Daisy" would also have been surprised if chucked unexpectedly under the chin.

Our host led into a large and luxurious sitting room. A window ran the full width of the room, giving a panoramic view of the snow-capped mountains. A central floor space was decorated with black and white marble tiles. Long sofas strewn with cushions lined the walls; all very sixties.

A waitress served us drinks. Margaret and Maria sat apart from us on a sofa, sitting stiffly but close together. Their apparent mutual disapproval didn't fit with their physical closeness. I had the strange feeling that if we'd left them alone together they'd suddenly start undressing each other, but then I have watched a lot of films on this subject and my experience of women is somewhat coloured by my time with Donna, who was not above commandeering some poor passing innocent at one of her parties and wrestling her to the floor.

At this point I noticed that our host was fidgeting. Actually so was Norman, but I knew the reason for this and it was food related. His hand hovered over his pocket but even Norman's underdeveloped sensibilities were alert to the possibility that to dive in right now might not be the done thing, so he fidgeted to express the agitation of the battle of manners that were going on in his head. Norman's heavily overpaid silk would be striking that pose of overconfident TV barristers, with the thumbs lodged complacently in the lapels. "I don't think we need trouble our learned friends with the false niceties of social protocol. The facts are quite simple and speak for themselves. My client is not only in considerable need of sustenance, but… and I would impress upon you, ladies and gentlemen of the jury, the need to commit this point to memory, for my learned adversary will certainly seek to divert your attention from it… My client has in his pocket, a bag of crisps – sour cream with spring onion and chives, if I am not mistaken, which I would like to bring before the Court as Exhibit A…"

The pertinence of this point caused Norman to twitch and dive his hand into his pocket, and I returned my attention to our host who was now staring intently at me. I should mention at this point – I'm such a crap storyteller; no, no, you're too kind – that we'd been served drinks: some sort of spirit with a strong pear theme but an even stronger ethyl alcohol theme. Our host blinked nervously and gulped down a large measure of this stuff, the strength of which would make an ancient Belgian bee nervous. His eyes were watering now which undermined the effect of the intense stare. I understood; I was myself shy by nature and I recognised the symptoms. I looked away to make things easier for him.

"Mr Curtis."

"Yes," I said helpfully.

"I know why you are here. I want you to know," he shook his fist half-heartedly, "that as long as I am president, the L.F.I. will never belong to the European Union." I think I must have looked slightly startled because he added hastily, "nothing personal you understand. It's just that I am the supreme power – a dictator if you will… Hobnob?" He thrust a plate of biscuits unexpectedly towards me.

I took one absent-mindedly. "Oh thanks. You don't approve of the application then?"

"No." He gulped down another glass and tears now streamed down his face.

I saw from the corner of my eye that Maria smirked and Margaret pursed her lips. It was a slightly strained moment, and the cat, who had re-entered the room, sensed the awkwardness of the situation and sought to relieve it by rolling on her back and patting at the air with all four paws. We all stared at her. Even by a cat's standards she was making an arse of herself. Our host looked pained.

"Do you play chess, Mr Curtis?"

I found myself nodding stupidly, surprised by this sudden turn in the conversation. Norman's hand moved to his pocket. If Clint Eastwood and Lee Van Cleef had been in the room, things might have gone badly for him. It was the sort of slick movement that a Romero or a Pedro (not necessarily known as "The Cruel," but very likely that way inclined by nature) would have made if up to no good. But Norman was just going for his crisps. The battle for the jury's sympathy had been won by an eloquent summing up.

"Ladies and gentlemen of the jury, you see before you a man accused – but of what? Of a hearty appetite? Of a passion that those with cold hearts, and I am looking at the prosecuting counsel as I say this, will never understand? The love of a bag of potato crisps whose very existence is fashioned for the sole purpose of that ultimate consummation; to have its cellophane bag slowly and delicately teased open… Ladies and gentlemen, if my client is guilty, then aren't we all indeed, in a very real sense, also guilty?" A loud clapping seemed to emanate from the general direction of Norman, which you might think strange, but stranger still was the sight of thirty-two naked women entering the room carrying soup plates, along with cigarettes, bottles of wine and handbags. I was surprised; Norman was surprised, even the cat looked surprised. I should mention that sixteen of the soup plates were black and sixteen were white. They positioned themselves on the floor which I now understood, as indeed I expect you do, formed an oversized chessboard. They knelt on the plates and produced paper headgear that defined the different pieces. There was a lot of fussing, giggling and twittering, even a little pinching and sporadic hair pulling; girls will be girls. With the distraction of so many bosoms and bottoms, reminding me of one of Donna's parties, it was going to be hard to concentrate.

If you've ever read Maxim Gorky's gripping autobiographical trilogy (and if you have, I would like to offer my severe condolences to you and your next of kin) you may remember the bit where Maxim and his student chums compete to push prostitutes kneeling on dinner plates as far as they can across a highly polished floor. This was a promising start for Maxim; I liked Maxim at this point; Maxim in the early days had a sense of humour; but this was only Book One, in Book Two, Maxim became serious, in Book Three, self-righteous, and by the end of it all I had lost all patience with him.

At any time after page 429, (which I feel was the critical point at which Maxim became decidedly prissy) Maxim would have thoroughly disapproved of this game of chess. He might have tolerated the opening moves; they may have even reminded him of his happy careless student days prior to page 428, but he wouldn't have approved of the giggling, the incessant chatter and the bottom wriggling which featured increasingly as the game progressed.

The girls were drinking heavily and high spirits turned to unruliness. Some of the pieces started questioning their moves, which is unusual in a chess game. I asked the Black Queen's Bishop politely if she would move to the D5 position. She gave me what I can only describe as a petulant look and said rather coarsely, "Oh for fuck's sake." I think she was cross because she was in the middle of a conversation with a white pawn – something about handbags. And of course as is often the way, others feel the need to show solidarity; a black knight's pawn told me that it was a crap move anyway, and the Black Queen stuck her tongue out at me.

I looked at my host to see how he was taking this. Several pieces had been even ruder to him and in the normal way national leaders are treated with a certain amount of respect, particularly dictators. Take A. Stambolüski for example: I bet he didn't allow for any insubordination amongst his peasants, even if they had dug potatoes together in their youth. As for Pedro the Cruel, "Yes, sir, no sir, oh absolutely, I couldn't agree with you more, sir – your wisdom is absolute and boundless; soap his testicles you think? Most commendable, most heartless, and dare I say, sir – most cruel. Thank you, sir." Henry the Navigator? Well, I expect there were some liberties taken. He was, after all, at the end of the day, only a navigator.

As for the President, he appeared not to notice. "Hmm," I thought to myself wisely: this is what people do when they have lost all authority. And my point was proved within seconds; the President made an "en passant" move, causing me to lose a pawn with brown hair, small breasts and cellulite at the top of her thighs.

The words "en passant" uttered by the President of the Latvian Fish Isles were greeted by a chorus of whistles and catcalls. The White Queen gyrated her hips, wobbled her breasts and made what I can only describe as a crude gesture. I realise that our own monarch has had to endure some fairly explicit tribal dances when visiting some of the remoter South Pacific islands, but I doubt if she has been witness to another queen lying on her back and opening her legs while gesticulating rudely with her fingers. To make matters worse, the triumphant black pawn who had displaced mine (the one with the brown hair, small breasts and cellulite at the top of her thighs. A note in red pen suggested at this point that I stopped banging on about cellulite. Personally, I think she has just drawn attention to the matter quite unnecessarily because there's nothing wrong with a bit of cellulite; I think it's womanly). Where were we? Oh yes – the Black Pawn was being triumphant, calling out, "En fucking passant," and as an afterthought, "bitch!"

The girl with the brown hair, small breasts etc. etc. wasn't taking this from a girl with blonde hair, larger breasts and no cellulite whatsoever (this was perhaps the root of the grievance; in my experience some women seem a bit touchy on the subject) and took the matter up with her by grabbing a handful of blonde hair. Other players voiced their opinions uninhibitedly with the exception of the Black King's Pawn and the White King's Knight who were snogging each other with what might be described as gay abandon.

Maria and Margaret exchanged glances. It was the first time I had seen anything like harmony between them, but there was a certain mutual weariness that suggested to the keenly observant (not sure why this has been crossed out with red felt tip – I've put it back in again), a subtext to this exchange along the lines of, "Here we go again."

Meanwhile our host was smiling. Someone somewhere must have given him bad advice. There is no record of Pedro the Cruel ever having smiled, even when his mummy made silly faces into his cradle. Henry the Navigator was too busy scanning the horizon with a look of keen anxiety to have even considered smiling. A. Stambolüski not only never smiled himself but took bloody revenge on anyone else who did. Stalin smiled it is true; but only in a wolf-like way when signing Kulaks' death warrants.

I shook my head; Norman shook his head; I wondered for a bizarre moment if Norman's thought processes had been following mine, there's a first time for everything – but, following Norman's gaze, I saw that he was occupied with the matter of the Black King's Pawn and the White King's Knight snogging each other. Things had progressed since I had last looked to some fairly serious heavy petting – number eight on the scale I had learnt at school, number two on the scale for lesbians that Donna had taught me. The cat looked dubious; she was busy with one leg in the air licking her privates and paused to survey the two young ladies uncertainly. While imitation was doubtless the sincerest form of flattery, there was always the possibility that these two were taking the piss – and cats have their dignity you know.

I digress and I sense your surprise. My point was, and indeed still is, that our host was beaming complacently at the scene of chaos before him. It was only when he started touching his fingertips together that I understood: he was pleased with his move. I shook my head. Whatever advantage he may have won was being rapidly eroded by a generalised lack of discipline across the board (and there is no reason to write, "ha ha" in red pen just here). It should be in the rules if it isn't already that chess pieces are not allowed to dance with each other (particularly with pieces of the opposing side) fight, smoke, snog, drink or generally muck about. In fact while planning my next move, I had a sudden pang of compassion for Lord Montgomery of Alamein. History varies in its opinions of Monty. His detractors complain that he was obsessed with fighting tidy battles with overwhelming superiority and in doing so missed out on certain opportunities such as closing the Falaise Gap. That's as maybe but it's all very well for these smug types in armchairs and velvet smoking jackets to rabbit on with a large caption under their chair saying "A Historian." They miss the point. A chap can't plan anything properly when the enemy won't keep damned still!

My opponent seemed to sense that I was struggling and stroked first his trousers and then his moustache significantly – a fairly obvious imitation of Stalin at the time of sending D. G. Egorov to his death on the Western Front (his western front that is; eastern if you were a German of course; not that I'm suggesting that you are, and even if I was: why not? It's nothing to be ashamed of in this day and age).

"You concede, Mr Curtis?"

I thought I might; I thought it might please our host, who at this moment was sporting the look of a cartoon villain, sniggering expectantly at the demise of DangerMouse or Muttley or Jerry. He also looked anxious. I caught Maria's eye. She nodded ever so slightly. I found this hint of complicity exciting and was delighted to oblige.

"I think you've got me."

Alex raised a fist and hugged an elbow in a charade of triumphalism in which the keenly observant (me that is – just thought I'd mention it in case you'd forgotten) might have noticed a hint of relief.

"You will take dinner with me."

Norman and I nodded politely. Norman always nods when you mention food – and also salivates and breaks out a fine array of sweat on his face. Our host frowned.

"It was not so much of a question as an order, if you will."

"Oh quite," I said, and now there was no doubting the look of complicity in Maria's eye as it met mine. Awkward bit of prose that; I mean eyes don't meet in the strictly social sense; it's more of an exchange of expression, requiring reflected light from Eye A to be received by Retina B and vice versa, and each eye needs to be focused... ("Unlike this sentence," is written in red pen. The woman has a certain drollness that some might mistake for humour).

To return to Maria's eye, then, it met with mine and the substance of the exchange was, "This man is a truly crap dictator." Students of Mussolini may mutter that their man had his off days, but it won't wash. Our host had entirely forgotten himself and stepped politely aside for us to usher us into the room. Ivan the Terrible would have marched in imperiously; Kim Jong Il would have insisted on the doors being fired through with machine guns before entering (he had a lot of enemies and the problem was that South Koreans looked remarkably similar to North Koreans with their clothes on and he considered it best to annihilate everyone just to be on the safe side). Even Henry the Navigator would have swept all aside as he strode forward with a roving eye. And as for A. Stambolüski, he liked to impale a few servants on pitchforks when entering a room. This is because he was a peasant leader and a peasant leader always has to impress on lesser peasants that he's more of a peasant than they could ever hope to be, otherwise they are capable of getting above themselves, or possibly below themselves, depending on how you look at it.

I won't bore you (no need for a red exclamation mark here) with a detailed description of the dining room. Your modern reader likes things to move along, as my researcher frequently informs me with a sigh and a yawn; she needs more sleep that girl. Suffice to say that it had a large table and we all sat around it. Wine was bought in by naked girls, chess pieces in a former life, and their various personalities persisted. The Black Knight's Pawn giggled every time she poured a glass of wine. The White Queen's Castle didn't even get this far; she swigged from a bottle, burped, squealed with laughter and retreated from the room in a dead straight line. The White King's Bishop arrived with a great heap of steaming plates, banged them all onto the table, burst into tears and exited the room diagonally.

Norman whipped the lid off his plate and surveyed the contents suspiciously.

"*Wienerschnitzel,*" announced Maria with a certain pride.

Norman licked his lips.

Margaret pursed hers.

Alex coughed apologetically; the sort of cough that announces speech and we all turned to look at him. He leaned forward and stared at me intensely.

"I should explain, Mr Curtis, that I am quite mad."

"Oh," I said. I wasn't sure what else to say; some sort of regret perhaps, but the look on his face suggested he would have preferred congratulations.

Norman paused in the act of hunter-gathering in the bread-crumbed regions at the edge of his *wienerschnitzel.* Something was going on in his head; possibly a fire drill but more likely an emergency debate called by conspiracy theorists: these bizarre events were proof that dark forces were at work whose real intent was to threaten the food supply – possibly a fifth column; Russians were suspected but one should not discount Japanese extremists.

Our host coughed again, "Criminally insane, Mr Curtis – sorry; me, not you. I have major psychoses: schizophrenia, manic depression and," he puffed out his chest, "I have nineteen of the twenty-two determining features of psychopathy." He thumped the table unconvincingly. "The last three elude me for now, but it is only a matter of time."

I saw his game of course. He'd already let on that the L.F.I. would only join the European Union over his dead body. He didn't know that this was fine by me. I'd get to keep my flat in Brussels, and maybe Mr Jones and Mr Patel would see their way to fixing me up with another night with Madame Wong as a token of their appreciation; but still, I had to go through the motions.

"I'm afraid that that in itself doesn't disqualify you for membership of the European Union. Most heads of state within the EU are criminals and several, insane."

Alex nodded gravely, at which point the cat which had been sitting secretly on his lap, climbed up his shoulder, settled on his head and leant over to pat his moustache. Alex pretended not to notice. I admired his equanimity, but inwardly grieved for him; he was a truly crap dictator. Presumably he had acquired this cat as a sort of fashion accessory; seeing himself as a Bond villain, stroking the creature on his lap while it stared out at the world malevolently through coal-black eyes, all the time restraining itself from purring. The trouble is that there are cats and there are cats. The sort that get their paw-print on a Cubby Broccoli contract have years of "The Method" behind them. They go round muttering to themselves, "You looking at me?" They cut their teeth as kittens on spitting and hissing and hooking goldfish out of bowls. Alex had been sold a pup. The cat now settling itself for a long nap on his head was the wrong kind of cat; it was the sort of cat that in a tense scene would suddenly dart off to chase a spider. It was capricious and lacked single-mindedness. You didn't know what it would do next. In fact I think Alex was wondering the same thing owing to the suspicious silence on the top of his head. He closed one eye and looked upwards with the other, which I must admit added a certain something to his claim to be barking hat-stand. It did look decidedly odd. He opened his other eye and looked at me with it, while the other was still engaged surveying the top of his head. I nodded in approval; he was getting better.

"I intend to read to you from my book, Mr Curtis. I wrote it myself and have decreed it to be the sacred writings of the Latvian Fish Isles."

Margaret and Maria simultaneously sank their head in their hands.

"It is called the Book of Fish." He turned his head slowly and imperiously towards Maria. "Assemble the staff."

The staff was duly assembled, although when I say staff, I actually mean thirty-two naked girls in various states of boisterous inebriation. Alex looked at them severely.

"I wish to address you."

I don't quite know why they found this so hilarious but evidently they did, judging from the increase in giggling. I don't think there is as yet a recognised scale for giggling, but if there were, it intensified from a background level of, say, 3.7 to somewhere around 6.9. This had the effect of waking Norman from some food-related internal reverie. He looked startled. I followed his gaze to two of the girls previously reported to my readership for indulging in a kind of friendship that I know the Pope disapproves of, but has a healthy following in boarding school dormitories, pony clubs, ladies' prisons, Girl Guide associations and, strangely enough, the Catholic Church. They weren't shy these girls; they sat next to each other, which was essential for what they were doing to each other.

Norman stared. Norman has a theory about lesbians and I expect you'd like to hear it. Norman describes himself as a modern man; he is broad-minded enough to concede that many men are a disappointment to women in matters of, erm, bedroom fulfilment. Norman knows this from a publication found under his third wife's mattress (they slept in separate beds after the honeymoon night) entitled *Skirt Lifters*. For this reason, Norman finds it entirely understandable that women should wish to combine underwear drawers and dispense with the services of men, except of course for moving heavy fridges and removing spiders from the bath. This seems fair enough so far. I see some of my more relaxed lesbian readers nodding warily and unbristling themselves. But you are wise to be wary, ladies, for Norman's theory goes on to assert that this behaviour is a sort of coping strategy (filling in if you like) by women who, however big their hands, are actually latent heterosexuals. And he will add, with a knowing smile, that none of the women he has ever "known" have been lesbians; he omits to add that several of them applied for membership shortly afterwards. The implication being… since you do not have the advantage of witnessing the revolting spectacle of Norman smiling at you in a sexually charged manner as he says this (refer to any of the gargoyles supporting the eves of Ely Cathedral for an illustration)… The implication being then (for those of you with short attention spans) that any lesbian, however dedicated to the cause, would return to frocks and frilly dresses, burn her baggy jeans, and reduce her visible intellect by a half, after a steamy night of passion with Norman.

Lesbians, please do not be offended; Norman has similarly dysfunctional views about the Renaissance, transubstantiation and string theory. Indeed, Norman feels that had he taken up football as a boy, we would as a country only need to rummage in a cupboard once every four years to fish out the World Cup, give it a bit of a polish and put it back again. Perhaps now you understand why Norman's ex-wives formed a club. It started as an informal discussion group, but grew over the years to include ex-girlfriends and "escapees"; girls who had been asked out by Norman in their formative years but had somehow managed not to succumb (the figure is already over two hundred, and there are believed to be as many again who have yet to come forward due to traumatisation). Now they have extended their activities to bring-and-buy, bric-a-brac stalls and lecture tours in the Third World.

Where was I? Oh yes: the President of the Latvian Fish Isles leant over carefully so as not to disturb the cat on his head, and picked up a large blue leather-bound book with a picture of a goldfish on the front. He opened it proudly at a page marked by a tasselled bookmark, which the cat, awoken by the movement, promptly hooked up in a paw and started playing with on our host's head.

Alex coughed modestly and began to read. "The story of the Sardine." A promising start I thought, but you might not want to hear my thoughts on the matter. Here it is then; unabridged and uninterrupted.

"And it came to pass that a family of sardines were assembled in a rock pool and their discussion strayed from its usual course, which tended to dwell on food: the relative merits of plankton found on the ocean floor as opposed to free-floating, and the toxic properties of spirulina-chlorella, to give you just two examples, although there are many more available, because sardines have strong opinions on such things. Their conversation had turned to theology. The youngest sardine, who I shall call Jim, although that is not his real name, had been misbehaving; a not uncommon problem amongst young sardines. He had been swimming in an ostentatious manner and leaving some of the less appetising, although more nutritious, plankton on the side of his plate.

Sardines are predominantly Hindu. There are some Jewish sardines but they tend to hide under stones having evolved a flashy silver stripe on their underbelly that brings them unwelcome attention from predators. Muslim and Christian sardines are a rarity due to dietary restrictions and there are a few Catholic sardines (Saturdays to Thursdays only). Hindu sardines believe in reincarnation, which was a source of great anxiety to Jim's mum because Jim's behaviour taken overall led to a general concern that Jim would return to the pool not only as a lesser species, as if that wasn't worry enough, but quite possibly a lower genus. And Jim's mum, not being the sort of girl to keep her mouth shut (particularly when swimming in a nice ocean current rich in plankton) was pointing out to Jim in no uncertain terms that what he was likely to come back as was not going to be a credit to her reputation within the shoal – and Jim was opening and closing his mouth in a rather uncouth and rebellious manner, suggestive of, "yeah, yeah, yeah," when Jim's dad interceded. This in itself was a surprise because Jim's dad did not spend much time with his family. Rumour had it that he spent most of his time at the far end of the pool, floating upside down, one centimetre from the surface; just to impress the girls, some said.

Jim's dad cleared his throat, resulting in an impressive stream of bubbles, and Jim prepared to listen. Sardines are misogynist as a species and pay far more attention to males than females, mainly due to the superior length of their dorsal fins.

"Jim lad," said Jim's dad, "you must change your ways – my son," he added proudly because he had only 433 other sons. "You want to be a pilchard in the next life, don't you, son?" Jim nodded meekly. Who didn't? Two centimetres extra body length, superior colouring and camouflage, longer pectoral fins, a larger operculum, extra gill slits – and the girls… Jim swallowed and ingested a small piece of seaweed.

"Yes Dad."

Jim's dad flipped a dorsal fin and rolled over one hundred and eighty degrees in order to survey his son with the left eye, because the right one was getting tired. He shook his head sadly, which caused him to propel himself sharply backwards.

"Not the way you're going, son. Carry on as you are and you'll come back as something utterly insignificant, lower altogether than any form of ocean-going, rock pool or even pond life."

Jim gulped nervously and adjusted his camouflage to a brighter shade of pink.

“Yes,” Jim’s dad pressed home his point, “an investment banker or an estate agent, or even worse: some form of parasite.”

“Not a hedge fund manager, Dad?”

Jim’s dad nodded gravely. He was in an expansive mode and puffed up one of his swim bladders.

“*Homo Sapiens*, son.”

Jim’s mum sighed. ‘Here we go,’ she thought. Jim’s dad had an extraordinary knowledge of the outside world, obtained from his habit of floating one centimetre from the surface at the other end of the pool. Personally she would rather he had a little less useless knowledge and was of more practical use, but this is a general feeling amongst the female of the species towards the male.

“Absurd creatures,” began Jim’s dad reflectively. “They walk around on two legs most of the time but sometimes take to the air for no apparent purpose other than the extreme aimlessness with which they are afflicted.” At which point Jim’s mum would have bitten her tongue if she had one, in order to prevent her from saying, “As opposed to floating one centimetre from the surface of a pool all day.”

“It is essentially a wasteful creature,” Jim’s dad continued, “consuming vast amounts of electric power…”

“What’s electric power, Dad?”

“Think of the eel, son, and don’t interrupt.”

“Sorry, Dad.”

“There, you’ve done it again.”

Jim opened his mouth and closed it again, but since this was a fairly standard occurrence, no one was quite sure if he had intended to speak and thought better of it.

“Waste vast amounts of it, as I was saying, on unnecessary gadgets such as extractor fans in toilets. I see no reason why any creature should be ashamed of the smell of its own waste products.” At which point Jim’s dad rolled slightly on the vertical axis to avoid Jim’s mum’s critical gaze; she had seen him chasing his own excrement around when he thought no one was looking – and eating it! "Their judiciary is corrupt," Jim's dad continued hastily, "they have more concern for the rights of murderers and rapists than their victims. Wealthy thugs use the law to threaten and bully. Victims of domestic violence are ignored because judges are too lazy and misogynistic to take them seriously and yet the same judge will confiscate a young human's moped just for driving up and down with his legs off the pedals."

Jim began to fidget. He wasn't too sure about judiciary and had certainly never heard of a moped. He decided there and then that he would spend less of his life under stones and considerably more of it floating one centimetre from the surface at the other end of the pool.

"They enact unwanted legislation on crash helmets, smoking in bars and dropping apple cores, while ignoring the imminent catastrophe of environmental pollution that they have created for themselves. Life is transitory and it is as though by seeking protection from minor perils they can hide from the precariousness of their true situation, which we all know, is to bury one's head in the sand." Jim's dad fixed one eye accusingly at this point on a catfish emerging guiltily from the bottom of the pool. "Seventeen percent of them are starving and twenty-six percent of them have no access to clean water," Jim's mum rolled her eyes: Jim's dad had a bee in his bonnet about clean water, "while the rest of them drink exotic mineral waters or carcinogenic and fattening diet cola drinks out of bottles and use drinking water to flush their toilets and wash their cars. Their biggest problem is overpopulation and yet they do nothing about it." Jim's dad paused at this point and had the decency to flush bright red. Everyone knew that he could not pass by a clutch of unfertilized eggs without spraying his semen all over them. "Without control of their population, they face extinction from war, famine, pollution, disease and the destruction of their environment."

Jim couldn't contain himself. "I know what an apple core is, sir," he said respectfully, and waited apprehensively in the hope that this outburst had not annoyed his father It was hard to know because sardines cannot frown or smile, and accordingly Jim was left in the dark on this matter.

Jim's mum, meanwhile, was beginning to think that, delinquent though her son may be, he was still her son, and enough was enough. It was one thing to issue a reprimand and a warning, but to put the fear of several Hindu gods (each with twenty-eight hands) into him, was another matter altogether, and could have unforeseen consequences such as bed-wetting and experimenting with hallucinogens. She coughed, which unfortunately propelled her backwards and rotated her slightly clockwise.

"I think it's past your seabed-time young fish," she said tactfully. There was no point in causing a scene.

CHAPTER 9

"And that," said the President, closing the book reverently and crossing his eyes, "is the story of the sardine." At which point the cat woke up. She had begun yawning at about the time of the discourse on sardines' religious persuasions and had finally nodded off at the point that our judiciary had been described as corrupt. Now fully awake, she slid forward from Alex's head and attacked the tasselled bookmark viciously with both paws as she fell, evidently holding it entirely responsible for her losing her balance. She settled herself in Alex's lap and blinked up at him with a look of exaggerated innocence.

Alex frowned at the cat and squinted at his audience with an expression of complacent satisfaction. I was impressed; it seemed a fairly insightful view of humanity. In fact, as my eye happened to alight on Norman, who was looking particularly vacant, I was grateful for the fact that there were no sardines in the room to use this particular specimen of the human race as representative. I knew what was wrong of course: Norman was thinking, and unfortunately Norman's brain requires its full processing powers for this activity, and all those other motor functions which we so take for granted, required to keep the mouth closed, the tongue in the mouth and animate a relatively intelligent gleam in the eyes; all these were absent from their post and out to lunch. It was some moments before they returned and opened up shop. Norman frowned, coughed up some breadcrumbs and observed.

"One centimetre from the surface you say?"

Maria shot him a look worthy of Medusa, which I must admit made me jealous; I could do irrelevant and banal, but my heart sank as I saw the look of glazed stupidity on Norman's face – he was the master and I, just a novice. I lost myself in a daydream at this point. I imagined myself married to this magnificent woman. We'd just been shopping; I was so laden with carrier bags that I could hardly walk. Maria walked in front of me carrying a silver handbag. I struggled to pull my car keys out of my pocket and promptly dropped them down a drain. Maria raised her right arm – did I mention she was carrying a riding crop?

"Mr Curtis." I looked up to see Maria looking at me irritably. Well, it was a start I suppose, but nothing like the look she had treated Norman to. "Are you coming?"

I nodded and fell in beside Norman. "Where are we going?" I asked in a loud whisper.

"A bar," said Norman. "Weren't you listening?"

"My attention sort of slipped. Whose idea was that?"

"Mine," said Norman proudly.

"Tell me," I said. "Was it my imagination or was Maria standing over me with her hand raised?"

"Well, she was sort of adjusting herself if you know what I mean – I think she did raise her hand."

"I don't suppose she was holding a riding crop?"

"I don't think so." Norman didn't look surprised, which is one of the brilliant things that distinguishes Norman from the rest of the human race.

As we walked towards the town, I had visions of a sweaty nightclub, a tango blaring out, Maria in leather and me with a rose between my teeth. Reality, as is so often the case, was different. I think the most obvious difference was that the place was swarming with police. I guessed there must have been some appalling crime for there to be so many of them. But it only took a second glance to see that these police were behaving strangely. Some were relaxing against the bar with drinks in their hands while others shimmied around on the dance floor. They were chatting to each other in a way that didn't so much suggest, "And where exactly were you when you heard the first shot?" But more, "So how long have you been an interior designer?"

Yes, you're there before me: this was a gay bar and the theme was – police. Maria was the only woman in the place and was treated to many admiring glances. There is some strange quirk in the gay gene which causes their owners to admire the wide-hipped and full-breasted female form. Something in their glances said, "Ooh, look at her," in the literal sense rather than the usual ironic.

Maria led us to a table away from the dance floor. A sulky looking waiter with a pronounced sway of the hips took our order and flounced off. Norman looked around him with the first signs of curiosity. He'd just noticed the, "boys in blue," theme. Blue is perhaps an appropriate term because some of the officers were missing their trousers, the dancing was decidedly intimate, and there seemed no respect for rank whatsoever.

By the time our drinks had arrived, Norman's suspicions had developed from embryonic to five months gone. He leant over towards Maria and whispered loudly:

"Are some of those men homosexuals do you think?"

Maria gave him another crushing look – lucky so and so. Why should he be singled out for this special treatment? What was this X factor that Norman possessed to so inspire women in this way? I decided that one day I would dress as a woman and infiltrate one of his ex-wives' jumble sales to learn his secret.

I took a sip of my beer. Norman persisted:

"They're all dressed as policemen." Another stroke of genius from Norm; I couldn't hope to match him; it wasn't just stating the blindingly obvious, he had that look about him that told you this had only just occurred to him, and he was rewarded with an even more crushing look than before.

"They are policemen."

"Oh." Norman frowned. Norman disapproved. Perhaps he felt that trousers were an essential part of a policeman's uniform, or perhaps he feared that custodians of the law would not command the full respect of the populace while wobbling their testicles in time to Abba's, *Dancing Queen*.

Maria sighed wearily and turned to me. "To be perfectly frank with you, Mr Curtis, they aren't much good as policemen."

We were interrupted by some sort of fracas on the dance floor. A large moustached inspector (he was large and so was his moustache before you ask) in a very tight shiny uniform, possibly latex, was arguing with a slightly built sergeant. Snatches of the argument reached across the dance floor.

"You did – I saw you looking."

"What if I did – there's no law against looking."

"There ought to be – when you're COMMITTED to someone: soliciting trade with disgusting licentious looks."

The onlookers joined in.

"Why shouldn't he look?"

"Well you would say that wouldn't you?"

"Hark at her."

Someone burst into tears but most of them just carried on dancing. A massively built constable started laughing and a diminutive sergeant slapped him limply around the face, which seemed to make the constable laugh all the more; I rather suspected he was on some sort of medication. The sergeant suddenly collapsed and started hugging the constable's knees while sobbing uncontrollably.

"I hit you, I hit you – it's unforgivable."

Another officer with, "Forensics," written in sparkling sequins on the back of a fluorescent pink jacket, started taking flash photographs, and suddenly the flow of bitter recriminations stopped as they all started preening themselves, pushing and crowding around to get in front of the camera.

Maria shook her head. "They'll go on like this until four in the morning."

"Extraordinary," I said, "but shouldn't they be out on patrol?"

Maria snorted. "At night! They won't go out after dark – they say it's too dangerous. The problem is that they are employed by the Council and have to comply with all their regulations. If they ever get as far as locking anyone up, they can't hold them for more than two minutes because every cell has to be fitted with a fire door. They're forbidden to investigate serious crime because it has a brutalising effect on the force." At which point she directed a contemptuous look towards the dance floor. "Can you imagine any of that lot being brutalised?"

At this moment, the music changed to, Tammy Wynette's *Stand By Your Man*, and the dance floor erupted into *Sometimes It's Hard To Be A Woman.*

I saw her point.

"They refuse to arrest anyone except for the most trivial crimes. They say they're trying to improve the quality of their prisoners. In the event of a serious crime, if they can't get away with ignoring it completely, they wait twenty-four hours to make sure the criminal isn't around before visiting the scene. Then they draw chalk lines all over the place and call for the police photographer – you can see him over there..." She pointed to the Forensics man with the camera, who was taking shots of a chief inspector amusing himself and everyone else with the old elephant trick.

"You won't be surprised to hear that when he does eventually drag himself away to attend a crime, they all start posing for photos. They used to surround the area with yellow 'crime scene' tape, but the Council have manipulated the figures now to such an extent that they claim to have eradicated all serious crime and they changed the tape to: 'scene of a hurtful misunderstanding' in pink letters on a blue background."

Norman nodded sympathetically. "It's getting that way back home."

I looked at Norman curiously. Sometimes he makes remarks that sound thoughtful and almost intelligent completely by accident.

"I'm surprised they don't dispense with them altogether," I said.

"Oh no – that wouldn't do at all." At this point Maria gave me a strange quizzical look as if taking my measure to check if I were worthy of a confidence. Evidently I was. "They are a major source of revenue. The Council have introduced more and more trivial crimes to raise cash for the new Town Hall – failing to pay tax on growing rhubarb, exceeding the speed limit for pushing a lawnmower, replacing a light bulb without a certificate of competence."

"Ridiculous," said Norman emphatically. Strange that he should have waited until then; he didn't raise an eyebrow at rhubarb tax.

"Failing to be insured against insured losses…"

I had to stop her there. "Failing to be insured against insured losses?"

"Exactly – all losses must be insured."

"What losses?"

"Any losses – it doesn't matter – you've heard of a protection racket?" I nodded. "Same thing only they call it insured losses. You have to be insured against all losses, and then, if for any reason the insurance company fails to pay up, you have to be insured against that."

"Why shouldn't they pay up?"

Maria looked surprised. "Because of the small print usually."

Norman looked knowing. "Ah – the small print."

Maria and I looked at him until he began to fidget. Nervousness you might think, but more likely hunger: it had been a couple of hours now since his last intake.

I looked at Maria contemplatively. “And it is the Municipal Council that is so keen to join the European Union?”

“Yes – you see the Council are not having it all their own way. They have to bribe the Lord Chief Justice to get their legislation through, but even he rebels at some of the more extreme laws.”

“More extreme than rhubarb tax?”

“Oh yes – refusing to salute a council official on a bicycle, crossing a cycle path without looking both ways, failure to attend neighbourhood watch meetings – and loads about council railings; they want to criminalise leaning on them. It’s already a serious offence to actually do anything to them.”

“And how is joining the EU going to help?”

Maria appeared to study my face, which I found enjoyable, although it can’t have been pleasant for her.

“I need to explain a few things to you about this place, Mr Curtis. Our council leader, Sir Winyard Hall, is a genuine maniac rather than a fake one.” We exchanged a look of mutual understanding. “He also loves bureaucracy, and although I mean no personal offence…” She wrinkled her nose in my general direction which suggested to me that actually she did, “the European Union is the spiritual home of bureaucracy. He reads all the latest directives. He writes letters to the Commission proposing new regulations. The Council recently fined a woman for allowing her baby to make faces at a council official and wheel-clamped her pram. Sir Winyard wrote to the Commission suggesting that they should incorporate this into a new directive. Quite frankly, Mr Curtis, he doesn’t want to just belong to the European Union, he wants to dominate it. He disapproves of what he sees as a half-hearted approach to regulation. He sees himself as its natural president, spurring it on to greater heights, covering the whole of the Continent in gold-coloured railings, high kerbstones and new town halls…”

At this point we were interrupted by a loud chorus of cat-calls and boos. Four policemen in bomber jackets had just entered and made their way to a table nearby. Their jackets were emblazoned on the back with "Serious Crime Squad."

Norman looked puzzled. "I thought you said they ignored serious crime?"

Maria shook her head. "They do."

I looked at the group of men more carefully. One was sobbing quietly into his hands, another stared into space with an expression of deepest gloom; another picked out a blue-coloured tablet from a plastic bottle, stared at it glumly and swallowed it solemnly, while the fourth withdrew a book from his pocket and opened it. I glanced at the title: *Maxim Gorky – The Autobiography Translated by Isidor Schneider*. From the position of the book, I could see that it was well past page four hundred and twenty-nine and now understood entirely the unusual sense of the word, "serious" intended by the message on the back of their jackets.

"Tell me," I said, "you said the Council was trying to raise cash for a new town hall. Why do they want a new town hall?"

Maria gave me a look of complete non comprehension. "What an extraordinary question – that is the very reason town council's exist: to collect money to spend on town halls. They build one, then they pass new health and safety legislation and building regulations to render it noncompliant so that they have to build a new one."

"But what's the point of it all?"

"Mr Curtis!" Maria appeared shocked. "For an EU commissioner, you appear extraordinarily naive: the backhanders on the building contracts of course. I mean, admittedly, they do well out of cycle paths and railings – and of course paving and kerbstones are good regular income because they deliberately lay them so badly that they have to keep digging them up on a regular basis – but town halls are the real earners."

Norman looked at me indulgently. He appeared equally shocked by my naivety. "Think of it as infrastructure on a smaller scale, Curtis – Spanish motorways that end in a roundabout in the middle of nowhere – mind you…" He dug me in the ribs knowingly. "All those roundabouts have got a prostitute on them." He coughed nervously after a curious look from Maria. "Think of Rumania, Curtis."

This was Norman at his most patronising, but I had to concede that having worked in the EU for years, his knowledge of corruption was vastly superior to mine. A look of something loosely related to intelligence flitted across Norman's features.

"And of course, the new European Parliament Building in Strasbourg… ouch."

"Sorry," I said, "my foot slipped."

Norman looked hurt, probably because he was. We were, after all, ambassadors for the European Commission, and it crossed my mind that we knew very little about Maria.

"I take it then," I said changing the subject, "that Sir Winyard has his heart set on a new town hall?"

Maria finished her drink. "You'll see for yourself tomorrow." She shrugged her shoulders as if dismissing the subject from her mind. I would have liked to continue the subject of Sir Winyard and his town hall, because I liked it when Maria shrugged her shoulders, but at this point she got to her feet. This action did not go unnoticed on the dance floor. The LFI police force suspended some sort of synchronised routine that looked like an Esther Williams number, and froze in a reverential salute as Maria progressed to the door.

We returned to the Presidential Palace and Maria showed Norman and I to two adjacent bedrooms. I was relieved at this. Norman's first wife had confided in me what it was like to share a bed with him. Norman has dreams you see, and whereas most people are content to lie back with their mouth open snoring gently and let things take their course, Norman likes to be an active participant in his dreams, which is unfortunate for anyone nearby because these dreams are invariably about food and sex, often at the same time.

CHAPTER 10

I got into bed and was curious to see a TV remote control on the bedside table, marked, "LFI TV1." This was the only button; LFI TV2 was presumably still in the conceptual stage. I pressed the button and an antique-looking TV in the corner burst into glorious Technicolor black and white.

A glamorous lady newsreader wearing thick black spectacles sat stiffly upright at an old wooden school-desk with an inkwell in the corner.

"The price of sodium fell dramatically today after a further turbulent week of trading. A spokesman from the LFI Metal Exchange who wished to remain anonymous blamed heavy selling by the LFI Town Hall. We were granted an interview earlier today with Sir Winyard Hall."

The screen flickered with black and white zigzags and reconstituted itself into an extraordinary figure standing on the front steps of a huge gothic structure with "Town Hall" chiselled into a marble plinth above him. There was something about this figure that made me wonder if Batman had found a new adversary. He explained in a glance the whole mystery of Alex's trousers. Sir Winyard was well over six foot tall, and the first five feet were betrousered. I couldn't find this is in a dictionary so I lay claim to this word and when someone finally gets around to it, I would like it to read: betrousered (beetrowserd) pp. "Completely covered in trousers, trousered up, utterly swathed in trousers, so completely swamped in trousers that they form the focal point of one's consciousness."

I had wondered since first hearing of Sir Winyard, how it was that he had earnt his knighthood in this far off place. I now knew: it was for services to the trouser industry. A word about these trousers: they were fawn, generously cut and billowed gracefully in a light breeze. Knowing what I now know about Sir Winyard, it hurts me to admit it, but he wore his trousers well, and it was painfully obvious that Alex had attempted to outtrouser him and failed miserably in the attempt. What is wrong with these dictionary people? Outtrouser (owttrowser) vt "To wear ones trousers in such a fashion as to attempt to ridicule, belittle, or generally thumb ones nose at another chap's trousers."

There is a lesson here in extreme trouser wearing: the wearer of the extreme trousers should not be short, he should not look intense or anxious; a long Gallic nose to stare imperiously down while his trousers billow is desirable; there is a maximum ratio between trouser length "L" and breadth "W". (L = 2.74W). Last but not least, the extreme trouser wearer should not at any time allow his trousers to be patted pawed or pumbled by a Siamese cat, however much it purrs and rubs itself against you. Just a few guide lines there.

You probably have some idea by now as to the appearance of Sir Winyard Hall. He had that arrogant dishonest look of an ex-president of France. My lawyer (Ms Simpson) got a bit tense about this, in fact she said, "Fan ma brow." (I think I told you she was American.) This was followed by, "dang nabbit," and she ended up calling me a "bozo." I had to explain that I wasn't referring to any one particular ex-president, which she said would be, "cool beans," because it would be difficult for all the ex-presidents to bring a group action on the basis that at any one time some of them are likely to be dead or in prison.

He was speaking now, this rather unpleasant-looking man: "Shameful speculation there, Sue, and quite possibly slanderous."

Sue looked smug. Girls are better at looking smug than men partly because it is a little known tertiary female characteristic, and partly because they have more to look smug about.

"When you say, 'shameful speculation,' Sir Winyard, are you by any chance referring to the activities of the Town Hall?"

I don't know what sort of trousers Sue was wearing, if indeed any at all; the chances are that she was outtrousered – but certainly not outwitted. Sir Winyard looked annoyed and his trousers stiffened. Obviously I can only give an estimate but I would expect his wind resistance to have increased by at least seventeen per cent. The temperature of his cold stare, which had started off fairly chilly, dipped to the point that you could have used it to make ice lollies for the children.

"I believe in free speech, Miss Townsend – anyone who suggests otherwise will be sued immediately – but pernicious allegations of this nature shall not go unchallenged. The LFI Municipal Council exists solely as a benefactor…"

"So you deny that the Town Hall short sold large blocks of sodium?" cut in Sue, (or Miss Townsend if you were in a strop with her).

Sir Winyard was now seriously rattled. In fact the last time I heard anyone this rattled was when a certain ginger Welsh fellow European Commissioner was asked by a radio presenter (also a very sharp-witted girl) whether he personally drew the full amount of expenses under the system he said needed reform. He admitted reluctantly, after a very long pause, that he did – but he wasn't going to answer any more questions of a personal nature. He was very very angry and his name was… at which point my legal team interjected with, "No, no, Mr Curtis, please!" This was the start of a long legal lecture and I ended up giving in. They wear you down, these bods. If only Ms Simpson hadn't been busy tucking into a bowl of Lucky Charms, Fruit Loops and Pop Tarts, I would have gotten away with it.

Sir Winyard was trying to look offended but there was a gleam of anger in his eyes.

"With all due respect, Miss Townsend…"

I switched off. I wasn't looking forward to meeting Sir Winyard Hall the next day.

CHAPTER 11

I awoke refreshed and went down to breakfast to the pleasurable sight of Maria wandering around with a coffee pot. She turned a supercilious glance in my direction and pursed her lips. She looked stunning. She wore a white tailored blouse and a black skirt that fitted tightly over her massive hips. She evidently did not take fashion advice from the loathsome creatures that infest the world of breakfast TV who insidiously feed the insecurities of decent-sized women by telling them to "disguise" or "flatter" or "divert the eye from."

Maria did none of these things: she drew the eye and having done so successfully, fixed me with a frown of disapproval. I sank to the breakfast table with a groan. I remembered my first impressions from the day before: I hadn't imagined it: I was undoubtedly falling for this woman.

Norman acknowledged my presence by nodding, coughing and pointing a piece of toast with a large bite-mark out of it in my direction. I returned his nod silently so as not to encourage him. Conversation with Norman over breakfast resulted in something like an indoor firework display of toast crumbs.

Maria leant towards me to pour coffee. I averted my eyes for medical reasons.

"We have an appointment with Sir Winyard for lunch," said Maria.

"Ah." I said. I kept my eyes averted. The truth was that I had just remembered the most depraved dream I had during the night

– and it's no good asking me what it was, because it's all been lined through in red felt tip. I actually went to see my editor about this because I felt it was artistic and imaginative and shouldn't be excluded just because of some sort of misguided prudishness. I told her about my dream. She is normally an even-tempered woman and I was surprised when she slapped me hard around the face – although she apologised immediately and explained that it was merely a reflex reaction which I quite understood. She went on to explain that since the publication of *Lady Chatterly's Lover* there had been a steady relaxation of censorship. On current trends, she thought that my dream could be considered for publication some time in the second decade of the next century, but she explained that by that time both polar ice caps will have melted, causing penguins to live in fridges; tungsten filament light bulbs will have been outlawed and a religious sect will have formed in devotion to their memory, praying regularly to the fossilized remains of a 100-watt pearl with bayonet fitting. So I left her office rather unsure of her position on the matter.

This will give you some idea though why I was finding it difficult to look Maria in the face; I just managed a quick glance. Did I imagine that she was looking at me curiously? I found this hard to decide because most women look at me curiously, but I had the unpleasant feeling that she somehow knew about my dream and was looking at me censoriously – which I felt was unfair; after all, she was the one who had conducted the outlawed medical experiment on me in the first place and forced me to do all the dreadful things that I couldn't possibly tell you about – particularly those that involve… I'm going to draw a line under this now.

We set off after breakfast along the road towards the far end of the valley. We had not seen Alex at breakfast but a slowly moving red wheelie-bin high up on a mountain path betrayed his presence. Every now and then, the lid lifted and I caught a glint of sunlight reflected off binocular glasses.

I recognised in the distance the building I had seen on television the previous night. A sign before us announced: "The LFI Municipal Council welcomes careful pedestrians. For your own safety please obey our by-laws. Offenders will be persecuted."

Norman stopped to read the sign and frowned. One of the qualities I like in Norman is that in spite of his years in Brussels he dislikes bureaucracy, And he actually said, "Tchoh." I also frowned because beyond the sign was a great maze of galvanized steel railings. I was not far off from saying, "tchoh," myself. Railings are an insidious device that has crept up on us. They blight our lives. Back home, their only useful purpose is as a measure of the level of corruption in the council that erected them. Every November the local council holds a budget meeting; a serious affair because in spite of spending the first ten months of the year in an orgy of spending on useless extravagances such as illuminated road signs with inane messages, massive pay rises for useless officials and doubling everyone's pensions, they are still well short of spending the vast amount of tax they have collected from the rate payer. Councillors hire motivation consultants and spur their troops on for one furious spurt to blow the remaining money before Christmas – which is where railings come in. And of course, although no one wants them or needs them, they serve a second useful function: they are so ugly and depressing that unruly elements in the populace become dispirited and lose the will to throw bricks through the Town Hall windows.

There were rows and rows of them, separating the road from the pavement, the pavement from the grass verge, the grass verge from a row of front gardens. And then there were the signposts: "No radios to be played without a license from the Performing Arts Council." "It is strictly forbidden to access the LFI municipal highways by any means other than the authorised passageways." "Warning! Crossing the railings is a criminal offence."

Something popped in my head. I had a curious feeling of oppression and déjà vu. I was back at school. My class had been sent a new teacher. We had developed a fairly impressive reputation for insubordination which, casting aside false modesty, I take some credit for, and Anstruther felt that something ought to be done about it, in the shape of a nasty little bastard called Moran.

By modern standards, discipline was strict, but most of the teachers maintained their authority by throwing chalk at our heads with remarkable speed and accuracy, sarcasm and occasional use of the cane. These were the days of maths, physics and chemistry rather than media studies, knitwear, beauty therapy and golf course management. There were no professors of soap studies or obesity (I saw one of these on television recently who, despite having majored in cakes with a year in sticky buns, wasn't even fat!). We studied hard for exams that were tough to pass. This was before the educationalists decided that it was bad for little Johny to fail, so let's change that grade from, "embarrassing" to, "outstanding," and give him an Alpha plus for getting up in the morning and dressing himself, with a distinction for tying his own shoelaces. And as for those nasty difficult O levels, let's call them degrees and make things a bit easier by using jargon so meaningless that it can't be questioned.

You may have gathered by now that I rank educationalists almost as highly as economists. Modern teachers seem to have adopted the inane and deceitful language of politicians; you need a glossary when listening to them:

I am passionate about… (couldn't give a toss)
Let's have absolute clarity on this… (let's muddy the waters so that no-one can catch me out)
Driving the agenda towards… (I am a moron)

Delivering a vision… (I like sheep)
Engaging with the disengaged… (in fact I think I am one)
Focusing on… (it looks nice in that corner of the field where all the other sheep are)
The key issues… (Baaaaah).
Positive discrimination is equality… (*Arbeit macht frei*)

But to return to my story… (I think Madame had something to say on the subject but a red splodge suggests to me that UNFORTUNATELY her red pen has run out of ink – snigger). We did not love our schoolmasters but we grudgingly respected them; they knew their subjects, they had a sense of humour, albeit grim and sardonic, and they were fair. All this was lacking in Moran; he was uptight, humourless and unfair. He picked on boys for being clever or having mannerisms or just being different. I was a good-natured boy, kind to animals and old ladies, but I had a rather fundamentalist ethical code. I was more in the "eye for an eye" camp than the "turn the other cheek." When Moran viciously caned my best friend supposedly for continual interruption, but in reality for being Jewish, brilliant and odd, I judged that Moran should feel the full force of the law – my law; and blew up his car with a firmly stoppered gas pipe filled with weedkiller and sugar and detonated electronically from behind a wall. I had been generous with the chlorate and sugar; it was a truly massive explosion (I have heard that a terrorist organisation in the wilds of Waziristan still refer to it in their training manual). It blew out the windows of the new sixth form block and scattered bits of twisted metal over the hockey field.

Next day at assembly, old Anstruther made a ridiculous fuss about it, pacing up and down looking like Chamberlain. He wasn't necessarily trying to look like Chamberlain; it was just that he was a dead ringer for him and would have had to have worn a disguise not to look like him.

He told us that an act of terrorism had taken place and that if the boy responsible were found, he would be handed over to the Police and expelled from the school. Throughout this speech he stared pointedly at me, as did the rest of the school, masters and pupils alike. The whole thing was like one of A. Stambolüski's show trials (assuming that is that he had any; most peasant revolutionaries liked a few in the summer to take the place of garden parties). Everybody knew it was me; I was renowned for my explosions. I resigned myself to the retribution that would inevitably follow – and yet it never came. No one snitched; not even the music teacher who I had seriously annoyed by removing the castors from his piano.

A heartening story you might be thinking, but what exactly is its relevance? Well, I'll tell you: it was the road signs; the overbearing application of self-righteous, heavy-handed authority against utterly trivial offence was linked by association to that memory. My old passions were stirred. My right hand twitched and edged towards an imaginary T-bar. I stood still. Maria and Norman stared at me. All was silent except for the gentle purr of a motorised wheelie-bin somewhere behind us. There was a tense stand-off between me and the railings; the sort of tense stand-off you may have seen when Clint Eastwood and Lee Van Cleef are in a saloon, and Lee Van Cleef strikes a match on Klaus Kinski's three day old stubble. Perhaps not quite that tense, but these railings and these signs offended me. The railings were so close together that that you could reach out with both hands and swing on them as if they were parallel bars. Technically speaking, they were parallel bars; they were bars and they were parallel, and as a former gymnast (purely as a way of getting out of cross-country) I could not resist the temptation. I swang, or maybe it should be swung; who knows? Who indeed cares? I swang, I swung, I even swong (just for a bit), I salchowed and salsa'd and built myself up for a spectacular dismount with two full twists and a somersault to land against all odds the right way up in the road. I bowed to the assembled masses. Somewhere behind me came a noise that sounded like the clapping of a wheelie-bin lid. Norman as usual took all this in his stride. It was possible that given time he would exhibit surprise, but going on past form, I would not expect this until the following Tuesday.

The unmistakable sound of a motorised wheelie-bin drew near and we turned to see Alex throw open the lid and applaud. It was a strange sight, an undersized dictator standing upright in a vibrating wheelie-bin clapping his hands looking like a cross between a meerkat and a Spanish dancer.

But Maria's reaction was the greatest surprise to me; she stood looking at me with her lips parted, just staring, apparently completely unmanned, or in the specific case of Maria, unwomanned. You could not for one moment have suspected her of being unmanned for various reasons, but one or two in particular sprong to mind (sprang then, if you insist!).

"Mr Curtis." Her voice was changed completely from the usual imperious to faint and breathless – the sort of thing you would expect from Elizabeth Bennet on encountering that notorious bit of rough, Mr Darcy, coming out of the bathroom without his trousers.

She looked around nervously. "Mr Curtis, come back please. We are in the municipal area, it is strictly forbidden…"

I vaulted effortlessly over the railings – something between a half vault and a Fosberry Flop. And if you have been smiling indulgently during the last few lines and thinking that I have been deceiving myself with wishful thought, then you can now eat your words, or at least your thoughts and let that be a lesson to you, because at this moment I was witness to Maria patting her back hair! And if you are still doubtful it's because you haven't had the benefit of reading Desmond Morris's *The Naked Ape*. Women are subtle creatures you see – unless they're Australian of course. I remember a certain party in Melbourne. The sort of flirting that I was used to back home consisted mainly of eye fluttering and giggling, perhaps with the occasional hand lingering a while on the forearm – but at this party it consisted of a hand thrust down the front of one's trousers, and a coarse cry of, "Struth." But north of latitude ten degrees south, sexual behaviour tends to be more covert. You might think that the only significance of a lady patting her back hair is that she is concerned about its tidiness. To the student of Desmond Morris, this is the human equivalent of a lady baboon thrusting out her hips, changing the colour of her bottom from pink to bright red, and jumping up and down gibbering frantically. And if you have doubts about Mr Morris's *The Naked Ape*, then kindly consider the way she was looking at me; the usual steely look of disapproval was replaced by a slight smile, and she blushed – definitely blushed!

I was rescued from embarrassment by the sound of a dictator extricating himself from a motorised wheelie-bin. He strode forwards with an outstretched hand.

"Mr Curtis." He coughed. "Mr Curtis." He then flushed and looked embarrassed; mind you, I expect we'd all be embarrassed after having just flushed. He appeared to be struggling with some emotion and clasped my hand firmly but silently.

It was pretty clear to me by now that my spirited contempt for the Council railings had gone down well with my hosts. We moved on. We threaded our way through the steel railings. You may be interested to learn that in the LFI the galvanization process was what is commonly known as, "zinc and colour passivated," resulting in a brassy coloured finish as opposed to the usual grey; on the other hand, you may not be that interested, but I thought I'd let you know just in case you were.

CHAPTER 12

A high-trousered figure I recognised from last night's television awaited us on the steps of the Town Hall with Margaret at his side. Sir Winyard stepped forward with a flowing trouser movement to offer his hand. I shook it briefly – a strangely unpleasant experience. He looked down his nose at me and coughed.

"We've been expecting you, Mr Curtis." Now where had I heard those words before? At this point I noticed that Norman was behaving strangely. You might say that this was in itself normal, and if Norman had been behaving normally, then that would have been truly strange, but this was different; he was smiling broadly. The non-student of Desmond Morris would associate this with the close proximity of lunchtime, and would usually be quite right. Only a devotee of *The Naked Ape* or any one of Norman's six ex-wives would have recognised the danger signals, alerted the authorities and applied for an emergency injunction. This was Norman's sexually inviting smile, the same one I have likened to the gargoyles under the eaves at Ely Cathedral. This smile caused the corners of his mouth to turn upwards in a blatant leer that promised hours of bedroom passion. His eyebrows lifted in an arch gesture that challenged the recipient of the smile: if she played her cards right, all sorts of things were possible (some of them proscribed under the Sexual Offences Act of 1956), although the message was slightly confused by a disturbing likeness to Groucho Marx. The eyes flashed "come to bed" although again confusion was possible since I have witnessed the same expression on Norman's face when opening a bag of Zesty Taco/Chipotle Ranch Doritos.

Much as it disgusted me, I followed the track of this sex-charged love beam, and for a revolting moment thought that it alighted on Sir Winyard, but I saw that in fact it travelled past him, undiverted by his flowing trousers, and alighted on Margaret. I looked at her doubtfully; it seemed unlikely from her reaction to Norman yesterday that she would give him any encouragement. But suddenly, as I looked… Prepare yourselves for this; I know that certain snobby elements in the world of literature (who can usually be found with a red felt-tip pen about their person) look down their noses at particular literary devices: coincidence, repetition, or even dramatic suspense for that matter… cough… But please bear in mind, firstly that this isn't literature (she agrees with me for once) and secondly, what I am about to tell you is absolutely true… At the very moment the Norman sexual lighthouse beam fell on Margaret, she started patting her back hair! I would have liked some time to muse on this at length, but Sir Winyard had turned to lead inside.

I've only been in a town hall once before, to deliver a letter of protest about receiving a glossy pamphlet from the Council boasting about what they were wasting my Council Tax on. My point was not only that this document would have made Goebels blush, but also that it was a bit thick sending it to me of all people. If you have the misfortune to have your house broken into, the average burglar at least has the decency to make himself scarce and sell your worldly possessions discreetly on the black market. It's rubbing your nose in it to then send you a prospectus of all the things he's bought with the proceeds of the crime, and it's double rubbing your nose in it to make you pay for the brochure! That was my point.

Words alone cannot describe the opulence and tastelessness of the inside of the LFI Town Hall. I suggested an illustration to my editor but she has Scottish ancestry and just laughed and changed the subject, so I will have to content myself with a brief description: somewhere between a Roman temple, a Polish cathedral and a Turkish brothel. You can probably imagine most of these with the possible exception of a Turkish brothel. I may be able to help you there. Look up Al-Elefanti Sk in an Istanbul map. Approaching towards the town centre, from Asir Efendi Cd, you will come to a doorway on your left where a young lady will push out her breasts and beckon to you. Just make sure it genuinely is a young lady first – these misunderstandings can happen – then go to the grill in the door and ask for Mustafa…

Sir Winyard glanced sideways at me, I suspect to see if I was duly impressed. He looked expansive, particularly his trousers, which were flowing with a graceful ripple as if to remind visitors of their utter inferiority in amongst this tacky magnificence, whereas they (Sir Winyard's trousers) were completely at home here. You might feel that this discourse on the attitude of Sir Winyard's trousers is irrelevant; you'd be quite wrong – sorry to point it out so bluntly but there are times when the demands of honesty exceed those of tact.

Sir Winyard led us from a huge vaulted reception area into a long panelled room that I can only describe as being overwhelmed by trousers. Both sides of the room were lined by portraits, just as in Alex's dining room. I could see now that it was not just Sir Winyard's trousers that Alex had set out to parody; and, looking at the portraits, I understood and sympathised.

Sir Winyard followed my gaze and coughed with false modesty, a quite different sound to a genuinely modest cough; the epiglottis is raised due to the nervous tension (in the false cough this is) producing a more rigid structure and consequently a dryer and harsher sound – I think.

"My ancestors," announced Sir Winyard proudly and began to lead us down the assembled line of deceased Halls. Quite why he should have sounded so proud, I'm not sure; a more miserable collection I've never seen – all presumably having pursued a career in local government judging from the mean trivial grudging and dishonest features, and all trousered up to the armpits.

Sir Winyard announced each name proudly with boasts of spectacular feats of local government: "Percival Edgar Hall – the first councillor to introduce speed cameras to a cycle path. Stanley Archibald Hall – the first to have forced a central government volte-face on rate-capping, by closing the maternity unit of the local hospital and blaming the rate-cap." Sir Winyard droned on from what appeared to me one insignificant and wasted life to another. Finally, at the end of the line, we came to a picture some three times the size of the others. An imperious-looking woman stared down at us contemptuously down a huge nose above a sea of trousers.

"My mother," announced Sir Winyard reverently. "A wonderful, wonderful woman." I looked at him cautiously. There was no hint of irony in his voice. Good subject matter for Freud here, I thought. You see this in the world of showbiz: the would-be star obsessed with success, horribly driven, sacrificing all decent emotion on the altar of stardom – and then you see a picture of his or her ghastly mum, and all is explained!

Sir Winyard had now moved to the opposite wall and another line of Halls. My attention was taken quite suddenly to something rather peculiar. That's got you interested – this is dramatic suspense at its best, the very thing that publishers and their agents are so stuffy about, and here it is again, working like a dream, fascinating my readership… I will tell you: Margaret was sniffing at Norman – and I don't mean sniffing in the way that publishers and their agents sniff at the use of dramatic suspense; I mean sniffing with her nose extremely close to Norman's armpit.

"Aaaah," I thought knowingly, in the way that only a student of *The Naked Ape*, would. You see, due to a rich diet, Norman sweats a lot. You can actually tell what he's been doing by the pattern of sweat on his shirt; a bit of pottering around the garden shed produces a map of the Ottoman Empire from 1307-1359 (Istanbul can be found up near the left nipple). Should you wish to see how things changed in 1923 after the efforts of Kemel Atatürk, you need to ask Norman to do some light gardening; nothing too heavy or you will end up with a more or less faithful reproduction of South America with some appropriate blurring of the disputed territorial waters around the Falkland Islands. And what a terrible giveaway it is (never failing to bring a blush to whichever lady is in Norman's life at the time) when you see a 1:15,000,000 scale depiction of Asia Minor, with the Toz Gölü lakes featuring around the naval. When we see this, we do not need Norman to wink at us significantly or dig us in the ribs (which he always does) to know what he has been up to.

Norman doesn't wear deodorant. He says that his sweat is laden with phemerones and he considers it a blessing to female society at large for which, were he not a philanthropist, he would levy a small charge. And amazingly enough, there is a particular section of the female population (one has to include here, cats, dogs, small mammals and baboons with red bottoms) for whom this is true. Margaret was evidently one of them. I recognised the symptoms. One night, Norman and I found ourselves tailed by a petite oriental cat. Every time we turned around, she pretended to be conducting some local business in nearby shrubs, but she was fooling no one. She was stalking Norman, and the moment he picked her up, she buried her nose ecstatically in his armpit, purring so loudly that she dribbled. Come to think of it, she too was half Burmese.

Margaret, it was true, had a slightly tighter grip on herself, but I recognised the flared nostrils and the rolling of the eyes – not dribbling yet but it was only a matter of time. Norman was unaware that he had clicked. This is another of Norman's peculiarities. In the altered state of reality that exists in Norman's head, he has a host of admirers: women who crash their trolleys into him in the supermarket (accidentally on purpose), women drivers who flash their headlights at him because he has just pulled out in front of them (a feeble excuse), his bank manageress who wrote to tell him that his account was £57.43 overdrawn (as if!), the Vicar's wife who recklessly wished him, "good morning" (brazen hussy). The list goes on, and it includes several film actresses and lingerie models whose careers have been devoted to reaching out and enchanting Norman either by means of behaving provocatively on his TV set, or the blatant exposure of their semi-naked bodies in a Freeman's catalogue left so apparently casually on his door step. And yet when an enlisted member of the opposite sex (unlike certain inhabitants of Portsmouth who misrepresent themselves with names like Daisy) breaks ranks and heads towards Norman – he doesn't even bloody notice!

I had to discontinue my rumination on this subject because Sir Winyard was talking and I definitely heard the word, "lunch." Evidently so had Norman because he adopted a stance previously seen in Wellington's chargers at the sound of a nearby cannon blasting off in the direction of the French cavalry.

I made a sort of noncommittal noise of assent just in case I had misunderstood and he had in fact asked me if I had contracted any interesting venereal diseases recently, and was pleased to find ourselves being led into an adjoining dining room; I didn't particularly fancy lunching with centuries of Sir Winyard's ancestors looking down their noses at me, particularly Sir Winyard's mum, who I suspect may have had something to say about my table manners.

Sir Winyard sat at the head of the table, with Maria and I on one side and Norman and Margaret on the other. An elaborate menu wittered on about *Soup de jour, ciabatta goujons and cod parcettas* but Sir Winyard waved his hand in an expansive gesture.

"Order what you like, Mr Curtis – I think you will find the Town Hall kitchen will rise to the challenge." He smiled thinly, which is the only way to smile when you've just come out with something as slimy as that; he reminded me more and more of a James Bond villain.

Norman looked decidedly put out and I knew why: Sir Winyard had not once addressed him or even looked at him. Sir Winyard evidently believed in dealing with the organ-grinder rather than the monkey. Norman is generally complacent about his position as number two, content in the knowledge that he is the secret prime mover (he hung framed pictures of Rasputin and Peter Mandelson over his desk shortly after being appointed my assistant). But when treated as Sancho Panza rather than Thomas More, I imagine he feels rather as Red Rum after winning the Grand National, consigned to his stable for the night with only a congratulatory pat on the nose and an extra sugar lump, only to have his sleep disturbed by the knowledge that the little squirt who had been bouncing around on his back all afternoon brandishing a whip in a threatening manner and generally showing off, was now being sprayed with champagne, masturbated by a woman dressed as a nurse and, the greatest insult of all, being given a nosebag of powdered sugar lumps.

I wouldn't say that Sir Winyard's disregard put Norman off his main course (*Supreme de Volaille aux Langoustines. Ris de Camargue et Emulsion de Poivron* – with side dish of Cheesy Whatsits), but he was definitely not tucking in with his usual vigour.

Towards the end of the meal, Sir Winyard addressed me. "Mr Curtis, I would like to show you something of the new Town Hall after lunch. When complete, it will accommodate in excess of ten thousand people."

"Oh," I said.

Sir Winyard smiled thinly (again). "It seems a little excessive to you perhaps?"

"Mmm," I said, non-committally. This is probably the only useful thing a career in accountancy has taught me: always be non-committal.

Sir Winyard felt inspired to explain, "I have hopes, Mr Curtis, that when the LFI becomes the twenty-sixth member state of the European Union, our new complex will replace Strasbourg as the seat of the European Parliament.

"Aah," I said for a change, having said, "Oh," earlier, but wishing to remain equally non-committal. Bear in mind that my present exalted position was invented by my employers purely as a means of getting rid of me. It was unlikely that any representation I made would even be listened to. My purpose, if I had one at all (and modern psychologists suggest that it's a good idea to invent one if you don't have one already, or previously had one and lost it) was to maintain a pretence of considering any EU application. I did not like the fact that Sir Winyard appeared to be taking me seriously; a career in accountancy had not prepared me for this.

Sir Winyard continued, "Think of the benefits."

"Um," I said, but departing for a moment with rigid policy, suggested that none sprang to mind; in fact, without wishing to hurt anyone's feelings, knowing that people can be sensitive about these things, the LFI was somewhat off the beaten track for the conduct of European Government.

"But think of the benefits," Sir Winyard persisted.

For once, Norman got there first. He coughed or, to be strictly accurate, spluttered.

"A nine hundred mile return trip from Brussels; why, that's one thousand, seven hundred and twenty-five pounds per trip. I have always felt Strasbourg to be an unsuitable venue for the Parliament, Sir Winyard."

Sir Winyard smiled again (thinly I suspect but I wasn't watching closely). "Unsuitably close, one might almost say."

Norman looked pleased with himself. Not wishing to be critical but Norman can get quite exercised on the subject of, "fat cats", and yet here he was gazing upon Sir Winyard in a decidedly tubby feline manner himself.

I noticed at this point that Margaret was looking at Norman with an expression I have seen before in the faces of silent movie actresses about to have something unspeakable done to them (well it would be, wouldn't it – what with there being no sound track), which usually involved being tied to a railway line by a man in a straw boater and a sinister moustache. Straightforward so far you might think, and yet the look on her face was denied by the fact that her nose was almost buried in his passenger-side armpit. Her nostrils were flared. It is unusual to see such a mixture of horror and ecstasy all mixed up in the same face at the same time, unless you are a regular at Donna's parties of course. The poor girl was struggling; the forces of repulsion (watching Norman at work on his *Tarte fine aux figues et Pommes, Sirop de Muscat*) were in conflict with the forces of attraction (Norman's magnetic body odour). I sighed; I too was in conflict; my friendship with Norman demanded that I remain a passive observer, and yet Christian duty decreed that I should alert Margaret to those dreadful secrets that Norman's ex-wives have listed in a black leather-bound book (with brass clasps) and read aloud in African villages as a warning to the world's women. But in a choice between action and inaction, inertia always wins the day, as indeed old Anstruther pointed out so unnecessarily in my school report. Fate must take its course. I have no doubt that Odysseus' mum told him in no uncertain terms that that Circe was no better than she ought to be, and a fat lot of notice he took of her.

I was interrupted from this reverie by a low flying aircraft which turned out to be Sir Winyard.

"We are a small state, Mr Curtis, but our wealth measured per capita is the highest in Europe by a factor of seven point four six three."

"The benefits of being offshore, I suppose," I murmured.

Sir Winyard adjusted his nose, rather as a U-boat captain would turn his periscope towards a passing liberty ship, in order to look down it on me with pinpoint accuracy.

"Exports," he said emphatically; so emphatically in fact that he disturbed Norman from the final demolition of the duck and venison sufficiently for Norman to repeat with equal emphasis: "Exports?" – more than equal emphasis if you count the sheer weight of fig and apple debris that accompanied this utterance; some people do, others don't: I myself don't have a strong opinion on the matter.

Sir Winyard was talking again. The man was a menace to those of us who like to let our thoughts wander after dinner.

"Exports! The LFI has a university of unparalleled excellence, Mr Curtis, with a single faculty devoted to business management. On graduation, sixty-four per cent of our MBAs proceed to doctorates and pursue careers as management consultants throughout Europe and North America."

I couldn't help feeling sorry for the other thirty-six per cent: bitter for them to see their colleagues disporting themselves in mortar boards decorated with tassels and pontificating patronisingly to surrounding lesser mortals.

The throb of a fully laden Lancaster on a bombing run to Hamburg alerted me to the fact that Sir Winyard was talking again.

"Yes, a major source of revenue to the LFI in several ways."

Norman took a sudden interest in the conversation. This involved leaning back in his chair and raising both hands in what might have been an expansive gesture or possibly a throwback to schooldays when masters decided in the interest of class morale to ignore Norman's raised hand, inspiring him to raise both. We may never know, but the effect on Margaret was profound. Her eyes were wide open with an expression I have only seen once before: that of a Jehovah's Witness who had unwisely knocked on Donna's door on a Wednesday evening (theme night: "ordeal of the witch whore") and someone invited her in for a laugh. But here the comparison ends, because Margaret was dribbling slightly, whereas the Jehovah's Witness, wasn't. I'll finish this story if you don't mind because it has a rather unexpected ending. Once inside the door, the poor woman stood rooted to the spot, mesmerised, until a couple of passing poofs (not passing in a transient sense; they're still poofs; it wasn't, "just a phase", you see) put a large spliff in one hand and a tumbler of Scotch in the other. She dutifully took in a deep lungful of some Class A skunk, followed by an even deeper draught of Donna's finest single malt – possibly not strictly in accordance with the teachings of Jehovah, but then nor was ripping open her blouse, lifting her skirt, bending over and begging a leather-clad Donna to beat her unconscious. Jehovah still recalls the matter sadly in the snug bar of his local as, "the one that got away."

But returning to Norman leaning back in his chair with his arms in the air; what I was trying to explain was that this was an announcement that Norman was about to speak, and on a subject close to his heart. Norman, you see, used to give lectures on Business Management. He wasn't strictly speaking qualified, but Business Management is one of those peculiar subjects where qualifications are irrelevant for the very reason that if the people teaching it were any good at it, then they would be actually doing it rather than teaching it.

It all started in a modest way. Norman was treasurer of the Round Table. Members took it in turns to give half-hour talks on a subject within their competence, or in Norman's case, incompetence. Bearing in mind that Norman's single O level had been in Business Studies, Norman spoke with enormous authority, so much so that his audience quite believed he knew what he was talking about, as did Norman, as indeed do most lecturers in Business Management; belief you see, however misplaced, is the basis of the whole subject.

Unfortunately the member hosting the meeting had a daughter hovering around in the background, and she was a medical student. There is something about medical students, the association with sickness and death perhaps that when coupled with sufficient dosage of alcohol tends towards an exuberant attitude to life; a celebration of living, if you will, accompanied almost invariably by a warped sense of humour. And this young lady was not only in her third year at Guy's Hospital, but also had refreshed herself with half a bottle of something or other that should have been locked up in the anaesthetics cupboard.

She paid little attention to Norman's lecture at first. This is often the way of great speeches: they lull you into a false sense of security, building up from a modest introduction, and then jump out with the tub-thumping bits about, "having dreams," or, "*après moi* something twiddly in French," or, "*j'accuse*" (pithy that one) or just generally screaming at people you don't like in leather shorts. (She with the red pen intervened at this point and I think we all know why, but it is perfectly clear to the intelligent reader, which I am sure includes yourself, that one would not scream at people just because you think they look hideous in leather shorts, so I am NOT changing this sentence thank you.)

I am trying to describe to you the subtle mechanism by which this medical student's attention was captivated. Norman was getting into his stride. She didn't want to embarrass her father in front of his friends so she crossed her arms and squeezed herself tightly. After a while, she found that she had numbness in her fingers which worried her because she knew from her studies that this could be the symptoms of carpal tunnel syndrome, chilblains, multiple sclerosis or restless leg syndrome. After listening to Norman a little longer, she began to shake uncontrollably, which was even more worrying because she had just attended a lecture entitled, "convulsive rigors arising from acute nephritis," although of course she could not rule out Parkinson's disease, mercury poisoning or an overactive thyroid.

Further into the lecture, she broke into a sweat. It would be unusual for a twenty-one-year-old to start her menopause so early but medical conditions sometimes defied the statistics. Of course it could be nothing more than Swine Flu but she had to resign herself to the possibilities of Burkitts Lymphoma or Hairy Cell Leukaemia.

The palpitations started about ten minutes later; probably just paroxysmal supraventricular tachycardia, but a mitral valve prolapse was a more worrying possibility.

Towards the end of the lecture, tears were pouring down her cheeks in a way that suggested serious lacrimal dysfunction – and personally she suspected a brain tumour or at least sarcoidosis; she wasn't aware of being depressed and she ruled out nut allergy on the basis that she hadn't eaten a Topic or even a Marathon for at least a week.

By the time Norman had finished, she was seriously alarmed to feel a slight wetness in her crutch. This had to be serious; she was fairly sure she hadn't given birth recently and prostate problems were unlikely. If it wasn't bladder infection then it was almost certainly obesity – and she was only a size eight.

She just managed to pull herself together sufficiently to sidle up to Norman at the end of the lecture and ask innocently if he would accept a fee to give a lecture to a select audience at London University.

Norman's career went from strength to strength. He was booked solidly for months in advance. He told his daytime employer (a particularly nasty branch of a particularly nasty high street bank called National Midwestminster Barclaylloyds of Scotland, if I remember correctly) that unfortunately and most regrettably, he could no longer afford to work for them full-time due to other pressing commitments. He was mindful however of how dependent they were on him, at both branch level, and indeed at head office, and accordingly he would be prepared to contract his services to them as a junior cashier, providing of course that they fitted in with his other engagements and matched the level of remuneration that he enjoyed as a professional lecturer. He also felt that the bank could benefit from his skills and he would be prepared to give a half hour lecture at local head office to senior managers at a discounted rate.

This was Norman at his absolute best. High street banks in those days positively hated their staff to have any kind of independent means because it limited their power to browbeat and bully their staff (which was listed as a top priority in their "Management by Objectives") and here was Norman openly taking the piss out of them – except that he wasn't! You would have been and so would I, but Norman wasn't; he was breaking it to them gently because he knew what a body blow it would be to the bank to lose him, and he felt he owed it to them to tide them over a difficult time. He was even touched by the fact that his bank manager at their moment of parting should be red in the face and quivering with emotion. He could see that the dear man was close to tears and fighting manfully to hold back his tender emotions. Norman consoled him with a hug and of course in those days, when men's feminine sides were so repressed, Norman's bank manager reverted to type and attacked Norman with an executive paperweight.

Each lecture was bigger and better than the last; each ended in a hysterical rapture of applause that sometimes took half an hour to subside. Norman was pleasantly surprised but took it as his due. He didn't appear to notice that these gigs were all at London teaching hospitals or student unions; they just got bigger and bigger and the fees, fatter and fatter. It got to the point that just his appearance on stage was enough to have the audience up in their seats screaming for a full ten minutes – and the moment he opened his mouth to start his lecture, they were off again.

Quite how Norman found out that his business management lectures had become the number one attraction on the alternative comedy circuit, I don't know. Some say it was the invitation to appear at the Edinburgh Fringe Festival, others, an approach by Channel Four – but find out he did. He could have just laughed it off and continued on his path to becoming a multimillionaire; but actually he was seriously hurt and never mentions the matter to anyone who might be in the know. To complete strangers however, such as Sir Winyard, he would proudly lay claim to having been a particularly hot potato on the lecture circuit.

I might need to remind you at this point that Norman's interest had been aroused by the comment from Sir Winyard, that the export of business management graduates and post-graduates was a major source of revenue to the Latvian Fish Isles – to which Norman replied:

"Aah." Which may not perhaps indicate the level of his interest but I should explain that he said it with a sort of significant emphasis, rather as one might when rummaging through the wife's tacky silver handbag and finding a receipt from the Hotel Sleaze on a night when she was supposed to have stayed with her elderly aunt in Cleethorpes – not that I have a wife, and she doesn't think her silver handbag is tacky, even though everyone else knows it is and doesn't refrain from saying so behind her back.

Having said, "Aah" Norman lowered his arms, concealing the Islands of Java and Sumatra in the left pit, and Borneo and Sarawak in the right. Margaret looked disappointed and Sir Winyard continued:

"It is not just a matter of the direct revenue stream you understand. Our business managers have secured appointments as consultants to multinationals and governments throughout Europe and the United States."

I wasn't quite sure of the significance of this remark and my blank expression was not lost on Sir Winyard, and he smiled (guess how?).

"It is not a statistic you will see published, but conservative estimates suggest that each management consultant reduces a company's productivity by one point nought seven six per cent, and, in the case of governments, considerably more. In the medium to long term this feeds through to the economy at large and undermines the currency, giving the LFI considerable advantage. We do not employ management consultants, Mr Curtis, we merely train them and export them, leaving us with the hardest currency in the world, as I am sure you know."

I nodded intelligently; I didn't of course. I felt a bit of a fraud; here he was, taking me for some sort of serious eurocrat, when in fact I had spent my early youth, when not engaged in acts of terrorism, trying to impress girls using patent methods recommended by my brother, such as smiling insincerely, narrowing my eyes and sucking in my cheeks, and wiring a resistor into the circuitry of my Morris Marina to make the indicators flash very very slowly (this, in case you wondered, is a bit of psychology that works when you are drawn up alongside a couple in a Ferrari at traffic lights. The man will look annoyed and the woman, wistful, due to the subliminal awareness of your superior virility and endowment – apparently). And my later life, as we know, was spent trapped under the thighs of a dominatrix in between spasmodic acts of accountancy (up to the level of Part 1).

Fortunately Sir Winyard appeared reassured by my attempt to look intelligent, and moved on.

"Then of course there is taxation. We have the most punitive tax regime in the world, Mr Curtis, much of it in the form of penalties for the contravention of municipal regulations."

"Vaulting over council railings for example," Maria interjected, and her expression was deadpan. I had not until this point suspected her of possessing a sense of humour; now here she was, taking it for a walk around the block and letting it of its lead.

Sir Winyard did not appear amused. "As you say. We also have one of the most intense surveillance systems in the world, Mr Curtis," he said proudly. He waved a hand expressively towards the hall where his ancestors peered out meanly and grudgingly. "We owe much to my ancestors: speed cameras to enforce limits that have been reduced to zero; even the slightest movement now results in a hefty fine, traffic lights that are permanently red, the extension of penalties to pedestrians and pets. By the time the rate payer goes to bed at night, Mr Curtis, they have on average contravened sixteen point seven four regulations, and go on to commit a further eight point four in their beds if they are married, and twelve point six if not, followed by a further thirteen point two in their dreams – attracting penalties of 127 LFI dollars per day, give or take fifty cents."

This struck me as a rather peculiar speech. I looked across at Maria and saw that her lips were pursed in a disapproving manner. This was inconclusive because this seemed to be her default expression, so I looked across at Norman and was re-assured. Norman looked nonplussed. He raised his arms in the air again, and because it was a hot day the islands of Indonesia had been transformed into Western Samoa (left pit) and the Murmansk Basin (right pit).

Sir Winyard continued, "I think you will find, Mr Curtis, that the European Union will benefit considerably from the membership of its twenty-sixth partner."

"Really," I said. Impressive bit of dialogue this; some of us have it and others don't – just something you're born with I suppose – call it a gift if you like. I didn't want to encourage the man, not that he needed encouragement. He fixed me with a penetrating gaze. I've never been keen on being fixed with penetrating gazes; they make me nervous.

"And I do not refer simply to taxation, Mr Curtis. I refer also to the matter of democracy." He now fixed me with a significant stare, which is similar to a penetrating gaze but slightly different.

"Democracy, Mr Curtis is the malaise of our times. While I concede that the European Union has made some progress towards stifling it, we in the LFI Municipal Council have, I am proud to say, eradicated it completely."

Norman opened his mouth, possibly to protest or possibly as a reaction to a small piece of *Assiette de Sorbets Maison* left on the side of his plate. Either way, Sir Winyard took it as a coming accolade which he held up his hands in a gesture of modesty to forestall.

"It has not been easy. Like you, Mr Curtis, we have tried bribes and threats (I rather resented this) and found the need to move to blatant deception. Where you have gone wrong, if you will pardon my saying so, is to allow plebiscites – even though I know that you ignore any deviant results and repeat them until the correct answer is given. We in the LFI, however, have banned them altogether. We came to realise that ballots are an unwelcome interruption to the business of governance. We passed an instrument in council chambers, in closed session of course, to criminalise any form of vote, ballot or plebiscite. I think you will find a total of twenty-four such words, all meaning the same – we banned them all."

Sir Winyard looked at me down his nose, this time with affected modesty rather than hauteur. His nose, while being massive, was versatile in this respect. It seemed to adjust itself to a variety of expressions while being looked down. I wondered if there was a Lady Winyard who, in her courting days, had found herself rendered sexually defenceless by having a large nose manoeuvred into position and looked down in a decidedly fruity manner. Hmmm – best not to let one's mind wander too far sometimes. I was being looked at expectantly now, which while not in itself significant or penetrating, has distinct elements of both.

"But your application, Sir Winyard, I understand, is not endorsed by the President."

Maria gave me a look of approval, and Norman nodded with an expression that was neither penetrating nor significant. Norman often nodded just after lunch, and I knew from experience that this would soon be accompanied by heavy snoring.

Sir Winyard waved expansively and dismissively while looking down his nose contemptuously – definitely of French origin I decided.

"I wouldn't concern yourself too much about the opinions of our President if I were you, Mr Curtis," said Sir Winyard with smooth contempt.

I'm not that keen on the use of "if I were you." You might call me irritable (my Aunty Molly did when I was four and pulled her hair in protest against being kissed sloppily against my expressed wishes) but I find it patronising, and said testily:

"He is the President though."

Sir Winyard studied me coldly from down his nose. His expression was cold when it started its journey at perhaps minus thirty-seven on the Kelvin scale, and was then subjected to the chilling effect of a long journey across a high ridge (which shouldn't be underestimated; even the condor when cruising over the High Andes complains of it being a bit parky up there) and arrived at its destination at a temperature that could be useful for creating superconductivity in a particle collider; cold it was – decidedly chilly.

"This is not the United States of America, Mr Curtis."

Well I knew that of course even though geography was not my strong subject; in fact somewhere in my much missed school report were a few caustic remarks added to those of Anstruther by my Geography Teacher… Perhaps I'd better get on.

"No, I suppose not, but then again, I have to report back to the Commission, and I hope you will forgive me for saying so, but I am getting rather mixed messages."

Sir Winyard replied silkily: "I am confident that you will be able to leave the LFI in a few days, Mr Curtis, with a formal request for membership of the Union from the duly authorised authority." He smiled with an unpleasant smug complacency, giving me the strong impression that he had something up his sleeve. He arose to his feet.

"You must allow me to show you around."

CHAPTER 13

We followed Sir Winyard through those depressing open-plan offices to be found in councils all over the world, marked by the zombie-like milling around of the humourless and the self-righteous whose souls have been destroyed by preying on people who put their rubbish out on the wrong day. These offices seemed to extend for a mile or two. We eventually emerged from the back of the building into the open. A plethora of walkways to outlying departments were indicated by a clump of signposts: 'Ratepayer harassment office', 'Department of drawing lines around pot-holes', 'Department of creating cycle paths where they are not required and removing them where they are', 'Department of unnecessary pavement resurfacing with badly-laid fussy-coloured stonework', and one sign on its own pointing away towards the mountains, announced 'Olympic Village'. We took this path which led to a half-built stadium littered with earth-movers, concrete mixers and pile-drivers. Sir Winyard surveyed the scene contentedly.

"It was due to be finished ten years ago," he said proudly, "but we are hoping not to complete for at least another twenty years. The cost over-run is likely to be the largest on any capital project in history." He smiled… (you guessed it, but even more so than last time) "I think the LFI has something to teach you here too, Mr Curtis. I am aware that the EU has its own infrastructure projects that are successful up to a point in, erm, redistributing wealth. But an Olympic Project, if successfully mismanaged, beats them all, providing of course it is never successful in winning an Olympic bid and therefore, never completed. This, if you won't mind me saying so, is where your member states have gone wrong; they have on several occasions won the bid and then had the expense and inconvenience of having to host the games, and of course that entails actual completion of the project, thereby limiting the cost over-run and causing unnecessary time pressure and unwelcome public scrutiny. Besides" – a look of distaste spread over Sir Winyard's features – "it would not be pleasant to have our peaceful village infested by a bunch of hyperactive foreigners."

"Jumping over things," added Maria with a look of exaggerated innocence.

"Quite." Sir Winyard glanced frostily at Maria, who now appeared inscrutable. I wondered which of this formidable pair (Sir Winyard and Maria that is – just to avoid any possible misunderstanding) would get the better in an exchange.

We continued along the valley until we came to what appeared to be another construction project. There was a coming and going of people wearing hard hats in and out of site huts. A huge crater appeared before us; the foundations for the new Town Hall I presumed. We approached and stood before some railings to peer over the edge. These railings had some justification for their existence. They were the sort of railings that would slump into their chair after a long day and, when questioned shrilly by much smaller and younger railings as to what Daddy had done at work all day, would grunt and light a cigarette, while the female of the species told them (the sibling railings that is) not to bother their father because he'd had a hard day at work preventing people from falling into a very very deep pit.

Deep wasn't the word, or rather it was; the bottom was evidently floodlit but was so distant as to appear only as a dull pinprick of yellow light.

"Our new town hall, Mr Curtis," announced Sir Winyard, "or rather the foundations. Perhaps you would care to inspect them?"

"Yes please," I said in the sort of voice usually reserved for small children being offered large ice creams with two chocolate flakes sticking out of the top or shiny red bicycles with at least five gears. You see, I love holes and the deeper the better; they fascinate me. As a child I used to break into roadworks, pumping stations, sewers, disused air-raid shelters: absolutely anything in the way of underground workings. Fortunately child psychologists were rare in those days, otherwise they would have been around me like flies, with crackpot theories that I won't even speculate over, because even by my standards they would be disgusting, involving wombs and back bottoms etc.

Sir Winyard seemed pleased at my enthusiasm. He led us to a shining stainless-steel outbuilding that turned out to be the head of a bank of lifts.

"High speed, the fastest in Europe as a matter of fact; we will reach the bottom in approximately five minutes."

Norman looked nervous. He had just eaten a particularly dense meal. You could tell he was nervous by the sudden appearance of the Kuril Islands on the back of his shirt. Incidentally, the possession of these islands has been disputed between Russia and Japan for many years now, and while I wouldn't like to stir things up after all this time, the International Court might be interested to subpoena Norman's shirt (when anxious) in order to settle the matter; a distinct area of dampness under his left shoulder blade is undoubtedly a facsimile of the Russian flag flying over Ostrov Urup and I would have thought this put the matter beyond doubt.

In the enclosed space of the lift, I became aware of several things.

Thing 1) Maria's magnificent bosom was almost thrust up against me. I experienced a peculiar feeling in my stomach rather like a lift dropping like a stone – although come to think of it, the lift was now dropping very much like a stone, so that might have accounted for the peculiar feeling just described earlier in, Thing 1.

Thing 2) Sir Winyard was looking down his nose again but I wasn't sure why.

Thing 3) Norman's nervousness had increased, as evidenced by the sudden guest appearance of the states of Uttar Pradesh and Rajasthan between his shoulder blades, and a pungent body odour (which might explain the look on Sir Winyard's face, described earlier in, Thing 2).

Thing 4) Margaret's nostrils were flared wide open (probably due to the aforementioned body odour in, Thing 3). To a student of Desmond Morris, this was clear evidence of sexual arousal, but even the non-student might have worked this out by the appearance of the Punjab in a strategic area of Margaret that I am far too polite to specify.

And that is the end of the list of things; I'm sorry, I know you were enjoying them and would have liked some more, but that's all there are.

It seemed inconceivable that the depth of this pit was required for the foundations of a building. I put this to Sir Winyard who replied that the new Town Hall would be rather tall at two thousand and thirty-six feet.

"Good Lord," I said. "That'll make it the tallest building in the world."

"Really?" said Sir Winyard looking unconvincingly at his fingernails with a peculiar gleam in his eye, "I wasn't aware of that."

"But surely," I persisted manfully, aware of the fact that we had been progressing downwards like a space rocket for some three minutes now, "the foundations don't have to be **this** deep."

Sir Winyard surveyed me thoughtfully. "There are to be one thousand floors below ground level, Mr Curtis, reserved for the most vital municipal functions. The Town Hall must be able to operate in the event of a nuclear attack."

I was too polite to say that I couldn't think of any function of local government that was even necessary, let alone vital, except possibly rubbish collection, but Sir Winyard put me wise.

"Obviously all the functions of the council are essential, but some have to be given priority… The Department for the Erection of Unnecessary Roadsigns, the Department for the Laying of Absurdly High Kerbstones that didn't need replacing in the first place, the Department of Confusing White Lines and Proliferation of Mini-Roundabouts. These are but a few that spring to mind; there are hundreds more. The Department of Railings alone will occupy one hundred and twenty-seven floors, Mr Curtis."

"I see."

"And then there is the small matter of my mausoleum."

"Ah."

"Yes – the LFI Municipal Council, at an extraordinary meeting, unexpectedly saw fit to pass a resolution that the new Town Hall should be named 'The Sir Winyard Hall Memorial Tower' and that at the very base of its foundations, an area not less than seven hundred and forty-one square metres and not exceeding seven hundred and forty-two square metres, should be set aside for the mortal remains of the said, Sir Winyard Hall, in the possible but not inevitable event of his demise." Sir Winyard laughed. I'd rather he hadn't, it took me by surprise, I didn't know he could laugh. "A flattering resolution, Mr Curtis – implying, as it does, that the committee look on me as something rather more than mere mortal."

We landed with a spectacular deceleration, sometimes known as a bump; peculiarly appropriate I thought: just what was needed for Sir Winyard's delusional ramblings. I felt sorry for Alex at this moment; there he was hamming it up as a nutcase and making a pretty poor job of it, up against a bloke who turned out to be an Olympic standard megalomaniac. I was reminded of the words of a Harley Street psychiatrist I got to know through Donna's parties. He had a particular thing about dressing up as a schoolboy and being nagged at by a dinner lady for not eating up his pudding; the whole business escalating out of control to its inevitable conclusion where she screamed at him at the top of her voice, kicked him viciously in the testicles and crammed cake into his mouth. "The thing is, dear boy," he explained (while waiting for a certain lady solicitor to change into a dinner lady), "I spent nearly a year of my degree learning the classification of mental disorder; there's DSM-IV and ICD-10, there's descriptive versus somatic, there's groups and sub groups – hundreds of them, and every now and then, one gets sneaked into the wrong pile and they have to reclassify it – loads of red faces, ruined reputations and thousands of poor buggers on lithium carbonate when they should be on valium. And what's the point? That's what I say: what's the bloody point? You only need one word, dear boy… Fruitcake!" At which point he laughed hilariously like the naughty schoolboy he was, quite unconscious of the irony that in a very short time he would be having a full three pounds of the stuff pushed into his face.

We exited the lift onto a floodlit gallery circumventing the pit. No one appeared to be at work, but I could see people moving around through the windows of a ring of site huts. Strangely, they were all wearing suits and appeared to be shouting. Sir Winyard surveyed the scene with an indulgent smile.

"Our managers at work, Mr Curtis."

"What are they doing?" I asked.

"Ah," said Sir Winyard, which irritated me because that was my line. "Hopefully not much. I think I gave you the figures for the effect of managers on productivity, Mr Curtis. We don't let ours touch anything. We bring the workers in at night after they have gone home."

"So they work without management?"

Sir Winyard looked surprised. “Of course; they have the occasional supervisor I believe.”

“Ah,” I said, pleased to get my line back, “but why are this lot pacing up and down and shouting?”

“Mobile phones,” explained Sir Winyard. “There is no signal down here, but they don’t seem to have noticed. Mobile phone conversations tend to be meaningless, and we like to encourage their use in our managers. There is a danger, albeit only a remote one, that they could become mildly productive without them.”

So saying, we approached one of the site huts. A power-dressed young woman paced into view.

“If you’d just go to the cheese counter like I asked,” she shouted crossly into her phone and passed out of sight to be replaced by an anxious-looking young man, also shouting at the top of his voice.”

“Where are you? This is a terrible signal.” He frowned at another young man who flitted past, also shouting. “I don’t know why people have to shout.”

The young man paced out of sight. In fact there was so much pacing up and down that the whole hut pulsated. We moved away. It was a blessed relief to get out of earshot, but it was only a brief respite. As we approached a scaffolding tower, I became aware that it was swarming with managers in hard hats, draped around the uprights or pacing the boards. They too were shouting into mobile phones.

Sir Winyard surveyed them proudly. When I say, surveyed, I don’t mean that he estimated their height and weight, or even marked their position using a theodolite, I mean that he pointed his nose in their general direction and looked up and down it at them.

“We run a course for shouting into phones up scaffolding, Mr Curtis. They start on short ladders and work their way up.”

Norman laughed suddenly. Either his usual time delay system was malfunctioning or something had tickled him two or three days ago and had just filtered through.

Sir Winyard continued, "One of our postgraduate students was sent to China for advanced training on the Taipei 101 building and unfortunately was blown off the one hundred and first floor by a high wind." Sir Winyard looked upset. His expression suggested that a two minute silence would be held across the length and breadth of his nose. "Yes, a sad loss, a particularly stupid young man – a great loss to the world of business management; we had hopes of placing him in J. P. Morgan Chase Manhattan."

We watched and listened for a while. It was an eerie sight, standing at the bottom of this vast floodlit pit, watching the managers in their yellow hardhats, scurrying around and gibbering into their mobile phones. It reminded me of my earlier days back home when all the trees in our road were taken over by noisy twittering parakeets.

We made our way back to the lifts and started the long ascent. Margaret had by now all but given up the struggle; her nose was almost buried in Norman's armpit. Every now and again she let out a sort of bleating snuffle, but her widely dilated pupils expressed horror and suffering. Norman appeared unaware. It seemed now only a matter of time before her resistance failed and she threw herself upon him. I knew how she felt; not about Norman's armpits obviously. I wish I had worded this differently now. I would like to make a categorical denial of the sort that an errant MP makes outside his garden gate with his family gathered around him, to announce to the world that he had never heard of the "Open Flaps Go-Go Bar", and certainly not visited it, had never met, Fifi McFlayingpost, and had no idea how the apple had got into his mouth in the first place. That sort of thing – only in my case, more like, "I have no interest in Norman's armpits whatsoever and even if I were to even think about them for a moment, my only desire in the matter would be that Norman washed them more frequently."

No, when I said that I knew how Margaret felt, what I meant was that I myself was close to being overwhelmed by the close proximity of Maria who was standing behind me, and that certain part of her anatomy which I mentioned earlier was now brushing gently into my lower back. In spite of the fact that it gets no mention by Desmond Morris, this was evidently a lesser known erogenous zone. The situation reminded me of a time some years ago when I visited a wine bar up in town with some friends. It was that, "eyes met across a crowded room," cliché – and what eyes! They commanded me to break into her bedroom as soon as I had finished teaching that bull a lesson it wouldn't forget in a hurry (she looked a bit Spanish). I didn't obey their commands in full, but I did order an extra-strong pint of lager, which made me feel sufficiently dynamic to start edging myself in her general direction while studiously looking the other way (another useful technique from my brother's extensive repertoire). Slowly but inexorably our bodies touched, caressing lightly, back to back, buttocks and shoulders. The pressure increased; she pressed harder; I hardly dared to breathe; the woman was brazen. I felt my excitement build to fever pitch. I knew where this was leading. True, I had been given false encouragement at times in the past, but there was no possibility of misunderstanding here – and as if to prove the point, the young woman prodded me in the most intimate of places, and at last I found the courage to turn and face her…

In order to follow the ending of this story, you have to understand that I had followed my brother's instructions to the letter, and in the process of looking away determinedly, I had allowed a slight navigational error to creep in. I had in fact spent the last half-hour frottering a hat-stand. I doubt if there is a law against it and it gave me probably one of the most erotic half hours in my life, but Spanish beauty it wasn't and I wasn't even going to offer to buy it a drink. My friends informed me that the Spanish beauty had indeed been looking at me, but more in a, "why is he rubbing himself against a hat-stand?" type way rather than anything sexually inviting.

I wasn't going to make the same mistake twice. I did not delude myself that Maria was deliberately caressing me with her unmentionables. A simple volumetric calculation was all that was required to verify this. Estimating the width and breadth of the lift wasn't too difficult; it was the size of Maria's bra that was the problem – sharing the end of the alphabet with the grades in my school report. And thinking about it wasn't going to help solve the problem in my trousers. I decided to look at Sir Winyard's nose to help calm things down a bit. He was peering down it at me in a peculiar manner; I can only describe it as conspiratorial.

This was explained moments later when we stood again on the steps of the Town Hall to make our farewells. In the normal way, I would have contented myself with some sort of pleasantry such as "Must dash, thanks for showing us around," but Sir Winyard was looking at me expectantly. I did my best.

"Thank you for your hospitality, Sir Winyard. I will of course consult with your President and report back to the Commission." Rather glib I thought; I liked it, it had a certain gravitas. I looked at Norman to see if he looked impressed but unfortunately the lights were out and there didn't seem to be anyone at home. This was not an unusual state of affairs with Norman, whose thought processes tend to take time off in between meals.

Sir Winyard smiled again in a manner that was thicker than usual. He withdrew a long brown envelope from a trouser pocket. Perhaps indeed this was the reason for the overgenerous trousers; for all I knew they were stuffed full of brown envelopes. He tried to hand it to me. At which point, as they say, I made my excuses and left. As I walked away, I became aware that Maria was looking at me. I found myself flushing with embarrassment and tried to think of a diverting topic of conversation: pantie girdles, bras and the price of sodium came to mind, none of which seemed appropriate. I felt foolish; I felt sure that A. Stambolüski in a similar situation would have risen to the occasion with an oily smirk and a raised pitchfork, while pocketing the capitalist blood money on behalf of the revolution.

Maria interrupted my thoughts. "Why didn't you take it?"

How could I explain to her that I was only a PE1 qualified accountant, and this sort of thing is covered in PE2. I did my best.

"I couldn't take it. I've never been any good at that sort of thing – probably never will be," I added sadly.

"But you're a European Union Commissioner!" She sounded amazed.

"Special Commissioner," I protested feebly, "but I know what you mean. The truth is I have no aptitude for it. They did their best, they sent me on courses, even gave me extra tuition, but some people just don't have what it takes."

CHAPTER 14

It seemed to me that all of us were a little preoccupied that evening. I briefed Alex on my meeting with Sir Winyard. I would have expected him to show some interest, but he just stared at me blankly, blinked several times and ticked the cat off for getting above herself (she was licking his ear at the time). He then excused himself on the grounds that he had to give an important speech in a nearby graveyard.

Norman also appeared unusually quiet. Margaret had perched herself next to him, sitting primly with a straight back, facing slightly away from him with her hands crossed in her lap – all very Jane Austen except for the laboured breathing and occasional flaring of the nostrils; in fact she looked like the trick question for advanced students of body language.

I retired to bed early but couldn't sleep. I switched on the television and what looked like a shopping channel appeared. I recognised the train driver and conductor from the day before. The conductor was talking.

"Well girls, another gripping night of shopping." He yawned widely. An inappropriate heavy rock sound-track accompanied his words with a throbbing bass line. The presenter shook his head.

"LFI's premier rock group, 'Wild Medicine', which, would you believe I just happen to have on video."

He gave a mischievous wink at the train driver, who was giggling, pressed a switch, and the camera zoomed in on a video screen. I recognised the "legend in his own trousers" syndrome that infects so many rock stars. Usually this is just embarrassing as anyone who has been to a U2 concert will know, but it acquires additional comic value when performed in a pub or a mall or, best of all, on a shopping channel. The lead singer had the statutory coloured sunglasses and had forsaken all earthly love except for himself. He pouted heroically at the bass player, who obediently dropped to his knees and started strumming even more ostentatiously than before, at which point the camera panned out and back to the studio. The presenter's desk was overturned and he had disappeared from sight except for a comfortable-looking pair of suede shoes drumming on the desk. You might have thought some sort of accident had befallen him were it not for the hysterical laughter coming from behind the desk. The camera was now shaking and a sort of suppressed snorting noise told that the cameraman too was losing control. After a minute or two, he abandoned his post to join the two presenters rolling around on the floor clutching their stomachs. The presenter finally controlled himself sufficiently to manage a few words while desperately looking away from the others.

"That was er Wild Medicine…" He had attempted speech too early. He caught the train driver's eye and let out a great shriek of laughter, and they were all off again. My theory about the gay gene is that one of the suspect regions on chromosomes seven, eight and ten contains a double helping of giggle DNA; mind you, people taking themselves seriously is sublimely comical. Back in my youth, I had a friend who used to hold parties devoted to watching macho Hollywood actors in films about gangsters, hustling or anything requiring them to look mean and serious – and just at the sight of Robert Redford, Steve McQueen or Paul Newman (the list goes on) everyone would start falling about. It left me with a distorted view of the cinema: I took it that all Hollywood films were comedies; it came as a surprise to me to learn that some of them were intended as serious drama, and unfortunately I have never quite been able to adjust to that view.

The presenter had now mastered himself; in fact he looked at the cameraman rather snootily as if he was to blame for the whole disgraceful incident.

"Good evening, shoppers – and have we got some bargains for you!" He shook his head dismissively. "Doubt it." He looked even more irritably at the cameraman who was now rolling an oversized cigarette, and whispered loudly: "Do you mind?" The cameraman shrugged and the presenter turned back to the camera. "Yes, some fantastic bargains for you. I'd stay by your phones if I were you." He rolled his eyes. "Not that you get out much." He walked over to a bright yellow vacuum cleaner. "Well what have we got here, shoppers? Hmmmm – looks like a vacuum cleaner doesn't it? But not just any old vacuum cleaner. This is a very special vacuum cleaner." He kicked at it viciously and looked even more crossly at the cameraman who sniggered and puffed hard on his cigarette, concealing his face in a cloud of smoke. "This vacuum cleaner, shoppers, is particularly expensive. Now why should you pay so much extra? I hear you ask, shoppers. Difficult one that…" He stood for a moment with one leg curled around the other and a finger to his lips. "I mean it's not as though you're stupid, is it? Well, let me explain: first of all, it draws twice as much power as an ordinary vacuum cleaner which is particularly good at getting rid of all that nasty electricity. It also means it will burn itself out in a year or two and you can buy another one that isn't such a gruesome shade of yellow. Secondly, when you switch it off, it's such a relief, because of the ghastly fucking noise it makes…" He put his hand to his mouth. "Ooh, did I swear then, shoppers?" He turned to the cameraman. "Did I swear, Sean?"

Sean raised both thumbs and drew deeply from his cigarette, leading me to wonder at the nature of the tobacco he was smoking.

"I did, I did, and I'm so sorry. I've let myself down, and I've let you down, my lovely, loyal, gullible, sad shoppers. Thirdly, and most importantly, the almost unbelievable feature of this overpriced, over-powerful vacuum that sucks all the pile out of your carpet is that: it – doesn't – have – a – bag!" He paused for dramatic effect, while Sean stretched his legs across the desk. "Isn't that great! Isn't it such a bloody nuisance having a paper bag to collect all the shit, when you could have it scattered around inside your vacuum cleaner making it a nightmare to clean." He stood shaking his head. "Oh, God give me strength."

I switched off at this point. I felt he had been a bit hard on the bagless vacuum cleaner. I mean, it may be that it is a completely useless invention; certainly compared with the self-defrosting fridge or the self-untying shoelaces (of which I am the proud owner of several pairs) but you can't expect people to keep buying the same old things just because they work well and are cheap; this would put thousands of marketing executives out of work. Bear in mind that in a few years' time they will re-invent the vacuum cleaner with a bag, double the price and everyone will be happy.

I settled back into bed. I wasn't remotely sleepy though. I'd like to leave a significant pause at this point – just here in fact… What is it that young men (well, relatively young) do in bed at night when they can't sleep? Quite! Yes, it is embarrassing and rude, and I'd suggest that sensitive or easily offended readers skip the next three pages, better make it four to be on the safe side. Right then, hopefully no one is reading this now. I discussed this with my editor and she stared at me thoughtfully and said she thought this quite likely.

Anyway, there I was lying in bed with myself, as it were, looking at the ceiling, my hand resting across my stomach, and well, one thing led to another. I know that the act of self-love is generally frowned upon by certain sections of society: nuns, bishops, priests, imams, a large percentage of wives and girlfriends, and most definitely by the school secretary who caught me at it in the narrow space behind the prefabricated sixth form classroom. She had unambiguous views on the subject which she shared with me (possibly the source of my fascination with dominant women). But then again, there is another section of society who should come forward and own up to being ******* (apparently this word is offensive to women with red pens)... All those awful architects who nearly bust a blood vessel when Prince Charles quite rightly points out that they've built nothing but monstrosities for the last forty years – oh and of course those appalling people in the BBC who jury rig children's competitions and then can't see what they have done wrong! (Lie to children, if they are still wondering.)

You will understand that under these circumstances my thoughts turned to Maria... This is getting really embarrassing now; not only are the boundaries of good taste shortly going to be dug up and replanted, but I have been advised in red felt-tip that I could find myself in trouble with the law. Accordingly I would like to distance myself from myself and have asked my legal representative to recount my following actions, but she just said, "dang nabbit," and refused because she is having her breakfast at the moment – waffles I think, with eggs sunnyside up. So I had to make do with one of the other cowardly lawyers from xxxxxx, xxxxxx, xxxxx and Simpson.

"My client," (I shall refer to him henceforth as, 'My client,') whom I would rather not represent, but being a lawyer and therefore not having too many scruples, I shall just take the money. Being accused of something or other and tried under the 1861 Offences Against the Person Act (amended 1885), I shall cite as a precedent, the case of William Joseph Barnabus v Reading Parish Council, bought to trial under the Metropolitan Commons Act (1866) at Newbury Assizes in 1903, because I feel it sufficiently irrelevant to have no bearing on the case whatsoever.

“My client then, was lying in bed, and freely admits to pleasuring himself in a gentleman’s way. He asks for several thousand previous offences to be taken into consideration, starting from the age of ten or possibly eleven – he alleges that his memory isn’t entirely clear on this matter, but that it was definitely in or around the potting shed.

“His thoughts, while engaged in this act of self-pollution, turned to a certain, ‘Maria’, who was persuaded, in his depraved fantasy, to behave in a shameful and sexually provocative manner purely for the perverted and licentious purposes of my client’s sexual gratification, which frankly disgusts me, as I am sure it does, your lordship and other members of this court. Maria was dressed as a traffic warden and was engaged in gripping my client by the testicles and hissing in his ear – and I quote: ‘Who’s been a naughty boy then?’

“My client… I’m sorry this is so disgraceful that I feel I can no longer represent my client directly, and shall therefore be myself represented by another lawyer, with even fewer morals, who will act as an advocate – and wishes to give testimony from behind a screen in order to protect her identity.”

“Good evening. I act on behalf of my client’s client, Mr, er, Curtis, although I would like to point out to the court that I also would refuse to represent him directly in this matter due to the depravity of the charges if he were on legal aid. Let it be said quite plainly then, that my client’s client was lying on his back, indulging in, not to put too fine a point on it, masturbation, presumably with malice aforethought, when a strange thing happened…”

I think I will take over from here if you don’t mind, legal fees being what they are. I was at a critical point in these proceedings. In the world of aviation, this is known as "V1": the point where one has trundled up the runway to take-off speed but could still slam on the brakes and stop at the end of the runway – but once past this point, it's too late to stop and you will come to what might be described as a sticky end. In my case, I was hammering up the runway, just past "V1", braced for flight – and the bedroom door opened!!! (That's three exclamation marks), And in came Maria (let's add another four)!!!!

When I say, "in came Maria," this requires some clarification. We are dealing here with fractions of a second. You have probably seen a photo finish at the races; it was a bit like that. I saw the door open; I desperately tried reverse thrust; it was touch and go, but Maria's anatomy came into play at this point. Most people entering through a door seem to marshal their anatomy through more or less simultaneously. Not Maria! There is an advance guard of bosoms to announce her presence. I understood at this moment Einstein's theory of relativity, which had eluded me at school: time slowed to a trickle, the mass of bosoms appeared infinite, and I exploded into the bed sheets with a velocity just short of the speed of light.

The rest of Maria appeared around the door. In my state of utter confusion, it took what seemed like an age to interpret the expression on her face as she approached me. I was expecting the school secretary scenario to be replayed: the wagging finger, the hissed admonishment, in which the words, "dirty boy," featured largely. School secretaries possess psychic powers in order to discover small boys behind prefabricated classrooms, and even more spectacularly to tazer same small boys with a disgusted look when their thoughts wander anywhere near a bra strap or stockinged area.

So, you will understand that being doubled up in bed, my face the colour of an over-ripe beetroot, I expected the worst – and was relieved and surprised when Maria spoke.

"Mr Curtis, I hope I didn't wake you, and I hope you will forgive this intrusion."

"Aaaaah," I said, and yawned expansively to cover the fact that I was still out of breath. I stretched my arms as I yawned. Shame there weren't any cameras around. When you consider the rubbish acting on these soap operas, they could have learnt a thing or two from me. There is more to acting than sighing deeply, looking angry and sounding depressed in a regional accent. But then I shouldn't be too critical; they probably didn't have the benefit of several years' experience in the Harrow and Pinner Amateur Dramatics Society, (regularly reviewed in the *Harrow and Pinner Gazette* – circulation including parts of Rayners Lane).

"Ah," I said again, but with a totally different intonation; minimalist but laden with significance – pure Olivier. I patted the side of the bed and she perched primly on the edge.

"The fact is, Mr Curtis, I have decided to trust you."

"Ah," I said (Brando this time).

"It was when you vaulted over the railings; I realised then that you weren't, one of them." I wasn't quite sure what she meant. I've never been, "one of them," although there was a time somewhere around puberty when I had a particular interest in other boy's testicles; these things happen at public school. That's probably not what she meant though and I don't want to dwell on the subject. Instead, I said:

"Ah." (De Niro, in case you wondered.)

"And then you refused Sir Winyard's bribe – and I knew for sure."

"I see." (Gielgud with a touch of The Master [Coward].)

"We are in great peril, Mr Curtis. Sir Winyard is not the suave gentleman he appears."

"More of a dangerous lunatic," I returned.

She looked at me directly and I have to say it shook me. To date, I have mainly spoken about Maria in a way that would make any self-respecting feminist bristle; but this was one of those defining moments. I had a peculiar feeling in my stomach. Actually I had a peculiar feeling on my stomach too but I put this down to the endothermic effect of vaporisation.

"As you say, Mr Curtis – you're, erm, more perceptive than perhaps I gave you credit for."

I nodded my head and tried to look wise (Ian McKellen as Gandalf).

"He's up to something," said Maria.

And I knew what. You see, my dad used to read Shakespeare to me in bed. Most four year olds get nice bedtime stories full of talking bears and bunny rabbits with Christopher Robin thrown in as a reality check. I got Scottish witches and Danish princes, all up to no good with a distinctly unhealthy blood lust for their fellow citizens – and if ever the part of Brutus comes up for audition at the LFI Amateur Dramatics, Sir Winyard is the man.

"He is going to try and usurp Alex."

Maria looked impressed and grabbed my hand impulsively, which worried me in case it was still a bit sticky.

"How did you know?"

"Elementary." (Basil Rathbone) "It was his remark about the EU application coming from a duly authorised authority; not only that, but he was smirking as he said it."

Maria squeezed my hand, which my stomach took as an excuse to perform some sort of floor dance.

"We have to act. There's a lot you don't know about this place, Mr Curtis. Alex may seem strange to you…" I didn't know what to say to this; the awkward truth was that he didn't seem that strange to me. "–But he is actually a decent man and our only defence against Sir Winyard and the Municipal Council."

"Some sort of fascist dictatorship?" I ventured. "And when you say, 'we must act', what do you have in mind?"

She gripped my hand even more firmly. My stomach decided to close for refurbishment and reopen as the big top at a circus. I tried to sober it down a bit by giving it a lecture on the curing properties of anaerobic adhesives – there was precious little oxygen now between my hand and Maria's; I had visions of a surgical separation and some awkward explanations.

"Margaret," she said thoughtfully, "knows something. I can read her like a book. The difficulty is going to be getting it out of her. Do you have strong views about violence against women?" She looked at me hopefully. "I mean, I expect there are EU directives against that sort of thing, but perhaps you could stretch them a bit under the circumstances."

I do have strong views about violence against women, and they are not the same as Donna's. I also hold views on hunting with hounds: chase a bag of sausages on a string pulled by a Range Rover, instead of a fox; not keeping horses tethered on open land; and hanging people who beat donkeys or anything else with fur on it, even glamour models in stoles, but I sensed this wasn't the moment to discuss them. Maria was looking at me expectantly, possibly imagining me tying Margaret to a chair, pointing a lamp in her face with something in excess of a one hundred watt bulb (with tungsten filament) and being generous with the back of my hand. I didn't want to disappoint her but I wasn't really her man. It is true that I have on occasions lashed out at a wasp with a rolled-up newspaper (and making rude remarks in red pen about this sentence is fatuous: whoever heard of a wasp going around with a rolled-up newspaper?) but I usually miss and on the rare occasions when I get one, I feel pretty damn bad about it for several days afterwards – thinking of Mrs Wasp waiting back home with a brood of excited larvae saying, "When's Daddy coming home, Mum?" And when a couple of his workmates covered in jam tell her glumly that he is missing in action and was last seen in a dogfight with a rolled-up newspaper and she mustn't get her hopes up – and she has to break it to the kids… It doesn't bear thinking about.

But I had an idea. I knew that Margaret was in a nearby room. Being a stooge of Sir Winyard, she was almost certainly keeping tabs on me. I suggested to Maria that she should be the one to wake Margaret up and restrain her if necessary. These things are best done woman to woman, especially if you are a devotee of a particularly mucky type of novelette. I told her to await my arrival. I tried to look confident with just a touch of Pedro the Cruel. You might be wondering if I knew what I was doing. "But of course," is my answer. I had it all planned out in stages. Stage 1 was to sneak into Norman's room and pinch his smelliest shirt. I was relieved to find that my hand disengaged easily from Maria's.

I found myself at Norman's door – not immediately of course; there was bit of pottering around required beforehand. I decided not to knock. Norman likes his sleep and takes it seriously. I remember an anaesthetist explaining to me that there are four levels of anaesthesia; stages one to three are useful for keeping your mind off things during tooth extraction and general surgery. Stage four, on the other hand, is best avoided due to the severe drop in blood pressure, kidney damage and brainstem death. Norman asleep flits from stage three to four, in what could be described as a near death experience. In fact one of Norman's recurring dreams is hovering in a dark tunnel, brightly lit at the end, with his great granny (who died back in 1962) weaselling around in the background.

Sure enough, as I sneaked in, Norman was spreadeagled on his back, both palms hanging out of each side of the bed in a sort of supplicating Al Jolson position, but I was pleased to see that he was still hanging on to life albeit by a thin thread. It is generally unnecessary to call for the undertakers when the corpse is muttering a list of Twizzlers flavours to himself. I was immensely surprised though to notice, as I sneaked past his bed, that his eyes were open.

"Ah there you are," he said, rather as though he had been expecting me.

"Yes," I said, "just popped in to borrow one of your shirts."

"Ah, well help yourself, Curtis – it is Curtis, isn't it?"

"I think so."

"Jolly good – thought it was."

This was followed almost immediately by heavy snoring; the brief visit to level one was over and he was back at death's door. It would now need a defibrillator to restore him before his eight hours were up. I grabbed Norman's discarded shirt and sneaked out to embark on…

Stage 2. I had high hopes for Stage 2; they involved striding in a manly and menacing manner towards Margaret's door in order to execute Stage 3. But at this point I had reservations – not the habitats of Native Americans, nor indeed the advance booking of tickets for something utterly banal and tasteless, which is all you get in the West End nowadays. No, my reservations were more to do with the thought of using coercion on Margaret. It was my upbringing that let me down. If I were descended in a direct line, or possibly even an indirect one, from Pedro the Cruel, this would be the high spot of my day. But I wasn't; my hereditary aptitude for this task was what old Anstruther, when referring to my mathematics paper, described as, "pitiful."

One example should be enough to make my point (more than enough, you may be thinking, in which case I'd rather you kept it to yourself because a certain word count is required to achieve the cover price on this book). This example, and a particularly fine one I think you will find it, is my father's attempt to administer corporal punishment on the occasion of my having blown up his potting shed with weedkiller and sugar – again.

The trial was held in the kitchen, and summary justice was issued by my mother in the form a directive to my father: "It's time you gave that boy a good hiding; you let him get away with murder and see where it ends up."

I protested on several counts. (Count 1) I had not been given any opportunity to defend myself. (Counts 2 & 3) No one had bothered to listen to me and even by the standards of a kangaroo court this was pretty damned unfair. (Count 4) I had no one to represent me since my brother was in the garage rewiring the windscreen wipers on his car to crawl across the screen at a snail's pace, which was another guaranteed way of impressing girls apparently. (Count 5) In fact the whole thing reminded me of a show trial that I had just read about in Solzhenitsyn's *Day in the life of Ivan Denisovich.* (Count 6) So there!

I was ushered upstairs. My father asked me awkwardly if I wouldn't mind awfully just bending over a fraction, if it wouldn't make me too uncomfortable, old chap. He then lay about me with a slipper – just! I was embarrassed for my father. I thought I'd make things easier for him by wincing with pain and rubbing my bottom, for which he looked grateful, and so one day would the *Harrow and Pinner Gazette* (distributed also to certain parts of Wealdstone), for this was the foundation of my acting career in the Harrow and Pinner Amateur Dramatics Society.

"Erm, I don't suppose you could manage a bit of bawling for your mother's benefit?"

He had come to the right place. As is so often the way, history honours the wrong heroes: Stanislavski strutted around taking credit for, The Method, when in fact it was created in an upstairs bedroom in Rayners Lane. I let out a blood-curdling scream. The next moment my mother stormed up the stairs, flung open the door and stared with speechless accusation at my father, who didn't help himself by looking guilty, but then again he always looked guilty.

"Beast!" She slapped him sharply around the face and disappeared in a flood of tears. And that, my dear long-suffering reader, was the strange part of this drama: no one had ever seen my mother cry proper tears before; she would ham it up every now and again over some contrived indignity, but everyone knew this was because she was angling for a new mustard-coloured sofa to compete with the orange flowered monstrosity that the neighbours had just bought. This, however, was the real thing and my father and I both tiptoed out into the back garden (even though there was no potting shed to hide in) because we couldn't cope with it.

And with this pathetic heritage I am supposed to find it in myself to start using strong-arm tactics on a defenceless woman!

Stage 4. We'll skip Stage 3 because she with the red pen deleted it all and wrote "BORING" in large red letters in the margin. I've noticed she's been a bit jumpy today. It would be just tactless to mention the time of the month. Let's just say "I'm with Chico," which may offend my extensive readership in Brazil but hopefully will not cause any offence over here. Stage 4 it is then: I opened Margaret's door gingerly to see her all wide-eyed and bound and gagged in her nightdress, with Maria standing over her looking ruffled. I approached with the sinister weapon of forbidden torment behind my back, which to the best of my knowledge and belief, Norman had not changed since we started out from Brussels. I admit to being nervous; if this ever got out, I'd be up at the Hague, indicted on several charges under the International Human Rights Act, and at least a couple under the Geneva Convention. The accusing phrase "cruel and unusual punishment" echoed in my mind. I'd often wondered about that charge. I imagined some poor soul in a South American jail being descended on by a bunch of uniformed sadists with particularly nasty moustaches, wielding a red-hot branding iron twisted into the shape of a duck. The cowering prisoner suddenly perks himself up, folds his arms smugly and says: "You can't do that – that's unusual that is." The moustaches bristle cruelly and there is much muttering of "testiculos", but they eventually slink off knowing when they are licked.

Possibly, possibly – but in my case, Maria was looking at me expectantly and somewhat curiously. I knew what I must do. I felt the eyes of the portraits in the room downstairs upon me. Pedro the Cruel raised his thumbs with an evil smile; Ivan the Terrible winked; A. Stambolüski shook his pitchfork approvingly, and King Ludwig of Bavaria saluted a nearby tree.

I withdrew the garment from behind my back and a waft of it caught my nostrils. There was no doubt that what I was about to do was both cruel and unusual. I just hoped that if I got caught I could share a cell with someone nice.

Margaret's eyes were now like soup plates. I drew the two armpits together and held them in front of her. Her nose twitched and flared. The only time I had seen nostrils that wide was in some World War One footage of the Russian Front when someone had just let rip with a forty-pounder somewhere in the vicinity of the rear quarters of a cavalry officer's charger.

Margaret writhed moaned and whimpered, but I was resolute. I nodded to Maria and she began the interrogation; not so much: "Where were you when the Partisans blew up the railway line from Archangel to Smolensk?" More: "What exactly is Sir Winyard up to?" Margaret began to convulse and I slowly withdrew the offensive garment – which did the trick.

"I'll tell you, I'll tell you, but please…" Even though her wrists were tightly bound, she managed to beckon with a finger. Norman's shirt began its descent and I let her have it, both barrels, right in the face. She moaned and heaved and finally was still. I withdrew the garment, which, just as a point of interest, was stained at the back in the unmistakable shape of the Windward Isles, which told me exactly what Norman had been up to before he had retired for the night – and frankly I found it disgusting.

Margaret's face was now bright red and her hair stuck out as if struck by lightning. I recognised her facial expression from that of a Mother Superior in a rather smutty film I had once seen, entitled *The Nun and the Gardener*, when approached unexpectedly from behind, presumably by a gardener; it was hard to tell without clothes.

Margaret began to sing like a canary. I'd better give you the gist of it because the real dialogue was a bit patchy, punctuated with, "no, no, please," and "yes, yes, oh yes," as Norman's shirt rose and fell; actually rather similar to the soundtrack of, *The Nun and the Gardener*, now I come to think of it.

Sir Winyard was indeed up to no good. It seemed that he was planning a spectacular coup in every sense of the word. He was about to appoint himself Emperor of the Latvian Fish Isles! On hearing this, Maria interjected with the sensible objection that the LFI didn't have an emperor, to which Margaret replied sulkily that it soon would have. I suppose we shouldn't have been surprised – after all, Sir Winyard had already knighted himself; an unusual procedure for a mere council leader, although from my experience of councillors, most of them would be down on one knee like a shot, given the opportunity.

It appeared that the only obstacle, up until now, to Sir Winyard's bid for power, had been the Lord Chief Justice, who, Maria explained while pushing Norman's shirt comprehensively into Margaret's face, was a crusty old gentleman who not only disliked and distrusted Sir Winyard, but was kindly disposed to Alex, who had once complimented him with the utmost sincerity on the luxuriousness of his hair, which in fact was a very obvious wig. This went down well with the LCJ who was aware that most people refused to look at this item directly, taking only sidelong glances at it when they thought themselves unobserved.

This news then was particularly shocking to Maria and she was vocal on the subject while stuffing Norman's shirt diligently into Margaret's face. The big question was: were we too late? Apparently a constitutional document had been drawn up and was due to be signed by the LCJ; and Alex, as a mere president, would have no say in the matter.

"We have to act tonight," said Maria absent-mindedly poking bits of Norman's shirt into Margaret's nostrils; not that she appeared to mind. We left her happily tied to the bed. I wasn't worried; with the jaundiced view of life acquired from attendance at Donna's parties, I have observed that most people tied to beds seem quite happy with their situation.

Maria felt that we should, there and then, at one o'clock in the morning, break into the Town Hall and steal this document. She seemed quite definite about it. I, on the other hand, wasn't that sure, but on balance I felt that if a woman with a very large bosom takes hold of your hand and leads you off into complete darkness, one should go with the flow, or even be compliant (for any of my readers who work in the area of quality control).

It was a dark night, and the looming shadow of the Town Hall looked particularly brooding and gothic, but then again the situation had its compensations: in the darkness, I found myself colliding with the various moving parts that comprised Maria's anatomy which was an immensely pleasurable experience. It reminded me of a time when my father had taken me to a fair. We went on a thing called, *The Rotor* and to date it qualified as the most exciting experience of my life, but... I see you have anticipated me... Yes, this was altogether in another league, and not just in the area of sensuality. Consider the fragrance of edelweiss infusing the night air, the stars twinkling against the snow-capped peaks... you'd rather not? Oh, very well then. Bear in mind that the previous emotional zenith in my life had been set by my primary school teacher: a certain Miss Davis, she with the legs and the radiant smile, who took it upon herself, while in a particularly exuberant mood, to plant a kiss on the head of the most adjacent six-year-old. I was that six-year-old, and I should warn these young women of the world – because I expect this sort of thing is still going on in Rayners Lane and certain parts of Pinner even as we speak. What is it I should warn them of? I appear to have lost my thread... Oh yes, watch out for those careless kisses; they form a definition (or benchmark if you are still working in quality control) of love in a young boy's heart, from which he may never recover.

It was, then, in a sort of ecstatic muse (this is going to get worse, I warn you) that I reached the Town Hall. Maria had thought to nick Margaret's keys out of her handbag, and we let ourselves in. The hall was in darkness but there was something horribly forbidding about the place and, as we sneaked through the dining room, moonlight cast upon the portraits of Sir Winyard's massed ancestors. Quite apart from the various expressions of municipal meanness and small-mindedness, there was a universal expression of disapproval which was particularly forceful due to the extreme number and length of the noses that were looking down on us.

Evidently Maria shared this feeling because I found her small and shapely hand inserted again into mine. I felt a sudden feeling of immense gratitude to Sir Winyard's ancestors for their lifelong devotion to civic misery.

We sneaked up a staircase and along a hallway. Margaret had described the room where the document in question was last seen. The problem was that the room was not empty. I realised this only after I had opened the door and we were faced by a frightened-looking young man working at a desk. Fortunately I recognised the expression on his face; it was very specific, found only in young rabbits dithering around in the beams of oncoming cars' headlights, and in young accountants living and working under tyrannical circumstances. I was sufficiently sure of myself, having worked at Poulters' and having done a lot of night driving, to stride up to the young man and demand:

"And what exactly are you doing, might I ask?" I frowned, completely against my will; I wanted to pat him on the head and offer him a cigarette and a swig of brandy – just like we used to at Poulters'.

"Accounting, sir."

I folded my arms. "I can see that, young fellow, but whose accounts and why in the middle of the night?" I bent down and lowered my voice. "I'm from the European Commission, you know."

The lad nodded. "Yes, sir – I'm on punishment detail, working on the Council Railing Expenditure Accounts." He looked slightly puzzled. "Are you auditing our accounts, sir?"

"You could say that; you could say that indeed," I added with extra significance. I was bought up to be truthful at all times, and it was true that you, or anyone else for that matter, could say that if they liked. I inspected the young man's ledger and recognised at a glance the form of accounting that is widely used in the EU.

"These accounts appear to be completely bogus."

The young man breathed a sigh of relief. "Thank you, sir."

I ran a practised eye down the ledger; I needed to turn the conversation around.

"And why are you being punished?"

The young man looked surprised. "We're all being punished, sir."

"Ah," I said (the old fallback).

"I left the top off my felt-tip pen." (Excuse me interrupting, but I sometimes wish someone else with a felt-tip pen would leave it off.) "They said it was an act of anarchy against the Municipal Council."

"I see." (I like variation in my dialogue) "And the others?"

"The others, sir?"

"You said: you're all being punished."

"Oh yes, sir." He got up and led us to a rear window. We looked out on a throng of construction workers, all beavering away under arc lights.

"Hmm," I said, "And what have they done?"

The young man looked frightened. "Serious stuff – putting their bins out on the wrong day, leaning their bicycles against railings, dropping apple cores – all sorts."

"I see." I handed him back the ledger, pointing to a column as I did so. "This cross balances."

The young man looked visibly shocked and stammered an apology. “I’m terribly sorry, sir – I must have overlooked it.”

I smiled; it was time to be magnanimous. “These things happen, but you must check your work. You have applied to join the European Union, you know. Our accounts haven’t balanced for sixteen years.”

The young man looked impressed. “Cor.”

I winked. “And we mean to keep it that way; the one thing we cannot afford is transparency.”

The young man looked shocked. “No, sir – of course not.”

“Good man – now then, we need to see the document box next.”

I was pleased to see that the young man looked unsurprised at this remark.

“It’s gone, sir.”

“Gone!” This was Maria chipping in. I thought I’d mention it because otherwise you might have thought it was me. She didn’t look pleased. She sort of drew herself up, and the young man looked daunted, possibly due to the vast expanse of bosom confronting him. It impresses young men, this sort of thing.

“They took it earlier,” he explained.

“Where to?” Direct this girl; no pussyfooting.

“The LCJ I did hear.” He was still looking unsurprised, slightly daunted and impressed, but was also rather red-faced – the bosoms again, I suspect.

I felt that we’d been rather hard on him, what with finding fault with his accounting and confronting him with Maria without any sort of warning. I did what we used to do at Poulters’: ruffled the chap’s hair in a generally pally and supportive sort of way.

“Good chap – now keep this visit to yourself. We like to keep the element of surprise in our inspections.”

“Yes, sir – of course, sir – thank you, sir.”

I gave his hair a final tousle and we left.

We slipped out of the Town Hall and started making our way back. I felt sorry for Maria. I would have liked to help but it seemed as though we were too late, which all goes to prove that you should never underestimate a woman; a point which was made moments later, when I noticed that I was being led off the main boulevard into a dark back street on the north side of the valley.

"Where are we going?" I whispered loudly.

Maria stopped suddenly. Her face, in the moonlight, appeared animated by some emotion.

"To the Lord Chief Justice's house – the rat."

"Oh right," I said. Presumably this meant that we were to break in and steal the document. There didn't seem much point in demurral. After all, when 617 Squadron were briefed to fly across Germany at night, drop to sixty feet and lob experimental bombs into some dams, all you heard was the enthusiastic lighting of pipe bowls; there weren't any disjointed rumblings about, "Not fancying this one very much."

"Mr Curtis?" My thoughts were interrupted as they so often are.

"Right here," I said helpfully.

"Did I imagine it or did I see you tousle that young man's hair?"

"I think I did a bit – didn't want him getting depressed," I explained.

"I see." She shuddered slightly. At first I thought it was the cold, but then I saw that she was laughing. I was bemused. Bear in mind that my experience of women was limited. Donna considered laughter to be some sort of character defect that should be beaten out of people. I suppose I must have looked surprised, which is always fatal in these situations. The poor woman was just trying to quieten herself down when she happened to glance at me and lapsed into a fit of giggles. Thinking about it, if she ever finds herself short of work, I'm sure she could find a job in publishing; it seems an important part of the job description: to burst into fits of uncontrollable laughter at the sight of yours truly. I was pleased for her though; she seemed to be enjoying herself – and felt moved to give her hair a good tousle. This succeeded in sobering her up. She stared at me with a peculiar expression – a peculiar expression that is, unless you are an expert on animal behaviour, either from having read a lot of Desmond Morris, or spent a certain amount of time chatting to cats sitting on garden walls. There is a certain type of cat (and person for that matter) who when tousled or even chucked unexpectedly under the chin, will be sufficiently nonplussed not to know how to react at the moment the abuse takes place, and to stand there thinking the matter over before either reporting the matter to the police or rushing up to an innocent neighbour in the next garden and savagely attacking her ankles for no apparent reason. As the regular perpetrator of such crimes, I know that look well, and recognised it now on Maria's face. She came towards me and I moved to cross my legs in an attempt to protect my ankles. But instead, I found that she placed her hand (small and shapely if you remember) in mine and began to purr – although there were a few words mixed up in there:

"We must hurry."

We did – through silent snow-covered backstreets. There was something magical about this journey which I know you would rather I didn't dwell upon.

We arrived at the Lord Chief Justice's disgustingly luxurious residence. It didn't look inviting; it didn't have that easy-going look about it that some houses have, that say, "Why don't you pop in and see if there's anything you fancy, after all when you think about it as a good Marxist Leninist, 'each according to his needs' – and, 'all property is theft,' and all that sort of thing." Not that sort of house at all; it looked as though it held uptight views on the subject of private ownership – just the sort of attitude you would expect from a house occupied by a Lord Chief Justice in fact.

At this point in my ruminations the front door gave in to the persuasion of one of Maria's hairpins. It surprised me that a Lord Chief Justice's front door should be so weak-willed, but perhaps one shouldn't question these things in too much detail; I know my editor thinks I shouldn't.

We were inside, tiptoeing across an exceedingly sumptuous carpet. In fact the place oozed luxury. I don't know what the average LCJ earns, but I can only hope that he gets stung heavily in the highest tax bracket. It seems a bit much for some wealthy old codger to spend several hours a day glowering at a bloke with a jemmy sticking out of his pocket, making hurtful and highly personal remarks about the bloke's morality, when he himself (the LCJ that is) makes a fat living out of burglars, and ought to be grateful to them, because if it weren't for them, he would be out of work, and where else can you earn a small fortune being a pompous hypocrite (except in government of course)? And to make matters worse, the poor bloke isn't even allowed to mention this. So much for free speech, I say!

I should mention in passing that we were now in the living room and Maria was looking in a proprietary manner at a red leather document case. You are probably thinking two things (maybe three if you are a woman, because they have more complicated minds). Firstly, Maria appears to be doing all the work in this affair, and that I am a mere hanger-on; you'd be right to be thinking this but don't gloat too much because I have a VERY SIGNIFICANT part to play in this drama, yet to come – so there! Secondly, everything appears to be going nicely to plan, which is a bit of a departure from real life. Thirdly… I only suggested that my female readers (and there can't be many) might have a third thought, but I haven't a clue as to what it might be, women's minds being the complex devices that they are – but I would hazard a guess that it concerns mustard-coloured sofas or silver handbags.

You have every right to think these things, but I can confound my critics on the second point. At the very moment that Maria was about to pounce on the red leather document case, we were disturbed by a noise. What sort of noise you might gasp? And I can be specific in reply: a regular thumping noise accompanied by a background rustle interspersed with occasional heavy clicks – not dissimilar in fact to the noise of a bad-tempered old boy in a nightshirt clomping down the stairs while loading a double-barrelled shotgun.

I wouldn't say I was afraid, but others probably would. Maria was made of sterner stuff. She expanded her chest (which took my mind off things) and looked decidedly annoyed.

"Well?" she said.

The old boy also looked annoyed. For a while the two stood there glowering at each other, giving me just time to give you a bit of a description of this old codger. Bad tempered and nightshirted, you know already; add to this then: knees just showing under the nightshirt (two of, both extremely knobbly) – slippers (brown leather, one right hand, one left hand) – nose (one, centrally affixed, offering good all round view of surrounding countryside) – eyes (one pair, mean and beady) – mouth (comprising one upper lip and one lower, sulky and petulant). Other interesting features included being about eighty and wearing the most extraordinary wig I have ever seen. In an Iraqi shop window it would have held place of honour as "the Mother of all Wigs!" 'Cos it was! Opulent, flowing, silky and adorned with a row of tight legal-looking curls.

We all stared at each other for a moment. The old boy was spluttering with some emotion that had evidently been troubling him for a while, and finally managed to spit out:

"What do you mean? Well?"

Maria wasn't having any of it. "I mean: what is it that you want, disturbing people in the middle of the night when you should be in bed, doubtless waking up the neighbours with your snoring?"

"Disturbing people!" I got the impression this remark had offended him. Maria definitely had him unmanned, although by the look of him I wondered if he had ever been fully manned in the first place. She pressed home her advantage.

"We know your game."

At this point, he showed the first sign of uncertainty. For all I knew she was bluffing. There was a certain lady who attended Donna's parties who made a regular income out of the local judiciary by this method. She explained that all JPs had particularly disgraceful private lives, and that just by telling them that she, "knew everything" she could sting them for ten thousand a year, or in the case of QCs she, "knew every disgusting detail," which was worth twenty thousand.

Maria continued, "And I thought better of you! What sordid, twisted, underhand deal have you struck with him?"

The LCJ was evidently losing this confrontation. He looked decidedly sheepish now. Maria pressed home her advantage.

"More wigs I suppose."

The LCJ rallied a little with a show of offended dignity. "Do you suppose for one moment that the Lord Chief Justice of the Latvian Fish Isles would allow improper influence to be bought to bear by the provision of suitably dignified headwear for the supreme judicial figure? *Pudoris super ista*, Ms Shine."

Maria gave him a look. I should mention that this is another example of masterful use of literary device, so little appreciated by certain short-sighted publishers; I refer of course to understatement. You will remember some pages back my allusions to some fairly disparaging looks loosed off in my general direction by Maria. While I found these stimulating, they also made me question my own self-worth and found that it amounted to something approximately three angstroms high (not to be confused with an Anstruther, who you will remember was my old headmaster). Looking at Maria now, I didn't know whether to feel hurt or gratified. The look that she had just fired off at the LCJ was of a far greater calibre than anything she had discharged at me. The part of me that felt hurt was weeping like a baby and complaining, "She never looked at me like that," and it was true, she hadn't – not like this. Her lip curled, her eyes burnt down on him; her expression as a whole, could be said to snarl in disgust. He shrivelled before her. Assuming his self-esteem to have started out at say, twenty angstroms high, it shrank now to something less than one and a half (or three Anstruthers which I personally reckon to be approximately half an angstrom; it is just a shame that the scientific community as a whole has failed to recognise the Anstruther yet as an official unit).

I wondered how much more the old boy could take. His knees hadn't struck me as particularly strong in the first place and were now beginning to knock together.

"Well?" she barked at him. I knew now that he would crumble. Every man has his breaking point. One of Donna's theme nights featured interrogations by French maids with feather dusters. Even hardened ex-SAS men cracked in the end, and there was a certain look on their faces towards the moment of capitulation.

"Well?" she demanded again.

He would have given her the blue print of the uranium enrichment process at this point. "Wallpaper!" he shouted, as if it was a relief to get it off his chest. He turned suddenly and beckoned us into an adjoining room. The walls were bare. A pasting table stood alone in the centre of the room. The LCJ gestured towards it. All resistance was gone now. He fell to his knees before the table in an apparent act of worship.

"You see?"

I did see. Draped across the table was the most extraordinarily tasteless, loud, tacky-looking wallpaper. Apart from the gaudiness of it, with a crushed velvet finish, inlaid with gold and silver thread, it was extraordinarily thick. I was just trying estimate this in millions of Anstruthers when the LCJ appeared to read my mind.

"Ten and a half millimetres thick!"

"Wallpaper!" This was Maria speaking. I don't go around shouting, "wallpaper!" at people in the middle of the night.

The LCJ shifted weight awkwardly and muttered, "*Ergo mea putare protius bellus ist*."

"*Sed polus nimium magnificus*," I replied.

The old boy appeared to notice me for the first time, which was odd because I had been hanging around for a while now. "I suppose you are this EU Commissioner I've been hearing about?"

I nodded and introduced myself.

He looked sourly at me. "Latin is strictly prohibited in the LFI!"

"Oh," I said, "it's just that you said: *Ergo mea*…"

He held up his hand with a pained look. I didn't think my Latin was that bad, although I must admit Anstuther had rather gone to town on the subject in my school report. It wasn't through lack of practice; the fact is that teaching of Latin at public schools was used as a method of inuring small boys to the tedium of life at the top for which they were being prepared. Extra instruction was meted out as a punishment to certain boys who got caught attempting to break the record for getting their penises out in front of the class with their eyes shut. The skilful part was judging exactly how long the Latin teacher would have his back turned writing things on the blackboard such as: "*Felis sedilis ab mattus*."

Unfortunately, although my record breaking attempt was heroic, it was also optimistic to the point of being foolhardy, at something over seven minutes, and unfortunately, the last five minutes were spent in full view of, "Mad Stevo," our Latin teacher, who had neither a sense of humour nor any homosexual tendencies (either condition might have reduced my sentence) and punished me with so much Latin homework that I became quite conversational in it. You can imagine then that I was disappointed by the reaction of the LCJ who was at this moment frowning at me.

"All our legislature is written in Latin, Mr Curtis. It is both inaccessible and unintelligible to the people – which is, after all, the purpose of the law."

Maria was growing restless. "Could we please get back to the point, which is: that this miserable Faust has sold his soul for the price of some moth-eaten wigs and particularly disgusting wallpaper."

The old boy opened his mouth to protest. I gathered from his expression that the penultimate insult to a Lord Chief Justice was to question his taste in headgear, and the ultimate, his wallpaper, but he met Maria's gaze and began to whimper.

It was at this moment that I was struck by a momentous revelation. I don't know whether any of my readership have personally encountered any momentous revelations. They affect people in different ways; with me, they cause a tingling sensation behind the ears. It was the expression on the LCJ's face: I recognised it, you see – I had witnessed it first hand at one of Donna's parties, on the face of the local MP (Liberal Democrat in case you are politically minded). Donna was having trouble with the local council over planning permission for a gazebo (possibly because it included a forty-foot-deep dungeon designated for the purposes of "cruel and unusual punishment," – not your average gazebo). Fortunately, the local Lib Dem was a "sub" (submissive) and Donna did a thorough job on him, which is where I return to the look on the LCJ's face; it was identical to that on the face of the local representative of the people of Harrow constituency (which included parts of Kenton and Wealdstone) when Donna appeared before him in tight leather, brandishing a bullwhip: sort of slavering anticipation.

I had sometimes doubted the relevance of my career to date to my position as a European Union Special Commissioner (as no doubt have others), but I saw now that my training in accountancy and having an ex-girlfriend specialising in bondage and sado-masochism were in fact essential requirements. I addressed the Lord Chief Justice.

"*Protractus flagritriba necessitas est*," I said, which translated, I hoped, as: "I think a thorough and vicious beating may be required, your worship." I was on the right track. The old boy's mouth fell open and he began to pant with excitement, which, incidentally, made me wonder if he had ever been a Liberal Democrat. I saw that he looked at Maria expectantly, which was not surprising; she looked particularly stern at that moment. In fact I wasn't particularly looking forward to breaking it to her exactly what I was letting her in for. "It's for your country," sprang to mind; men have been saying this to women over the centuries under all sorts of dubious pretexts, but in this case it would be the literal truth.

At this point, the old boy pottered back into the room holding a horse whip. You probably hadn't noticed that he'd left the room. Well, neither had I. People don't tell me everything, in fact they hide things from me.

Maria looked surprised. The LCJ ambled up to me and handed me the whip, at which point I also looked surprised – very, very surprised. I had taken it for granted in all this that his chosen chastiser would be Maria, for all the obvious reasons; in particular that she was a woman. Personally, I've never enjoyed being beaten by men. It happened quite a bit at school, and left me cold (apart from the selected areas which were left rather hot). Also, I had thought that the LCJ had been slavering in the general direction of Maria, but I saw now that she had been standing behind me and I had done that thing that Sherlock was always ticking Watson off for: making assumptions. Finally (minor detail) the old boy was evidently as queer as a coot.

"It's for your country!" My words floated back at me. It wasn't even my bloody country! I took the whip and whacked it into my hand purposefully. "If something is worth doing..." as my mum used to say – although I'm not sure she had in mind beating the living daylights out of a Lord Chief Justice from foreign parts, or indeed the foreign parts of a Lord Chief Justice.

The old boy tottered forwards and bent over a conveniently situated desk. I looked around at Maria with the thought that it might be seemly if she left the room. I'm sure at times like this in Jane Austen novels, all the ladies withdrew to smoke cigars and speculate on the length of the Reverend Collins' thing. Not Maria; she stood legs akimbo with her arms folded and with a curious look of anticipation on her face.

"*Inclino posterium*," I ordered.

The old boy lifted his nightshirt and dropped his pants. I hadn't intended any pant removal. Perhaps I should take a refresher course in Latin: I suspect it has changed a bit since I was at school.

I will not dwell too long on the painful details of what followed. I originally ran to sixteen lines on the subject – a very similar number of lines to those that appeared on the upholder of justice in the Latvian Fish Isles' bottom in fact – but there is enough violence on the television nowadays without me adding to it. Suffice to say that I let him have it. Well might you lift your eyebrows, but what you may not know (having lived a sheltered life outside accountancy) is that somewhere in the assembly stage of the "sub" persona, for reasons still unexplored by theologians, the Divine Creator shoved the purple pain wire into the green pleasure socket. I set about both buttocks viciously until the poor old boy was tottering around clutching his cheeks, muttering "*graphicus ecstasia*." This had the unfortunate effect of reminding me of old Anstruther (who tottered on his run-up due to extreme old age, infirmity and cluttering up brain cells with Latin verbs that were required elsewhere for maintaining balance). I let the LCJ have another six, closely grouped and all near the bull's-eye. Sublimating his image with that of Anstruther helped enormously – made me feel much better about the whole business, and rather the same for the LCJ I think. I'd like to retain a certain minimum standard of delicacy in this book (and my editor says she would like this too) so let us just say that should the LCJ have decided to spend the rest of the night putting up his wallpaper, somewhere around the fifteenth stroke he developed the resources with which to do it – all over the carpet.

And when all was done, the old boy continued tottering about in an Anstruther type way and his muttering became slowly coherent.

"Mr Curtis," he zigzagged his way towards me and grasped my hand. "Mr Curtis – no one ever – in all the world – I can't tell you how happy you've made me – can't express my gratitude..." Tears were now flowing down his cheeks and he absent-mindedly grabbed his backside; probably a mistake because he groaned in pain, then cried a bit more, and finally burst into a sobbing fit. The man was a mess.

"You will express your gratitude," commanded Maria.

"Of course," the old boy said absent-mindedly, "I will tear up the document right away."

I shook my head. "No."

Maria and the LCJ looked at me in surprise. Once again I was able to draw on previous experience: this time, my association with that cunning old bastard, Poulter. And boy was this cunning! Don't think for one moment that I'm going to tell it to you all at once. You know my views on dramatic suspense. In fact, just to keep you all fascinated, I will take a couple of sentences to describe to you some peculiar dreams I had been having of late about crop spraying. You probably know that there is a ban on the use of organophosphates for crop spraying. Interestingly... Leave it until Chapter Fifteen you think. Very well, if you are quite sure, in which case, I shall return to my narrative…

The unclassified part of my plan then, was to let Sir Winyard achieve supreme power, but this would be his undoing because when I appeared to be persuaded to accept his wish to join the European Union and produced the Accession Treaty for signing, there would be a lethal addition! The only problem was that I didn't have the Accession Treaty about my person and was concerned for a moment whether the old codger would be so compliant in the morning. But here is where the psychology of the, "sub" comes in. During the night, the Lord Chief Justice of the Latvian Fish Isles would be bound to roll on his back. This for most people would be a painful reminder, but for a "sub" it would produce yet another round of pleasure so that I fully expected the old boy to be in a state of ecstasy that would last through until teatime.

"We'll be back in the morning for your signature on the Accession Treaty," I said to him curtly, and was not surprised to see him look back at me in a decidedly huffy manner.

"*Sic vitae est*," he said snootily. "Incidentally, I assume this treaty to be in Latin?"

"English," I corrected him – "well, sort of."

The old boy looked appalled. "English! Dear me, anyone could read it."

I shook my head. "You obviously haven't seen any EU treaties. There are hundreds of pages of meaningless platitudes, but cunningly mixed in with them are the nasty bits. They are designed by industrial psychologists. A feeling of gloom sets in after page six; this progresses to morbid depression by page ten, a feeling of personal worthlessness by page fifteen, and horror and suicidal thoughts by page twenty. A coma is usually induced by page thirty and no one has remained conscious or alive in a meaningful sense of the word by page forty. I say that because French presidents insist on being able to read the whole document to make sure everything is to their advantage at everyone else's expense. So you see, a clause inserted near the end is quite safe from being read."

We took our leave. It seemed to me that Maria was thoughtful, and I caught her looking at me sideways once or twice. It wasn't the sort of look I was that keen on. The only other time I remembered being looked at in that way was by a previous girlfriend shortly before a significant conversation on the lines of: "I feel that at this time in my life I need some time by myself to determine my future path," which when translated, read as, "I've just met a bloke with a Porsche." But it couldn't be anything like that. You can't dump someone you are not going out with.

Lights from the Presidential Residence greeted us across the snow. We slipped inside, watched curiously by a couple of half-naked women lying propped up against the wall inside the door. One was smoking a pipe; the other was drinking from a bottle of rum. They looked as though they were on a break from filming, *Caligula*. The owner of the bottle wolf-whistled.

"Evening Miss." This was followed by a loud giggle, inspiring the owner of the pipe to remove it temporarily and observe.

"Phwooooar – she gets bigger by the day."

It is possible that the pipe-smoker would have made some additional comments, but a sound like a small calibre rifle shot decided her to rub her cheek instead. We left them in a heap of giggles. I was impressed to see that Maria remained entirely expressionless, but not for long; two minutes later we found that Margaret's room was empty; somehow she had broken free and Maria gave vent to a variety of expressions, requiring a broad spectrum of censorship: one "U", four "As", five, "Xs" and several, "thirteen, but only when accompanied by an adult." She went on to add cynically that there was no point in looking for Margaret except in the immediate environs of Sir Winyard. There was nothing for it but for us to turn in for the night.

CHAPTER 15

I had a dream that night – not of the Martin Luther King sort – not that is unless he was also susceptible to dreams about crop spraying with organophosphates (you see – I said I'd save it for Chapter 15). It is possible that he did, but if so he kept it to himself and stuck to the edited highlights when addressing the assembled masses the next day – in which case I have every sympathy with him because there is evidently a conspiracy in the world of publishing to keep people with dreams off the subject of crop spraying and organophosphates in general… My own have been struck through with a red pen several times.

I was trapped in a Bulgarian orchard, hiding from A. Stambolüski for some reason. He was standing on an orange box shaking a pitchfork at a load of peasants (which maybe explains why I was hiding from him) who were presumably revolting. It was a stirring speech. I could tell by the fact that the peasants themselves looked stirred; and they evidently agreed with much of what he said, because they shook their pitchforks and called out "Urrrr", in unison. I should point out, firstly that they were actually members of the Bulgarian Peasants Party, not Unison, which didn't even exist in those days – and secondly that, "Urrrr", is Serbo-Croat for "Arrrrrr", or "Oooooh-arrrrr", in dialect.

Well you know what dreams are like: it all ended up with me being chased around the orchard by Bulgarian peasants in

Cockshutt Model 30 tractors with crop-spraying attachments driven off twenty spline power-take-offs – which was completely ridiculous because A. Stambolüski died in 1923 and although the power-take-off had been invented in 1918, it was only fitted to McCormick-Deering 15-30s back then, and they only had 6 splines. Of course I realised this as soon as I woke up and laughed heartily at the whole episode, but somehow I could not get back to sleep just in case A. Stambolüski's lot were still lying in wait for me behind the apple trees. I decided on an early breakfast instead.

Norman of course, was already in attendance. It's one of those empirical laws that it is impossible to be down to breakfast before Norman. If Heisenberg and Schrödinger had studied Norman's breakfast habits instead of wave mechanics, they would probably still be friends. As it was, they ended up saying some extremely hasty things about each other: "I knew of Heisenberg's theory, of course, but I felt discouraged, not to say repelled, by the methods of transcendental algebra, which appeared difficult to me, and by the lack of visualisability." That was Schrodinger. "I had no faith in a theory that ran completely counter to our Copenhagen conception." And that was Heisenberg. From which you can see that there was no chance whatsoever of reconciliation even though their mums stayed friends and went shopping together. This is a general problem with scientists. Take those chaps searching for dark matter in a tunnel under the Gran Sasso mountain for instance; silly place to look if you ask me. Dark matter is notoriously shy, and you won't find much doing in the way of shyness in Italy. No – they should forget it and concentrate on something more definite, such as Norman being down to breakfast before anybody else. You could call it Norman's Law and give it its own formula (Pi would be in it somewhere).

And these certainties in life give comfort to a chaotic world. To see Norman at work on a blueberry and apple pie chased away the last ghostly images of rampaging Bulgarian peasants, although

I would have preferred Norman's pie not to have contained apples.

I poured myself a cup of coffee. Norman grunted a greeting – accepted as, "Good morning," in most countries of the world except Korea where they tend to say, "*Annyong-hi jumushyossumnikka*" instead.

"I had a strange dream last night, Norm."

The noise of a food processing plant working with the needle hovering around, "maximum safe intake" ceased suddenly; although activity further down the production line could still be heard as a sort of gurgling interspersed with the sound of singing.

A finger prodded me sharply in the ribs and a shower of delicious sugared piecrust exploded in my face as Norm announced:

"So did I!"

That was it really; it's another of nature's laws that a dream of Norm's takes precedence over anyone else's. Lucky that Norm wasn't anywhere in the vicinity of Martin Luther King on the 28th August 1963, otherwise a massive American audience would have found themselves bored rigid, instead of moved to higher things.

Norm leant over in a confidential manner, which wasn't entirely necessary since we were the only ones there.

"It was of a sexual nature, Curtis."

Now there's a surprise. Norm's dreams were usually fairly mucky.

"I was in bed." Good start, I thought, for a mucky dream, although there are other locations: hospitals, offices and bicycle sheds sprang to mind. "And I found Margaret lying alongside me." Norm paused for the impact of this to sink in. "She was sort of nestled up to me." Norm chuckled. "Funny things, dreams – she was licking my armpit."

You might just as well have said "rabbits" to a Jack Russell terrier for the affect this remark had on my ears.

"Did you, errrm?"

Norman looked at me stiffly. "You seem to assume, Curtis, that I would take advantage of such a situation purely for the purposes of gratification."

"Yes – but did you?"

He took my point as a fair one. "As a matter of fact…"

I was now extremely suspicious. In order to present my readers with a balanced review of the evidence, my lawyer wishes to present this case on my behalf. Unfortunately Ms Simpson is on her lunch (shuck beans, stack cakes and Southern fried chicken with tossed salad and a blueberry muffin covered in molasses) so one of her associates has reluctantly agreed to take the floor.

"Ahem," (sound of throat clearing) "M'lud, ladies and gentlemen of the jury – including the lady in the second row with the appalling hat with waxed fruit on the top – consider the evidence if you will and I think you will find it compelling. Do I really need to do more than bring to your attention the matter of the licked armpit? I – THINK – NOT. Even in this day and age of miniskirts, kiss-me-quick hats, edible pants and general licentiousness, how often is it that a young woman assails a strange young man lying naked and heavily unconscious in his bed in the middle of the night, by licking his armpits? One or two of you look dubious. I can't do much about that, but let me explain further. My client has already informed you that this young man's dreams were often of a sexual nature. He did not mislead you; indeed, the content of these dreams could have come directly from the script of, *The Nun and the Gardener*, but my client made one significant omission in his testimony. This young man's dreams, always and without exception, involved food! Ah! You might say – would I care to substantiate this allegation, and I think M'lud knows well enough that I would. Very well then; I have a list of this young man's dreams; allow me to distribute Exhibit A (a dream). I shall shout for the hard of hearing. Thank you, M'lud. In this dream, the young man, identified by several witnesses of impeccable character as, 'Norman', indulged in coitus with Marie Antoinette while eating cake with her. How? You wish to know, and it is my brief to enlighten you. You must take into consideration the fact that the young lady in question was French – a race to whom sex and food are no strangers. Norman was leaning over her shoulder helping himself, if you'll pardon the expression M'lud, with a confectionary fork. But this is not my point; one does not need to be a psychologist – I think the position is clear…"

"Norman," I said.

"Yes, Curtis?"

"How do you know that it actually was a dream?"

Norman chuckled. "It's funny you should say that, because when I woke up, I had this feeling in my scrotum. You know when…"

I cut him short. I hadn't started my breakfast yet. "Yes, yes – so maybe it wasn't a dream?"

Norman looked wistful and sighed. "I wish you were right. She's a lovely girl; she has…"

"Yes, yes."

"I know it was a dream, Curtis. It was all strange and muddled like dreams are, and I don't just mean the business of the armpits: it all started with you breaking into my room and stealing my shirt – you see what I mean?" He laughed. "Not likely in real life is it – you're not even my size."

I started toying with some toast. Altogether this was good news, and not just for Norman's testicles. On a more serious level (without any offence intended against Norman's testicles who, I dare say, are serious enough in that they do not read tabloid newspapers and watch soaps on television) this meant that Margaret had not sneaked off and betrayed us to Sir Winyard. This thought took me to the far right-hand corner of my piece of toast (when viewed from the rear; for'ard starboard for nautical types). I was just buttering up a second piece – not so much telling it that I found it attractive and that it looked young for its age; more, spreading butter on it – when I heard the patter of approaching feet, which turned out to be Margaret in a flimsy nightdress. She made a sort of pleasurable squeaking noise at the sight of Norman and immediately sidled up to him.

Norman's face was a study. This was too much for him. Somewhere in the mechanism, someone was trying to process this new development and right-clicked too hastily, causing Norman to crash. Margaret, meanwhile, was squeezing and stroking him. I've only ever seen such shamelessness in our family cat when my mum came back from the fish market (ginger with white splodges of course – you know the type: no self-restraint). It occurred to me as fortunate for Margaret that none of Norman's exes were in attendance, to save her from being marched off, strapped to an oak tree and read long extracts from the leather-bound book with brass clasps.

Norman was slowly rebooting. A huge smile littered with pie crumbs spread across his face. I was relieved. This is one of my nicer characteristics: I wish only the best for my pals, and I hadn't been sure how Norman would react to his altered circumstances, but apparently he approved. He patted Margaret in a proprietary sort of way and asked her in that intimate tone reserved for lovers:

"Would you like some of my pie?"

This question will remain, just as the whereabouts of the Higgs Boson Particle (unless it is also hanging around in a tunnel in Italy), unanswered, because at this moment, Maria entered the room. I should explain that at this point I was approaching the sixty-fifth parallel of my second piece of toast – up around the top of Finland – and about to bite deeply into a sparsely populated region of the Arctic Circle. But I suspended my plans and let the Husky's frisk around for a bit, for I too was overwhelmed. Maria was wearing a white blouse. So what? You might rudely interrupt; she always wore crisp white blouses, she probably bought them in bulk. Yes, but if you would just listen for a moment instead of jumping to conclusions, this blouse was different. Firstly, it wasn't a crisp blouse; it was a silk blouse that billowed around considerably. Secondly, it had two buttons undone, revealing a considerable length of cleavage. If one compares Maria's cleavage to something of a parable length such as the Mexican border, she was revealing an area from Guadalupe Bravos to Piedras Negras. I averted my eyes too late to prevent turning a bright shade of crimson and ejecting my toast onto the kitchen table – the whole of the Arctic Circle and a small area of the Kola Peninsula.

I noticed that someone was mucking about with time again. Possibly the scientists chasing dark matter had finally cornered the poor thing in its deep tunnel where it had thought itself to be safe cuddled up to the Higgs Boson particle. Or maybe the contents of Maria's blouse were themselves pulling at the very fabric of the space-time continuum. Either way, I felt that it was demanded of me to make an absolute arse of myself. There I was smugly describing Norm's brain malfunction but at least he had the good sense to shut the thing down; mine was going critical. It's all to do with the amygdala you see; this is the bit of the brain associated with pleasure and displeasure. A party had broken out in mine, with champagne corks popping, balloons, hard drugs – the lot. It was a City of London pub on annual bonus night – young bucks stampeding around with their ties undone, some of them blatantly manipulating themselves – disgraceful really, particularly in the presence of ladies, not that there are many ladies in my amygdala. They made their presence felt briefly during puberty, causing a fleeting interest in other young boy's testicles (note the words, "briefly" and "fleeting" please). Since those days, they have taken up lesbianism and see their main role as disapproval of most of what I do, and to cause occasional unmanly outbursts during piano concertos, and to express rampant disapproval at even a glimpse of a football match – oh, and they help me out a bit with my ballroom dancing.

The problem with all this partying was that it was right above the speech centre, which contains some delicate equipment, working at this very moment on sending an important message though the appropriate motor neurons to the effect that, if it wasn't too much trouble, would they mind contacting the diaphragm, shape the mouth and waggle the tongue a bit to produce the following sound:

"Good morning, Ms Shine, I trust you slept well," which unfortunately came out as a sort of strangled squawk. I don't blame anyone in particular; they all gave of their best. I decided to turn it into a cough. Norman thumped me helpfully on the back, which had the fortunate effect of spilling everyone's drinks in the amygdala and generally spoiled the party – and I was able to speak again.

"Good morning, Ms Shine, I trust you slept well."

"Erm, yes," said Maria distraitly. She had just observed the fact that Margaret appeared to be attempting to climb inside Norman. "And you?" she asked Margaret coldly.

"Oh yes," replied Margaret with a decidedly smutty giggle, while rubbing the inside of Norman's thigh. The poor creature was all over the place. It is always dangerous for a woman to transform from ice maiden to sex kitten without spending several hours in a decompression chamber.

Maria and I discussed the matter after breakfast. She suggested that we should make our move while Margaret's infatuation lasted, and present Sir Winyard with the Accession Treaty for signature. She was of the opinion that Margaret's infatuation with Norman was unlikely to survive another lunchtime, which was rather cynical I thought. But I saw a distinct danger in shoving a large document under Sir Winyard's nose and handing him a pen. For once my intuition was superior. You see, here I had the benefit of having worked for Poulter. If anyone asked him to sign anything, he would immediately summon a team of crooked lawyers (Messrs xxxxx Carter someone or other – very litigious – on the seventeenth floor) to pick over it looking for catches. Whereas Sir Winyard, having just made himself Emperor, would waste little time in throwing his weight around I felt sure.

"He'll call us," I said confidently.

The phone rang. Maria picked it up and handed it to me in silence, with a curious look in her eyes that I had never seen directed towards me on the face of a woman before (except for my three-year-old niece when I bought her a particularly large ice cream) respect!

There was the sort of noise one finds in a wind tunnel coming down the phone line, which I took to be a rush of exhaled breath from a particularly large nose.

"Ah, Sir Winyard," I said.

"Mr Curtis," he acknowledged, then coughed modestly. "It appears that the people of the Latvian Fish Isles have, in their gratitude for my relentless application to civic duty, been gracious enough to bestow on me the title of –" He paused for dramatic effect, which would not have pleased my editor or the world of literature at large, although I think you know that my own personal views are much more tolerant on the matter – and I see no point whatsoever in making objectionable and personal comments in red felt-tip at this point; it's not helpful, and more to the point, it's not my fault. I'm only describing the pause dramatis created by Sir Winyard; it's not as if I am in any way responsible for it. Don't shoot the messenger, I say.

"...Emperor!" Sir Winyard paused again for this to sink in. I thought I'd play along, rather as prostitutes do when confronted by particularly small genitalia (so I've heard): I gasped.

Sir Winyard cleared his throat. "You have a Queen, I believe, Mr Curtis?"

"Er, yes," I agreed hesitantly, "not personally you understand, but we do have one kicking around in a palace waving at people, that is when she's not doing the housework."

"Quite. Hmmmm – Your Majesty, Your Majesty." He appeared to be toying with this as a form of address. "I think not." I could hear the sort of wrinkling noise that a particularly large nose makes in the process of turning up. "I do not recognise your Queen, Mr Curtis."

"Well she has aged a bit – she's gone eighty you know."

"I think perhaps: 'Your High and Incredible Oneness,' is more appropriate – but you, Mr Curtis…"

"Yes," I said, finding time beginning to drag slightly.

"…Can continue to call me, Sir Winyard."

"Oh thanks – that's jolly decent of you." I think I sounded affable enough but actually I was a bit peeved. I'm rather fond of her with the handbag and gloves. I used to get strapped to a chair in front of the TV on Christmas Day as a child, and HM would give me a personal dressing down while staring directly at me – my parents nodding knowingly on the sidelines. She was polite enough but she knew exactly what I'd been up to in sickening detail – greed, (a whole bag of gobstoppers) selfishness, (taking the last custard cream out of the tin when I'd already had four) dishonesty, (telling Miss Davis that my lunch box had been stolen when actually I had scoffed the contents at eleven o'clock break). She knew the lot, HM! Only, being well bred, she refrained from clipping me round the ear or using any choice language – which is what separates royalty from the rest of us plebs.

This is not to say that I have at all times been as deferential and as loyal a subject as I might have been. There is the matter of the Golden Jubilee celebrations. Street parties were held. Thinking about it now, I can't think for the life of me what people were actually doing behind the barricades in the blocked-off streets, but something quiet and respectful I suppose, NOT driving a motor-bike through the barrier with an extremely pissed-up friend on the back waving a bottle of brown ale and shouting, "Up the Queen!" which could have sounded patriotic enough if he had not then sniggered loudly and roared, "Right up the Queen!" Fortunately I was able to create a diversion by failing to negotiate a pavement outside the Methodist Church, spilling us both over a low wall and giving my friend the opportunity to vomit copiously into the flower bed, announcing, "I needed that," before passing out. In my defence I would point out that I had consumed four pints of light and bitter and was not in complete control of my senses, my friend or my motorbike.

Anyway, my point is that while HM might tap the odd gloved fingernail or two at this, she should know that this was a single departure from a lifetime of loyalty. Indeed, some authors have been rewarded for their labours with a variety of decorations. It sounds a little presumptuous, but I can just envisage the situation…

"Mr Curtis."

"Maaam."

"Come now, there is no need to prostrate yourself."

"I think there is Maaaam – a most excellent cucumber sandwich. Did you make it yourself?"

"I'm going to knight you now."

"Oh thank you, Maaam. There's no need you know, an MBE would be quite sufficient, your Infinite Majesty."

"Not at all, Mr Curtis – I insist. You should see some of the peasants I have to decorate – crooked bankers, those awful Beatles and some perfectly dreadful football manager…"

"We still haven't got the chewing gum out of the bloody carpet – damned socialists – country's going to the dogs." (Prince Phillip – off stage left)

"Thank you Maaaam."

I mean to say, when you consider it: most of the recent presidents of major European countries have only been saved from a long spell behind bars by presidential immunity, whereas our Queen has never knowingly sold anything dodgy in a car boot sale, vandalised a telephone box or phoned her mates pretending to be a clap doctor with bad news – as far as we know. And here was Sir Winyard, turning his nose up at her! A bit of a cheek I call it.

The sound of a fairly well established hurricane (Norma I think, but possibly Catrina) sounded in my ear. It was Sir Winyard.

"Perhaps after the ceremony, Mr Curtis, you would like to call to receive the Latvian Fish Isles' formal signature on the instrument of accession to the European Union."

"Oh, er, yes of course," seemed the appropriate thing to say – not too enthusiastic. I put the phone down thoughtfully.

Maria suggested that she should deliver the treaty to the LCJ while I finished my breakfast

Some hours later, we set off for the Town Hall, Maria and I in front and Margaret and Norman bringing up the rear, cuddling each other nauseatingly. My mind strayed… A recent statistic claimed that men think about sex every fifty-two seconds. I wouldn't like to comment without my lawyer who is currently having her breakfast (kippers on rye with waffles, maple syrup and three eggs, sunny side up). I'm afraid that in the presence of Maria, this statistic worked in reverse: I thought about some subject other than sex every fifty-two seconds. At this particular moment, I was on one of those rather longer intervals in between not thinking about sex, and consequently started guiltily when I found that Maria was talking to me.

"Mr Curtis?"

"Yes," I said, trying to sound as if I had been thinking of woodwork, climate change and plant morphology.

"Can I ask you a personal question?"

"Of course," I said, praying that it would not be on the lines of, "What were you thinking of?"

"Are you married?"

"I don't think so."

"Presumably you would know if you were."

"I'm sure I would have been informed – I mean it is usual, isn't it? Are you?"

"Am I married?"

"Yes – are you married?"

"No, although I have been proposed to several times."

"I'm not surprised."

She stopped suddenly. "Why do you say that?"

The next few moments were spent disentangling ourselves from the overheated body parts of Norman and Margaret. They had been so absorbed in their study of field biology that they hadn't noticed that we had stopped, and in the resultant collision the dining car and sleeper had run through and mangled themselves in the first class. When order was restored, Maria repeated her question:

"Why did you say that?"

I fidgeted; it was an awkward moment. "Well, I mean, you're very… You're er, well, damned attractive."

She giggled unexpectedly; one doesn't expect goddesses to giggle. "You think so?"

"Does the Pope like peanut butter?" I'm not sure this came out quite as I intended, but Maria looked pleased.

"The trouble is, Mr Curtis, that some men are attracted to the exterior rather than the interior, if you follow my meaning."

"Absolutely," I agreed while sweating profusely. I felt more was required of me. "I mean, one of my friends, chap I knew at school actually, fell in love with his fridge."

"Fell in love with his fridge?" She was looking at me quizzically.

"Yes – chap called Maurice. He was always a bit obsessional; his first ever girlfriend used to cut the crusts off her sandwiches because she wore a brace, and he kept them all in a bag and couldn't bring himself to throw them away – that sort of thing. Then his fridge packed up, which was a major event because it had belonged to his parents who had been killed in a plane crash when he was four. So he had to get a new one and of course he resented it. At first he would only use the freezing compartment and even then the guilt would keep him awake at night. Then he found his milk was going off and he started slipping the odd pint into the back of the door, always with an apology to the old fridge which of course was witness to the whole sordid affair because he couldn't bring himself to throw it out. Well, that was the thin end of the wedge: cheese, eggs, avocados, yoghurt; slowly but surely he filled the thing up. His guilt was so severe that he had to go for therapy, and it all came out. I won't repeat it all to you because Freudian psychology is particularly mucky; it seems that the fridge represented his mother, the avocados were her breasts, the yoghurt, his semen, and I can't remember the frozen peas, Belgian pâté, horseradish or the sardine and tomato paste – just as well really. The long and the short of it was that he was trying to get his fridge pregnant. Mind you, his therapist was struck off shortly afterwards for diagnosing a girl with anorexia and spots as having a castration complex. But for Maurice things went from bad to worse. One day, he got horribly drunk and had a blazing row with his old fridge and put it out for the bin-men. True, he spent the next week searching the local rubbish tip, but the deed was done and there he was, finally alone with his new fridge. You can probably guess the rest."

"I don't think I can, Mr Curtis." It seemed to me that Maria gave me a strange look. I was surprised at her lack of intuition; women are normally much ahead of men in this respect.

"He stopped going out and on the rare occasions we persuaded him to join us in the pub, he would be looking at his watch the whole time. He wore his best clothes at home. A neighbour told us she had seen him through the kitchen window wearing a top hat and tuxedo. He'd sit by his new fridge, soft music playing in the background. Sad story really, but as long as they're happy."

"They?"

"I see your point. Can a fridge be said to be happy, particularly with a temperature regulated not to exceed 5 degrees in the main compartment and minus four in the freezer, depending of course on the star rating…"

"Mr Curtis?"

"Yes."

"Do you have any more stories like that?"

I was pleased by her enthusiasm. "I had another friend who developed a pathological fear of his slippers…"

"Could you keep it to yourself then? You're making my head hurt."

I obliged her with a dignified silence. It seems to me that women (particularly those in the world of publishing) are prone to mood swings. Maria was holding her head in her hands as if in some pain.

"And the relevance of that story was?"

"Ah." She'd got me there. I'm sure there was one but I couldn't put my hands on it for the moment.

"Perhaps that he fell in love with the fridge itself rather than its contents?"

"That was it." I tried to look intelligent. My brother had schooled me in this art. The trick was to turn both feet out so that you balanced on the edges of your soles as you walked. It required balance and concentration and was also rather painful – producing just the right level of seriousness and contemplation to one's expression. I tried it and I think it was working; certainly Maria was looking at me.

"I'd like to discuss this matter with you further, perhaps later on."

"Yes of course," I said, desperately re-working the signals from my speech centre that were coming out as: "foam, gibber, wibble."

We had come to the Town Hall and climbed the steps. The ceremony was under way in the main hall. Sir Winyard was crouched down muttering to himself, with the LCJ in attendance. The assembled ancestors looked down from their pictures with expressions that seemed particularly mean and serious.

Sir Winyard acknowledged our presence with a slight inclination of his head. The LCJ sidled over to us. I noticed that he walked stiffly, wincing with each step.

"Ah, Mr Curtis," he positively beamed, "such a pleasure."

"What's the old goat up to?" asked Maria.

The LCJ looked petulant. "He decided that he was the only one with sufficient authority to perform the ceremony."

As if on cue, Sir Winyard tapped himself on both shoulders with a ceremonial sword, popped an extravagant-looking crown on his head and got to one knee, announcing:

"Arise Sir Winyard the First, Emperor of the Latvian Fish Isles and all its dominions…"

"Its dominions?" I whispered to the LCJ.

"There's this goat hut…"

Sir Winyard directed a withering look in our direction, and it seemed to me that his ancestors turned particularly hostile glares towards us.

"Do you, Sir Winyard the First, Emperor of the Latvian Fish Isles and all its dominions, humbly swear at all times to serve yourself…?"

Sir Winyard appeared to hesitate. I assumed that there was more to come but apparently not. The LCJ whispered in my ear that Sir Winyard had decided to adopt the oath of allegiance used by local councillors all over the world. Sir Winyard faced his assembled ancestors with tears rolling down his cheeks. They appeared unmoved.

"I do," he said in a broken voice.

That seemed to be it. Sir Winyard turned to face us and raised his head slightly in order to look down his nose at us.

"Thank you, thank you," he said, even though no one had said anything. I felt that congratulations were in order.

"Congratulations," I said.

"Ah – Mr Curtis. You find my situation somewhat changed since our last conversation; I am now in a position to sign the Accession Treaty."

"Ah," I said, and made a fairly good show of looking crestfallen (derived from my stunning Romeo in Act Five, Scene One [Mantua. A street] on learning of the death of Juliet – well received by the *West Ealing Advertiser*, but the usual mealy-mouthed review from *The Harrow Gazette* – encompassing selected northern parts of Sudbury Hill).

"You shouldn't rush into it you know. It's a complex document with constitutional implications." This was not the sort of remark you might expect from an EU Commissioner, but this was my reverse psychology at work, and I was justified by a nasty sly expression from Sir Winyard.

"I've had it checked by our Lord Chief Justice, Mr Curtis; I am satisfied with the document, and I see no reason to delay; that is, after all, the purpose of your visit to the LFI is it not?"

"Oh yes, quite," I said – "it's just that…" I allowed myself to tail off into uncertainty in very much the same manner as my, dare I say, unsurpassed portrayal of a widow in *All's Well That Ends Well*, Act Three, Scene Five (Florence. Without the Walls. A tucket far off). I will not burden you with certain comments made by that insignificant gazette that bears the name of Harrow and yet doth…

Sir Winyard clicked his fingers at the LCJ, which I could see was the wrong note to strike. Lord Chiefs Justice in general like to think of themselves as unsubservient to all others.

"The Treaty."

The LCJ produced a large document. This was it! I knew that if I betrayed even the slightest sign of anxiety, this would arouse Sir Winyard's suspicions. This was a Clint Eastwood moment. I narrowed my eyes and rolled an imaginary cigar from one side of my mouth to the other while inwardly informing certain desperados that I was confident that they would make the appropriate apology to my mule. My nerves disintegrated; I searched desperately for some sort of inspiring thought to calm them. Strange how the history of mankind sometimes hangs on these moments; with Robert the Bruce, it was a spider dithering about; with me, it was a glimpse of the Mexican border. It just so happened that at this moment Maria leant forward to scratch her knee revealing the northern states of Chihuahua and Coahuila from El Paso to Nuevo Laredo. In the normal way, this would have put my nerves into a mincing machine and turned the handle, but in this instance it worked in reverse. I'm not sure why, I can only suppose by the same mechanism as electro-convulsive-therapy works on depression. You are feeling a bit down in the dumps and a couple of chaps in white caps strap some electrodes to your skull and pass four hundred and fifty volts through it – sort of distracts you and takes your mind off things – almost everything I should imagine. The world seems a better place, possibly because you can't remember what was wrong with it in the first place; also having forgotten who you are, what you're doing here, and who the little lad is, hugging your knee and calling you, "Daddy."

The Mexican border stretched out before me in its bounteous magnificence and I signed in an aura of calm. I passed the Treaty to Sir Winyard with a steady hand. He took it and removed a massive Montblanc fountain pen from his pocket and began to unscrew the cap. My nerves decided that this was just taking the piss. If you examine the thread-form of an expensive fountain pen you will discover that although it has typically a 12 t.p.i. (threads per inch) pitch, it uses a multi-start thread which engages in up to three places; this not only keeps it from running off the vertical axis but also enables it to unscrew completely in a few revolutions. Sir Winyard's Montblanc, however, appeared to be designed for the purpose of eternal torment. To my fevered imagination, it seemed that he had been turning it in slow motion for the past couple of weeks. His thumb and forefinger appeared the size of a couple of airships and his ancestors all leant out of their picture frames, wagged their fingers and clicked their tongues.

The cap finally disengaged with the noise of a hawser freeing itself from a windlass on an ocean-going vessel of five hundred thousand tonnes that had just broken its moorings, and the Montblanc nib (the size of a garden spade) began its descent towards the document – and then paused!

Time wandered off for a tea break. I fought back the temptation to start whistling and turned in desperation to Maria's cleavage, which had now extended from Agua Prieta to Matamoras on the Gulf of Mexico. Time returned much refreshed, burped a couple of times and settled back to work. Sir Winyard's pen continued its journey towards the spot marked "X".

And it was all over! Phew! Sir Winyard was looking smug. I was feeling smug, but had no intention of looking it until I was several light years away from Sir Winyard. Maria however had no such inhibitions and was definitely smirking. Women tend to do this when they've just put one over on a man; I've noticed this. See a woman smirking and you can be fairly sure that some poor bloke is throbbing in the background, having just had his credit card debited to the tune of £2169.67 for a four-seater sofa and accompanying pair of high wing chairs in tasteless mustard check. (Sorry Mum, but it had to be said.)

I shook my head with apparent concern. “I don’t know what the President will say.”

Sir Winyard now joined in the smirking – it was becoming fashionable. “I wouldn’t concern yourself unduly, Mr Curtis. Regrettably there is no longer a requirement in the LFI for a, er, president. I intend to dissolve the position after lunch. I shall issue an edict I think, or possibly a decree.”

Sir Winyard handed me the Treaty. I muttered some pleasantries while continuing to look resigned and anxious, made my excuses and left. Norm and Margaret followed in an autonomic way, rather as a dog follows a sausage on a piece of string. They were so wrapped up in each other that I doubt if they had any idea of what was going on around them. They were tickling each other somewhere around the kidneys, although it would have needed a CAT scan to find them in the case of Norman. It occurred to me that in the usual course of love, tickling in the area of the lower ribs is something like stage five in the courtship procedure (stage two in France). This leads on to playful wrestling, blowing in the ears, general frottering, culminating in stage ten, which I won’t describe because it’s rude (but not as rude as stage eleven [stage three in France]).

The whole process seemed to be working in reverse with Norman and Margaret. They had started on stage ten (probably! I don’t think Norman knows about stage eleven, and I have promised the ex-wives club never to mention it to him). The way they were going, they would regress to stage one – ignoring each other pointedly (for the English) or staring into each other’s eyes like a couple of intense sheep (for the French).

I was interrupted by Maria grabbing my arm. “You were brilliant.”

Funny she should say this; in fact, one in the eye for those supercilious halfwits in the *Harrow and* something-or-other. I didn't say anything though because she was stroking my arm and this was having an extraordinary effect on another part of my anatomy, which was reacting as though a French girl had just sidled up to it in a bar in Marseilles and offered it upstairs with a girl called Pascale who would go to stage fourteen for a Martini with two cherries in it.

"Perhaps we can continue that interesting conversation we were having," said Maria.

"Oh yes," I said. "Where were we?"

"You had just told me about a friend of yours who had fallen in love with his fridge."

"Ah, yes – more of a friend of a friend though." I didn't want her to get the wrong idea about me.

"And you, Mr Curtis, have you ever been in love? Excluding domestic appliances if you don't mind."

I paused. There was of course Miss Davis, and I duly told Maria about she who had once imprudently planted a careless kiss on a passing six-year-old.

"Then there was the hairdresser: tall, brunette, long bent nose – absolutely beautiful. She was working her way around the base of a pudding basin at the time, and nipped my ear sharply. I whinged a bit and the next thing I knew she had hugged me to her bosom and kissed the top of my head, very close to the area reserved for Miss Davis in fact." I pointed out the spot.

"And you were then, five years old?"

"And three quarters," I added stiffly, because it seemed to me that Maria was smirking again. A place should be held open for her at that dreadful local newspaper – do you know, I've completely forgotten the area it was supposed to cover.

"And since then?"

"No." The answer to this question saddened me, but it was true: I'd never been in love with Donna. "And you?" I asked.

She looked at me sharply. It struck me that she was reluctant to answer.

"I have had admirers, Mr Curtis – some, although not all, handsome, intelligent, generally eligible, but all with one vital missing ingredient."

I tried to look questioning. Not difficult to a chap whose talents were once so tragically missed by that – what was it again – some sort of provincial free paper?

"I need to respect a man, Mr Curtis. My admirers were all very willing to spread their cloaks over puddles, open doors for me, and – forgive me if I sound conceited – worship me. But I don't want devotion, Mr Curtis."

"No, quite," I agreed with a sinking heart. "I mean, who does? There's nothing worse, I always say, than devotion."

She looked at me rather intensely I thought. "I know all about your ex-girlfriend, Mr Curtis. Norman told me…"

Someone walked into the party in the amygdala and announced that all city bonuses were withdrawn due to a spectacular collapse of the Hang Seng. In a daze, I turned to see Norman tickling Margaret in a place where she probably kept her gall bladder, and carefully withdrawing what looked at a distance like a chicken in a basket from his pocket. I had just decided to go over and shove the lot into his face with a bitter recrimination such as: "Oh look how easily it fits into that big mouth", when we were collectively disturbed by the sound of distant gunfire.

Moments later, the LCJ appeared from the direction of the Town Hall, sprinting down the road towards us, clutching his wig and panting like an express train.

"Referendum," he said, by way of greeting.

"Ah," said Maria, which I found flattering: imitation being… (you know the rest).

It was my turn to look smug. This was the lethal addition I had appended to the Treaty. Sir Winyard had just signed up to have his own position subjected to confirmation by referendum! What was so devilishly, fiendishly cunning about this, if you don't mind me saying so, is that the last place in the world you would expect to find the mandate for a referendum, would be in an EU Treaty. I had caught Sir Winyard with his massive billowing trousers, somewhere in the vicinity of his ankles.

Maria looked at the LCJ accusingly. “He cottoned on a bit quickly.”

The LCJ shifted weight uneasily. “I might have just mentioned it,” but, breaking down under Maria’s critical eye, he added, “Oh all right, I thought he might give me a bit of a thrashing; I didn’t expect him to start taking potshots at me; which incidentally, contravenes the penal code of the LFI.” He looked up at us suddenly. “He’s not going to take this lying down.”

CHAPTER 16

I have to admit that my mind was not entirely occupied with the LFI's constitutional crisis as we made our way back. I had perhaps foolishly allowed thoughts of intimacy with Maria to play in my head. If only Norman hadn't opened his mouth. Maria had made clear her opinions on the subject of subservience. Her type of man was to be found fossilised outside a Mesozoic cave where he had died in an argument with a fellow in an adjacent cave about whether he had or had not been giving his woman (she in the leopard-skin jacket and matching accessories) the eye – NOT the sort of man to be found on his hands and knees at the end of a leash held by a leather-clad dominatrix from Harrow. And unfortunately, thanks to Norman, she was now in no doubt as to which particular subspecies I belonged. I bore no grudge, Norman meant no harm, but it seemed to me that Maria now walked at a distance from me.

We arrived to the sound of music emanating from the presidential residence. Maria explained:

"He's having one of his balls…"

I failed to understand this remark at first. It sounded rather like Sir Winyard's oath of allegiance: unfinished. To complete it required imagination: sellotaped to a coffee table? Shaved? Covered in milk chocolate? Imprisoned in a small metal cage? Lacquered? Tickled with a feather duster? It was hard to guess, but even as I mused, the music became identifiable as a Viennese waltz and the problem was solved.

As we turned off the main road, we saw that a municipal dustcart had set out from the Town Hall and was heading towards us at high speed.

We found the ballroom awash with young ladies prancing around gracefully. It had possibly started as a quadrille, but had been updated by the addition of beer bottles, cigarettes, missing clothes and a strong lesbian theme. Alex was not to be seen at first, but appeared shortly when spun around from behind a young lady, who appeared to be leading, and sported a shaved head, an eyepatch, full sideburns and beard. The effect was surprisingly arousing (which probably doesn't surprise you, but it surprised me). And before anyone starts making dubious remarks about my sexuality in red felt-tip pen, I would like to point out that the President of the LFI also appeared impressed. He was smiling all over, and his trousers were billowing magnificently.

Maria was at my side. "Do you know?" I asked, and at this point she probably didn't, but would shortly, "I think he's clicked."

Maria was about to reply when the door burst open and Sir Winyard appeared, surrounded by a large something or other of police. I'm not sure of the collective term here. I know it's a parliament of owls, and a frug of vicars, and a villain of wasps... But as for gay policemen: how about a gossip? Not sure, but there they were, cluttering the place up and looking not so much impressive as impressed by the splendour of the ball.

The music stopped. Sir Winyard drew himself up to his full height, pointed to Alex, and commanded imperiously:

"Seize him."

The LFI police force fidgeted nervously. They weren't trained for this sort of thing. I'm not an expert but I would say they wavered, and I think Sir Winyard suspected the same, because he roared:

"I command you as your Emperor!"

The force was impressed. An emperor is after all rather lavish. I like to think that a chance remark from yours truly had a turn in events.

"Subject to a referendum," I said.

And the force, who seemed at that moment poised to chassé into action, were distracted. Note: a distinct weakness in the LFI Police Force was their susceptibility to distraction.

"Oooooh," said one.

"A referendum," hissed another, as if impressed.

"What will you go as?" asked a third.

"I'll wear my gold top," answered a fourth.

I would say that at this point the whole thing hung in the balance, and the deciding factor was Alex's trousers; I think I told you they were billowing magnificently and I did not exaggerate. Not only did they billow, but they were of a sort of rich Harris Tweed trimmed with silver chaff which caught the light and sparkled with reflected light. In a struggle for the hearts and minds of a police force, various complex factors come into play, but in this particular instance it was the nature of the gay gene that turned out to be the determining factor. You could see the force scrutinising, first, Sir Winyard's trousers and then Alex's. To you or I, Alex's trousers were loud, gaudy and kitsch; they were over-the-top; they were the sort of trousers that made people mutter that the wearer was an upstart and a Johnny-come-lately. Sir Winyard's trousers were tasteful and reassuring in comparison. But this is the judgement of straight people! The gay gene shares one of its spirals with the Jewish gene and isn't having any of it. These trousers were magnificent, and Alex rose to the occasion and worked his trousers. I'm sure that if Desmond Morris had been in attendance, he would have smiled significantly and pointed out that Alex's superb generalship of his trousers owed much to the bearded lovely at his side, smoking a pipe. I had not seen Alex so confident. He stood arms akimbo and rotated at the waist so that the silver braid in his trousers caught the light and flashed around the room like a mirror-ball at a disco.

It could have been a moment of high drama. I'm sure if Shakespeare had got his hands on it, he would have made some sort of a tacky play out of it (which would have no doubt impressed the critics on that North London rag people used to line their cat litter trays with, who are so easily impressed with over-acting, and so unmoved by realistic depiction). But there was no showdown, just a gradual melting away of the force as they took to the floor in pairs.

There was no chance of an arrest, only several polite enquiries as to where Alex had obtained his trousers as they all pirouetted around the dance floor, leaving Sir Winyard high and dry. The part of an imperious emperor issuing edicts and decrees relies heavily on a supporting act of lackeys and enforcers who are NOT dancing in a quadrille, chatting excitedly about this and that.

Sir Winyard slunk off. We learnt afterwards that he found his municipal dustcart surrounded by hostile locals clamouring for a referendum, and he made a hurried and ignominious dash for the border in his dustcart, pursued by eggs and tomatoes. Good riddance to bad rubbish one might say.

Meanwhile, I'm not quite sure how it happened, but I found myself caught up in a dance with Maria. I wanted at this point to leave a page or two blank, rather than just say that words failed me, but my publisher advised against it on the grounds that it would be even more of a waste of paper (not sure what she meant by that remark) and also, this device has already been used in The *Life and Opinions of Tristram Shandy*, by Laurence Sterne – which I have read and enjoyed, but found difficult because the author has got a bad habit of wandering off the point. Suffice to say then that Maria in the flesh was a severe strain on the amygdala: the feel of her, the warmth of her, and of course the uninterrupted view of the Mexican border from the Pacific Ocean to the Gulf of Mexico.

I hope you won't mind a brief digression at this point, on the subject of cleavage and why it affects me so severely. It was all explained to me at one of Donna's parties by her psychologist friend. I was put under deep hypnosis, which involved mixing vodka with Austrian rum I seem to remember. He said I was particularly easy to regress, which I found flattering. It all came out, going back to when I was about three months old, scrabbling around on the floor in that world that babies occupy, trying to stroke the cat and articulate the word, "pussy cat," using the allowed syllables, "goo" and "gaa" in any required sequence, in between smiling and bubbling mucous. I was applying myself to this task when my favourite Auntie Doreen tripped over me.

To understand this, you have to think of it from the child's perspective; there you are on the floor occupied entirely with trying to enlighten a large tabby cat as to its generic name, when, all of a sudden, the ground starts to shake and a huge pair of red stilettos bear down on you. Auntie Doreen had shapely legs and disported them proudly in an assortment of high-heeled shoes. This is the stuff formative sexual experiences are made of: a bright red shiny stiletto cut low across the toes, bearing down on yours truly and catching me squarely in the high nappy area.

The physical damage was negligible – a bent safety pin and some sort of greeny-yellow deposit in the nappy – but emotionally this was a roller coaster. An approaching lady's shoe at floor level displays a deep cleft between the big and second toe; this is followed by a sharp blow and a certain amount of pain, followed immediately by cuddles, hugs and kisses, which, it was explained to me, in later life causes the sexualisation of pain and anything with a cleft in it – mountain passes, sausages being grilled in a row, severe fluctuations in the stock market, and of course, cleavages.

"Mr Curtis?"

I was being spoken to. It was Maria. Not surprising really; we seemed to be dancing in close proximity. I sighed deeply which didn't help matters because it just caused her chest to press tightly against mine.

"Mr Curtis." She had my attention. "To continue the rather interesting conversation we were having earlier…"

"Right." I agreed, but without much enthusiasm. I had a horrible feeling it was going to follow the lines of so many previous dialogues (often monologues actually) that I had as a teenager, so varied in their composition except for the closing lines, "I shall always think of you as a friend." If only Norman… But Maria was talking and demanded my attention, which was tending to wander between possible misfortunes that might befall Norman and the feel of hot soft woman against me.

"When I first met you, Mr Curtis, I was not impressed."

I nodded understandingly; we all make errors of judgement every now and again. You only have to think of that suburban handout with its small-minded and inexperienced… If only Norman…

"Under the circumstances, you will understand that I was not well disposed to any sort of bureaucrat or to any application to join the European Union, which after all has the tyranny, triviality, corruption and wastefulness of a local council on a grand scale."

"Oh quite," I said. This was going well – if only Norman…

"Also, Mr Curtis, I hope you won't be offended when I say that you seemed a rather insipid young man. I remember shaking your hand; you appeared to tremble like a leaf and could not look me in the face…"

I felt this was unfair: Perseus had a similar problem with Medusa and had to use a mirrored shield to view her with – and I bet she didn't have anything like Maria's cleavage. Besides, I couldn't face the embarrassment of appearing to wrestle with a boa constrictor in my trousers. This has been crossed out in red and replaced it with "asp". Perhaps we could agree some sort of compromise here with a somewhat larger than average grass snake. Bear in mind that when being fitted for my first suit, a very camp tailor asked me, "Does, sir dress on the left or the right?" Well I didn't know what he meant and he hissed at me suddenly with that glassy waspish stare that only a practised homo can produce, "Where does sir like to keep his big cock?" So there.

At this stage, we had fandangoed to the end of the ballroom and back level with A. Stambolüski. I suspect that in the duration Maria had enlightened me as to some of the other deficiencies in my character that had impressed themselves on her, but somehow I seemed to have missed them.

"And then, I saw another side to you, Mr Curtis; you jumped over the council railings in a gesture of defiance, and I confess quite freely to you that this was a turning point in my feelings."

I was interrupted at this point by the sound of singing; *My Lord, What a Mornin'* by the Morriston Orpheus Choir I think, coming from the amygdala, and as some sort of reflex action, I squeezed her in my arms. She might have pushed me away; she might have squeezed me back; she might have giggled or blushed. She did none of these things; she looked into my eyes directly with what might be described as thoughtful intensity – but I'm afraid that someone in dispatch sent a stirring signal directly to my testicles. (A certain rather cynical woman has written in red pen "What a surprise!" in the margin.)

"Yes, Mr Curtis, Norman told me about your relationship with your ex-girlfriend. I wouldn't want you to think..."

At this moment, a member of the local constabulary cut in on me and twirled Maria off in the direction of Pedro the Cruel. I didn't know how I felt about this. I would miss her of course, but then again it gave me the opportunity for an urgent conversation with Norman which I felt was overdue. Also, it was a godsend for those of us who like dramatic suspense, causing mutterings of, "Bravo," and "Masterful – quite masterful".

I found Norman between Mussolini and Ivan the Terrible. I wasn't sure what he was doing at first, but one glance at his shirt was enough: the display of the northern coast of Canada proved that he was dancing (I think without this information I would have called for an ambulance). Margaret was stuck in an area of armpit around the Hudson Strait. It was no wonder she was stuck; anyone with any maritime knowledge will tell you that the North West Passage is not negotiable at this time of year. I freed her gently but firmly and cut in. Norman laughed but did not look particularly surprised.

"Are you leading, Curtis?"

This is another of those brilliant facets to Norman's personality. How many straight men do you know, take up a vigorous foxtrot with one of their pals without batting an eyelid?

"Norman?" I said.

"Yes, Curtis," he replied, concentrating on his footwork.

"What did you tell Maria about Donna?" Norman chuckled. "Ah – it worked; we saw you dancing together."

"What worked?"

"A little psychology, Curtis, goes a long way with women. I told Maria that you used to beat Donna."

"What!" Or it may have been: "Whaaaaaaat!!!!!!"

"Yes, I told her that you were a bit of a disciplinarian, and that if Donna crossed a certain line, you would chastise her."

"Chastise her?"

"Across your knee with a hairbrush, for minor misdemeanours..."

"Oh my God!"

"And a riding crop for more serious infringements."

I looked at Norman in dumb horror while chasseing between Stalin and Henry the Navigator.

"You may not realise it to look at her, Curtis, but Maria is the sort of woman who likes a man to dominate her."

I stared at Norman in disbelief while we glided past Vlad the Impaler in a stylish Cajun Jitterbug and two-step. Norman smiled condescendingly.

"You don't have much experience with women, do you Curtis?"

"True, but then again I haven't got six ex-wives and numerous ex-girlfriends touring Venezuelan villages demonstrating to the natives though interpreters and flip charts how to defend themselves if you ever come near them."

"Hmmmm – Venezuela you say; I thought they were somewhere up near the Mexican border."

"Norman."

"Yes, Curtis."

"Please promise not to mention the Mexican border – not when we are dancing together anyway."

We were at this moment doing a nifty passé double past George Bush and Tony Blair when I was disturbed to find myself having thoughts about Norman which I have not entertained since that BRIEF moment of testicular fascination at school, and I was immensely relieved to discover the reason for this: Maria had cut in on Norman. She was wriggling herself against me provocatively, which caused a general stirring in the amygdala. People had taken a break during my dance with Norman and started a conversation about hedge funds and interest rates.

"Cheeky beggar asked me my bra size." She chuckled, evidently amused. I broke into a foxtrot in a desperate attempt to create a diversion. Certain factions had broken out in the amygdala. A pinstriped stockbroker was pushing his luck on the pinball machine (over in the corner by the bar).

"Mr Curtis?"

"Yes," I said because, after all, when all is said and done, I was.

"Our conversation was interrupted."

For which I inwardly thanked God, who, in spite of having made the world in seven days, was at times not as attentive as I would have liked to the care of my personal fate, but was absolutely on the ball today.

"I was saying that I had cause to revise my opinion of you; not just for jumping over railings, which was impressive in itself, but I have come to know that you are not as you appeared to me at first…" She went on to describe in some considerable further detail how I had appeared to her at first. This ran to several pages, but unfortunately there are times when an author has to do some ruthless editing to keep his work from wandering off the point. Content yourselves with the knowledge that we had passed King Ludwig of Bavaria twice, first in a tango, and secondly in a Moroccan tea dance, before she had finished and the dialogue became worth reporting again.

"You were in fact, decisive, powerful, masterful and, when it came to your dealing with the LCJ – brutal. I saw a snarl on your face that said: cross this man at your peril…"

I must interrupt Maria here to point out to my readers (if I still have any) that this snarl was in fact a wince of sympathy for the poor old boy's backside. This is a weakness I have detected in the opposite sex: while fostering a generally low opinion of the male of the species, when they do latch on to one, they tend to overcompensate, ascribing that essentially imperfect specimen with all sorts of qualities that only Mrs Superman (née Lane) could have claimed, providing of course that Mr S had been off the kryptonite (which I can't find in the Periodic Table).

Maria was talking again. "Of course I expect you've had plenty of practice?" I wasn't sure how to answer this, so I decided to close one eye, cup my chin and attempt to look thoughtful (another classic from my brother). "From handing out thrashings to your ex," continued Maria with a glint in her eye. I tried to look stern; difficult when one's chin is cupped and one eye is closed.

"Only when she deserved it."

"Norman told me that you used a bullwhip on her for breaking a vase that you particularly treasured: a blue one with a large red handle. Art Deco I believe."

This could have counted against me in The Hague, but at this moment I felt Maria's upper thigh press into an area marked, "Private." This considerably agitated the chap on the pinball machine in the amygdala (in the corner by the bar) who was now shoving viciously at the flippers. A "tilt" now seemed only a matter of time.

Certain things that happen between a man and a woman should, I believe, remain private. I would not wish to go into too much detail about what happened later that evening when Maria and I left the ballroom… And in fact the few tasteful details I saw fit to release have been removed and vandalised by she with the red pen, who accosted me in the corridor outside her office.

"Mr Curtis," she started in an accusatory tone, "you may have noticed that certain pages have been removed from your manuscript."

"One hundred and forty-seven actually – didn't you like them?"

"I did not."

"Oh."

"I have a husband, Mr Curtis."

"Congratulations," I started, but she fixed me with a hostile glare.

"We've been married for twenty-four years – twenty-four difficult years, in which the matter that you deal with almost exclusively on pages 176 to 304, has reared its ugly head on several occasions, and is referred to euphemistically by my husband as 'cuddles'. We have two beautiful children, Mr Curtis, as a result of 'cuddles'. My husband, like most men, is easily stimulated. I have had to change his newspaper to the *Financial*

Times, sew stronger elastic into his underwear and put a hammer through his satellite dish to prevent any further outbreaks of this sort of unpleasantness. Should my husband have picked up your novel, unlikely as that may seem, I could foresee a request not just for 'cuddles' but for 'special cuddles'," she shuddered, "which I will not go into other than to mention that it is still illegal in Canada. I have fourteen percent osteoporosis in my right hip, Mr Curtis. I took those pages of yours and I burnt them; after I burnt them, I crushed their ashes with a mortar and pestle, before dissolving them in acid; I then flushed them down the toilet on a particularly stormy night."

So that was that. Here we are on page 196 (of my original manuscript that is) which I shall refer to as page 304 as a form of protest, and I find myself three weeks later, transported as if by magic, back to Brussels, entering the office of Mr Jones and Mr Patel, with Norman in tow.

"Mr Curtis!" Mr Jones arose to meet me with what appeared to be genuine warmth. This was a surprise to me; Mr Jones, you may remember, was a bit of a cold fish. But it wasn't my imagination; I felt my hand gripped firmly (instead of the usual feeling that someone had just wrapped it in a decomposing lettuce leaf) and, as if that wasn't enough, he looked directly into my eyes – a focal length of some eighteen inches, some umpteen light years shorter than was usual. Not that this was a pleasant experience, and I suspect it was a great strain on Mr Jones because he almost instantly relaxed his gaze to a point somewhere in the region of Ursa Minor.

"Mr Curtis – congratulations are in order. A cognac perhaps?"

I accepted gratefully. I was glad he was pleased. I like to please people, and when I tasted the cognac and found it to be best vintage rather than the usual "hospitality" stuff, I realised that he was very pleased.

"We are very pleased, Mr Curtis." (What did I tell you?) "We understand the Latvian Fish Isles have withdrawn their application. This in itself is good news, but in addition, there is the matter of your expenses."

"Magnificent," added Mr Patel who you will remember didn't like being left out of things. Mr Jones was evidently in such a good mood that he refrained from glaring at Mr Patel almost completely – in fact there was a twinkle in his eye, probably from Alpha Centauri but possibly Pollux – I'm not too sure.

"Magnificent indeed. You have claimed in the last three weeks for a fact-finding tour of the Mexican border and a thorough exploration of the Amazon Basin." He shook his head in wonder. "And to think that only a few weeks ago, we were pleading with you to plan your trips across Brussels via Rome or Madrid – and the best you ever managed was Luxembourg! See how you have come on."

"Most commendable," interjected Mr Patel, getting away with things while he could.

CHAPTER 17

So this story, unlike so many lesser ones, draws to its close on a high note. It just leaves me now to bring you all up to date.

Norman and Margaret are an item. Norman has lost a lot of weight due to an executive decision taken by Margaret on his behalf to limit his food intake – something to do with Cholesterol apparently. Mr Patel, who himself wears his stomach on the large side, asked Norman enviously if he had acquired an exercise machine. Norman considered this question for some time before answering that he rather thought he had,

Alex proceeded with the referendum. Dictators in general (even crap ones) don't approve of referenda; they claim they are against their principles – but they can sometimes be persuaded on the strict condition that they are the only candidate. Alex appeared to enjoy himself, although he let himself down by hugging alternate elbows and making Mussolini-type salutes from within his wheelie-bin. And as for his love life (because I know some people are interested in such things in which case I think they should write in and let their opinion be known), you may remember that he was last reported dancing with a statuesque young lady smoking a pipe. There is something about a tall attractive bald girl sporting a moustache that I find... And consider also that this girl had a willowy graceful poise and a magnificent beard... But I digress, and should point out that all the facial hair was artificial; she wore it for a laugh because she was a girl with a finely developed sense of humour. It was in fact this sense of humour that drew them together.

Alex had a collection of Hollywood films. Strangely, he had the same attitude to Hollywood films that I had been bought up on. They made him laugh; he fell off his chair three times during, *The Godfather*. My theory is that because Alex had spent his life unsuccessfully trying to be someone he wasn't, he divined instantly when other people were up to the same trick. The crucial moment came when she with the beard walked in on Alex giggling away at a film which must remain nameless, but features a diminutive scientologist (it is a cult isn't it?) playing the part of a Samurai warrior. One assumes that the casting office had advertised for someone particularly short, with odd religious beliefs and proven ability to look intense while standing on an orange box. Incidentally, my lawyer informed me in between sips of her sarsaparilla and root beer, that this was "Okallohi'ablutm" (which I had to look up, and the nearest I could find was 'O.K. ugly retard' – so it wouldn't be that – would it?) because there is more than one diminutive scientologist in Hollywood – and even though one is shorter than the others, I have not referred to him as the shortest, only diminutive, which sufficiently fudges the issue legally.

She with the beard's ability to suspend disbelief was measurable in seconds. She was on the floor in three, fighting for breath, her legs kicking in the air, tears rolling down her cheeks, and her beard hitched up around one ear. You know how it is with laughter: Alex found himself joining the young lady on the floor, and somehow in the process of rolling around together, that subtle but deadly process was initiated which bloomed into fully fledged romance when the cat, fascinated by the young lady's beard, started patting at it, attacked it viciously and ended up licking her face, being in general that sort of a cat, while the girl stroked the cat and played with her tail being in general: that sort of a girl.

Alex is very happy and says he owes it all to Tom Cruise. I don't know why he should say this and I haven't had the opportunity to ask my lawyer because she's sloped off to see some friends called, "The Nicks."

As for Sir Winyard, to say he made an undignified exit would not be entirely true. His passage through the border was dignified by a full complement of homosexual guards all in particularly tight fitting French Foreign Legion uniforms who insisted on standing at rigid attention for nearly twenty-five minutes before presenting arms... and flowers and pink fluffy gonks, all collapsing into a sweaty heap after Sir Winyard's passage, smoking cigarettes and asking each other, "How was it for you?"

Sir Winyard was graciously allowed to keep dominion over the Imperial Possessions of the LFI, to wit: one goat-hut and adjacent outbuilding with fine all round panoramic vista, extensive planning and development possibilities; an absolute must for the first-time buyer on a limited budget (I think Foxtons were given the account).

My brother is still unmarried, but he has recently uprated his electric bell battery pack to twenty-four volts, and has increased the diameter of his front chain wheel by eighteen centimetres, and he confidently predicts that there will be major developments with Fiona Cartwright shortly.

And as for Maria and I, you would have a much more complete picture of the state of our relationship if a certain lady who makes a clicking noise as she walks due to the sheer number of red pens in her pockets banging together had not removed certain pages that I am confident a certain local paper in North London would have described as, "tastefully erotic" (providing of course that they have replaced the poison dwarves in the arts review section with human beings).

But don't let me give you the impression that our relationship is merely physical. At the opposite end of the bar to the pinball machine (which did finally "tilt" on our first night together and has got an "out of action" card strung across it) in the amygdala, a group of stockbrokers have started up a poets' corner. They meet regularly, remove their jackets to reveal powerfully elasticated red braces, and spout poetry to each other, and not just superficial contrived stuff like Ted Hughes; I am talking the real Sylvia Plath, along with Byron, Tennyson, Emerson and others. They are having a crack at Milton as we speak.

There is only one fly in the ointment: shortly after we got together (so sensitively described in those pages, tragically lost due to the small-mindedness and... never mind, sometimes one has to let things go) Maria acquired a seemingly endless supply of reproduction Art Deco vases – blue with red handles – which with extraordinary clumsiness she knocks over on a regular basis, and bursts into giggles every time one smashes to the floor. And I of course, in order to maintain the persona that Norman invented for me, narrow my eyes, sneer threateningly (by pulling my hair back with one hand while lifting an eyebrow with the other – thanks to my brother for that one) and strong-arm her off to the bedroom to be dealt with by practices not usually found outside Anstruther's study.

The problem is that in spite of the fact that certain names and events have been changed in this narrative, not so much as to protect the innocent as the guilty, Donna is for real – and Maria must never ever meet Donna!